A collection of short stori
train, bus, or whilst waitii
All of the stories are not
              title suggests.

They all have a surprise ending.

This book is dedicated to my dear wife Davina, who has recently been diagnosed with the early stages of Parkinsons and I am raising money from the proceeds of this book to help with the research into the disease.

I would like to thank all my family and friends who have supported this technological dinosaur to get the book into print!

SHARPLY TWISTED ???

PERFECT OPPORTUNITY

THE INTERVIEW

THE RUNAWAYS

FACE AT THE WINDOW

LIVING IN THE PAST

IT'S ONLY A GAME

LOTTERY WIN

MISSING

NO TURNING BACK

THE WRONG SUITCASE

HURRICANES

A BUSINESS PROPOSITION

DEADLY SECRET

TRIGGER POINTS

REVENGE IS SWEET

THE INSPECTION

THE PERFECT OPPORTUNITY

CHAPTER ONE

The new neighbours down the street had just moved in, but I hadn't seen them yet, only the gleaming cars, that adorned the paved driveway. They were highlighted by the golden glow of the setting summer sun. Alongside the sleek and elegant black convertible 280SL Mercedes sports car was a red pick-up, with signage on the side. 'Man with a Van. No job too big or too small, just give me a call'. It had the telephone number and web site emblazoned beneath it. I had firstly thought that the van belonged to a builder, called in to do some work at the house, but Clive, our immediate neighbour, had told my fiancée, Robin, that the van in fact belonged to the new owners. As neighbours, I thought that I must introduce myself to them, as the man with a van may be useful to us when we eventually got around to refurbishing our house.

The house that they had bought was one the grandest, in this smart suburb of South West London, only ten minutes walk from The All England Lawn Tennis Club at Wimbledon, and wondered who they were, as houses on Somerset Road often fetched prices in the stratosphere. We were very fortunate to be left the very run down property in the will of Robin's late Uncle Harry, who had doted on her, as if she was his child. Uncle Harry had never married, and he took great pride in being her Legal Guardian. Robin's father Hugo and her brother Richard were killed in a senseless road crash on their way from a skiing trip in Switzerland, about 12 years ago. She was only 8 years old at the time. Her mother, had unfortunately died whilst giving birth to her. Robin survived the crash, after spending months in hospital, first in the Saanen Hospital near Gstaad, and then being airlifted to Stanmore Orthopaedic Hospital in North West London for treatment on her head and back, that had left her in a wheelchair. Her recall of the accident remains a blank in her memory, and the doctors have no idea whether this part of her brain will ever recover, nor indeed, whether she will ever be able to walk, unaided, again. She had been, and still is unable to help the Swiss police with their enquiries. The only thing that the police found at the scene of the accident were her family in the crushed and severely crumpled Jaguar, and a gold cuff link engraved with something like 'AV or HY', but it was difficult to decipher, due to the scarring on it. It didn't belong to her father or brother as their initials were HF, Hugo Fraser and RF, Richard Fraser. The other car in the crash, left blue marks on the Jaguar, but was nowhere to be seen. Just two sets of long skid marks on the road. It was a hit and run.

I had met Robin, who was still under her consultant, whilst I was also attending Stanmore Orthopaedic for a chronic slipped disc, in the winter of 2010. She was now 21 and I was 24. We had met quite by chance in the hydrotherapy pool, one Wednesday morning, whilst

I was still recovering, and needed to exercise my back, without placing too much strain on it, and had been making steady progress in the warm water of the pool. I was completing my routine on my back, when quite literally, I bumped into her, not realising that she had entered the pool at the shallow end, in the direction towards where I was heading. C. RUN. CH, our heads smacked into each other. I swallowed a mouthful of water, and spluttered an apology towards her, "terribly sorry, I said, I didn't know you were there", I coughed, and coughed, trying to look apologetic, but this only brought on a fit of hiccups. She just couldn't stop laughing at the idiot that she saw before her. In mock jest, she clenched her fist and gently tapped on my head. "What are those for? She said, pointing at my eyes, you should keep them open." "Next time, I shall be more careful", I just about managed to say between my hiccups. Her physiotherapist was standing at the edge of the pool, monitoring her programme, saw my obvious embarrassment, and suggested that I should leave the pool, and that I should be more aware of other swimmers in the pool. I didn't need a second invitation to get out of the water, and as I dried myself with my towel, I crawled on my knees to the edge of the pool, and spoke to the lady who I had collided with, and suggested that perhaps I could make it up to her, when she had finished her exercises. "I'll be finished; she looked up at the huge clock above the pool, in about 15 minutes. I suggest that you buy me a drink as an apology. Meet at the cafe in say half an hour?"

"That's the least that I can do, I replied, I'll see you later".

I showered, and changed into my clothes, and I went to the car park, to put my wet things into my sports holdall, which was in the boot. I returned to the cafe, sat down at a table and waited. I anxiously looked at the swing doors, and then back to the clock. 45 minutes had elapsed since I saw her at the pool. Perhaps, I thought to myself, that discretion had got the better of her, and she had decided not to show up at all. I couldn't really blame her if she was a 'no show'. I walked over to the service counter and was just about to order myself a cup of tea, when the doors swung open, and this rather attractive young lady, bowled through them in a wheelchair. It didn't register, at first that this was my appointment, as I hadn't really taken a close look at her in the pool, under her big swimming hat. I had no real idea who I had bumped into. "About to order without me?, she scoffed, I'm sorry, but it took me a lot longer than normal to get changed, than I had planned, and then rescue my wheelchair. Still better late than never". Initially, I was slightly shocked that she was in a wheelchair, but that feeling soon disappeared when I looked at her lovely freckled face. She had a mop of auburn hair in tight ringlets, bright green eyes that shone like emeralds, high cheekbones, and a wonderful smile. From what I could see, she had a curvaceous figure, under a tight fitting roll neck jumper and shapely legs, hidden by a pair of fashionable jeans. She wore designer trainers on her dainty feet.

"What would you like to drink? I asked. They do a very nice hot chocolate with whipped cream." "Not for me thanks, as I am watching my weight, just a cup of tea will be fine". I'll order a pot of tea for two, anything to eat? Those Chelsea Buns look great, she said. "Not watching your weight with them I see", I joked. "OK, she said. A pot of tea for two and two of those buns please, I ordered. Shall I wait here or will you bring them over to our table?" "Just a tick, love, I'll have them ready for you in a jiffy." I took a tray, and carried my order over to the table where she had parked her wheelchair.

"Let's start properly, I said, I'm Jeff Thorn, and you are?". "Robin Fraser, she replied". "Well, that's got the introductions out of the way. I know it's a daft question, but what's a lovely young lady like you doing in a place like this"? I could see that she was blushing slightly beneath the light make up that she was wearing. "Well thank you, kind sir, but I could ask you the same sort of question. You first". "It's normally, 'Ladies first', but as I can see that you are reluctant to start, then here goes. I am 24 years old, single, and live in a bedsitter in Kilburn. I work for a Property Company and am training to be a millionaire. She laughed and gave me one of those delicious smiles that I had seen earlier in the pool. I am here, because I badly damaged my back playing squash, which was diagnosed as a prolapsed disc, and whilst I have not had an operation, and I really don't want to go under the knife, I am here to try to strengthen my back, with physical exercise. Thus far the treatment appears to be working. Now you." She took another bite from her Chelsea bun, wiped the crumbs from the corner of her mouth, and started. "I'm Robin Fraser, currently unattached and have just turned 21. I live with my Uncle in Wimbledon. I'm at The London College of Fashion right now, training to be a clothes designer. I'm here for treatment on my spine that was damaged a few years ago in a horrendous road accident. The treatment is good, but I don't know if I shall ever be able to walk again. She turned her head away from me, pulled out a tissue from her handbag, and gently wiped away the tears that had started to well up in the corner of her eyes. Sorry, I don't know why I should tell a complete stranger my horror story, but you seem to have a trusting face, and I guessed that you might be sympathetic". "Do you know? I said, , that I had no idea that you were in a wheelchair, until just now. I can empathise with you, as I have a friend who I went to University with, who unfortunately fractured his spinal column, whilst playing Rugby, and although he was told that he may never fully recover, he is making great strides, if you will forgive my use of that word. Of course, he will never be able to play Rugby again, but he now lives an almost normal life, whatever that means." Robin, cheered up a little with that information.

We merrily chatted away, and were getting on very well, when she looked at her wrist watch and told me that her taxi was waiting for her to take her home. We exchanged mobile telephone numbers, and agreed to meet again next Wednesday for tea and buns. "Same time next week", she called out as she expertly manoeuvred the wheelchair, out of the cafe. "Do you need any help"?, I shouted back as the doors closed. "No thanks, I heard her call, and anyway, you told me that you are not allowed to lift anything heavier that a box of corn flakes, and believe me I weigh more than that." She was gone.

We met, thereafter, weekly at the hospital cafe for tea and buns. I had changed my swimming appointment, so that there would be no repeat of our first meeting in the pool. We were getting along like a 'house on fire', so after a few weeks, we decided that we would like to get to know more about each other, and meeting in a hospital was not really conducive to any sort of relationship. I agreed to take her out, on our first real date, and at her suggestion we went to the Dog and Fox , which is right in the heart of Wimbledon Village, as it had been for about 300 or so years. We continued dating for about a year and it became obvious to both of us that we had fallen in love. One weekend, I surprised her when I took her away to a country retreat just outside Bath, and in the time honoured fashion got down on one knee, looked her straight in the eye and asked her to marry me, which she accepted without hesitation. "You'll have to speak to my Uncle, who is my Legal Guardian, and although I am of an age that I can make my own decisions, it would be nice to seek his permission. I love you with all of my heart, and I will marry you, for better or for worse, but it would be right and proper to ask him first".

Uncle Harry, was a typical Country gentleman. I assumed that he was in his late 70's or early eighties, suffered badly from gout, and rarely got out and about much anymore. He lived in a large rambling Detached Edwardian house, with plenty of carved woodwork, typical of the era. Robin and I went into his lounge, which had antique furniture scatted all over this magnificent room that had a fresco ceiling. A collection of well known paintings hung from the picture rail. He sat in a large winged armchair, with his foot resting on a huge pouffe, and smoked a Sherlock Holmes style pipe. His tweed jacket, somewhat the worse for wear had little burns in it where the tobacco had fallen out of the pipe's bowl. With his fabulous bushy beard, and a full head of white hair that straggled down his neck, he resembled King George the Fifth. "I reckon I know what you two have come to talk to me about, he bellowed in a loud stentorian voice, you want to take my Robin away from me, don't you"? "You have a great insight of the workings of my mind, I answered in a slightly nervous voice, but you've saved me the trouble of reciting my rehearsed speech. To put it bluntly, I would very much welcome your consent for us to be married".

"Robin has spoken a great deal to me about you, and whilst she is still relatively young, you are her first real boyfriend, but if you can make her happy, and your prospects in the world of Property are as I'm led to believe by Robin, then you can most certainly have my blessing." Robin, charged up to him, in floods of joyful tears, and hugged and kissed him, whilst he shook my hand strongly. "Where and when are you planning to get married?, he asked, pouring out a large brandy for himself. Please join me". We took our drinks and told him that we would like to be married next year. "Why so long?" He enquired. "We are saving up to buy a small property, and we shall have enough money for a deposit, when we sell my flat, and although we can afford to stay there for now, it's not really suitable for Robin as it's on the first floor, with no wheelchair access. It's better to start married life, in something that we can adapt for Robin's use."

Uncle Harry, was clearly delighted, and we booked a table that evening at our now favourite local restaurant, The Dog and Fox, to celebrate. I booked a taxi to take us the 300 yards to the restaurant, as Uncle Harry was in no fit state to walk. Shortly after we arrived, Uncle Harry complained that he was not feeling too well, and that he would call for a taxi to take him home, but we must not let his condition worry us, and to carry on with our celebration. I helped him into the taxi, and gave instructions for the cabbie to take Uncle Harry into his house. I thrust a £20 note, far too much, into his hand to make sure that he did.

We decided to go back to my flat, and make a 'proper' celebration of our engagement, as long as I agreed to take Robin back home the following day. I carefully carried her up the flight of stairs to my flat. I opened a bottle of Champagne that I had been keeping for this special occasion, and we toasted each other and our future. We put our glasses down, and had a long passionate kiss. I took her hand and carried her over to the bed. Robin was nervous , as she told me that her sexual experiences were fairly limited, but if I would be gentle with her, she would consent to us making love. At her request I turned out all of the lights with the street light outside the window delicately illuminating my room. We undressed in the semi dark and as promised I was very tender with her, and helped her over her initial shyness. Our hands caressed each other, slowly at first, as we discovered each others' bodies, and made sensual love. "Wow, that was fantastic, she breathlessly whispered into my ear, let's do it again". The air was charged with a powerful chemistry that I had never experienced before. We had a great night, and we were both utterly exhausted. We eventually slept until mid morning. I slid out of bed, and took Robin into the bathroom. I sat her on a little stool in the shower cubicle, and whilst I was on my knees, we playfully squirted shower gel all over each other, and rubbed it into each others' bodies in a very provocative way. "Stop it, she mocked, you're getting me all excited again. Don't forget that you promised to get me back to Wimbledon this morning". "I haven't forgotten, I said through a soap filled mouth, I just don't want this to end." "It won't, I promise you, she said, but I think that just for now, enough is enough." We dried each other, and both of us reluctantly got dressed. "To be continued", Robin laughed. It took all of my will power to leave our love nest and take Robin back to Wimbledon. I drove ultra carefully, with my very precious passenger on board.

I pulled my battered old Ford Escort Station Wagon onto the circular gravel drive, that had a multitude of tall weeds all clambering for the light. The leaves had started to fall on the un-mown lawn, with the swirling wind scattering them to the four corners of the garden. We went into the house, and Robin called out gently to Uncle Harry, but there was no reply. "He must be sleeping, she said to me. I'll just go and look." Off she scooted over the polished parquet floor, and knocked on the door of his bedroom, which was now on the ground floor, as he certainly couldn't get up the cantilevered stairs anymore. "Uncle Harry, she called, but this time in a louder voice, and rapped on his door. It must have been the brandy, together with all of the excitement that tired him out she said to me. I'm going to go in." She pushed open the door. The room was in total darkness, as the heavy drapes had yet to be drawn. She went over to them, and in a practised hand, pulled the drapes away from the leaded light windows, that had stained glass inserts. The shaft of light acted as if it were a spotlight onto the bed, where Uncle Harry lay on top of it, still dressed in the clothes that he had been wearing yesterday. "Be careful not to wake him too suddenly, I whispered, a shock would be no good to his delicate system". She went to his bedside, and gently rocked him, trying to rouse him, but he just didn't move a muscle. I went over, and tried to feel for a pulse, but I couldn't find one. "Call the ambulance, quickly, I said, but I think that it may be too late to save him."

The ambulance arrived, and to our despair, we were advised that he was dead, and that he had probably died in the night. Tears cascaded down Robin's face. She was totally inconsolable. In effect this was the third parent that she had lost in the past 22 years. "At least he died happy, I tried to console her, in the knowledge that his niece was to be married". "I know, she said through continuous sniffles, but his timing wasn't too great. He would have loved to have walked down the aisle with me". He had suffered a massive heart attack. Uncle Harry had a short service at Queens Road Church, some two weeks later, and was buried in full military uniform, as he had requested, in the family plot in Wimbledon Cemetery in Gap Road. He had no living relatives, apart from Robin, so it was rather surreal that we were the only two people present when they lowered his coffin into the ground.

We agreed to let a few more weeks elapse, before Robin and I started to go through all of his possessions. We went to his desk in the library, and found sheaves of unopened letters, and bills. The letters that were opened had yet to be answered, as he had this habit of putting a large tick through those that we assumed to which he must have replied. There were gas and electricity reminders along with the Council tax and water rates bills, put to one side. Fortunately, he owed nothing to anyone, as we discovered that he paid all of his bills annually. "Do you fancy a cup of something to drink?", Robin asked me, as I pored over the mass of paper in front of me. "Yes please, tea will be fine." She went into the kitchen, and I heard the kettle boiling. "Tea up in one minute" ,she called out. Then I heard the crash. I rushed into the kitchen to find her face down on the floor, with the wheelchair on top of her. The cupboard door was wide open. From my position, it looked like she had stretched too far trying to reach the cups, and had toppled over. I picked her up, and put her back into the wheelchair, as she recovered from her fall. "You're a silly girl, I said, why didn't you call me, and I would have got the cups out for you?" "I didn't want to disturb you, as you were totally engrossed in all the paperwork". I made the tea, and we went back into the library. "I'm feeling very woozy, she said, I think I had better go and lie down. I must be getting a delayed reaction from the shock of Uncle Harry". I took her to her room, and she was asleep in less than a minute. It gave me more time to wade through the papers.

Amongst the clutter, I found a large white sealed envelope with the words 'TO WHOM IT MAY CONCERN, ONLY TO BE OPENED UPON MY DEATH', and was signed Harry Vaughan, and dated only a few weeks ago. I felt that it would be better to wait until Robin was awake, as she was the only living relative that Uncle Harry had.

I was in the library all day, until daylight started to fade, and I switched on the table light. I heard padded footsteps on the parquet floor, and called out "Who's there"? I wasn't expecting anyone, so I picked up the heavy glass paper weight from the desk, and hid behind the door. The door creaked open. I raised the paper weight in my hand above my head, when a little voice that I didn't recognise called out, "It's OK, It's only me". The door opened as far as it could with me hiding behind it. "Where are you Jeff? "The voice said. I revealed myself from behind the door, and STANDING, yes standing in front of me was Robin, speaking in a child's voice. I didn't know what to say first. I was flabbergasted to see Robin standing there unaided, and to hear her speak with a child's voice. "This is some sort of miracle", I yelled, not knowing how to react, and threw my arms around her and held her tight. "I have felt myself getting better daily, since our engagement, and I fell in the kitchen, trying to stand up on my own, she said, but my voice, even I don't recognise it".

I'm going to call your consultant right now", I said, with a huge smile crossing my face. "He won't be there now, and anyway I would like to celebrate, hopefully the start of my recovery, with you." Her voice was getting stronger, all the time, although she had to sit in an armchair as her legs had started to wobble. "I wonder, if the nerves in my back, have been woken up by all of our recent activity in bed, she grinned. Let's go to my room and keep the therapy going, she said with a slow sexy grin." Who was I to deny her the extra exercise?

The following morning, Robin telephoned Mr Schneider , her consultant, and related most of her story to him. "I think that you had better make an appointment, and I can check you, properly. I don't want to get your hopes up too high, as this condition that you are now experiencing, may only be temporary." We managed to get a cancellation, and went to see him in Harley Street later that afternoon. I was very lucky that a disabled parking space was available right outside his consulting rooms. Not wishing to tire Robin out, I insisted that she still use the wheelchair.

"Well now, young lady, you seem to have made remarkable progress since I saw you, Mr Schneider said, when was it,? he looked at his notes, ah yes, 2 months ago". Robin was standing upright unaided, and walked slowly across the carpeted consulting rooms, and sat herself down in an armchair. "Tell me he said, in your opinion, how you believe that this sudden transformation, has taken place. A deep blush formed on her face. "I'm not sure how to put this, she said embarrassedly, but there is no other way, but to tell you exactly how my life has changed over the past few months, and when I first noticed that I was getting some feeling in my lower body". She took a deep breath, and waved her hand at me. "He's really to blame, or should I say congratulate". "How so, said a bemused Mr Schneider, he's not a doctor, is he? "No, she giggled, but his therapy seems to have done the trick. It has been sex, and plenty of it", Robin gleefully blurted out. We've been at it like rabbits, constantly since our engagement, and each day my back seems to be getting better. "Well, if that is a cure, then I for one am all for it, but I'm not sure how 'The Lancet' will be able to report it, he replied with a chuckle. I'll make a detailed investigation on your condition before jumping to any medical conclusions." He carried out a most thorough examination, took x-rays, and declared that whilst at this stage he could not be certain, he was fairly sure that our sexual activity had released the nerves in her back, and in a very short time, Robin would be able to walk properly, but we must not rush her. We thanked him, and made a follow up appointment for 6 months time.

We were elated with the news, and guess what, we celebrated in our now customary way, when we returned to Wimbledon. I stayed at her home, as it was pointless driving backwards and forwards between Kilburn and Wimbledon, as there was so much paperwork to try to sort out. It took me nearly a week to put all of Harry's papers into some sort of order. In all of the excitement from the start, hopefully of Robin's recovery, I had completely forgotten about Uncle Harry's sealed envelope that I had found. "Robin, I called out, as she was busying herself in the kitchen, you had better come in to the library, as there is an envelope for you from Uncle Harry, that he wrote before he died." Robin walked slowly into the library, still with the aid of a silver topped cane, that had belonged to Uncle Harry. "Sit down, over there" I said as I pointed to her favourite chair by the window that overlooked the garden. I sat next to her and she carefully slit open the envelope. She quietly read the letter. "We had better make an appointment with Montagu Littlewood, his solicitor, waving the envelope at me, she told me, and now that his papers are mostly in chronological order, the solicitor can earn his fees, and deal with this". She had gone very pale, and started to cry. "What does it say"? I urgently asked, wrapping my arms around her trying to comfort her. Through quick gulps of air, and tears she said "It is a letter saying that Uncle Harry believes that my father and brother may not have been killed by accident. He goes on to say that he was suspicious at the time, and despite offering the Swiss police an insight into the business dealings of my late father, they largely ignored him. Here, she said, handing the envelope to me, you read it and see what you think."

My first priority was to calm her down. "I'll make us a drink, then I think that it would be prudent if you were to take one of your sedatives, and rest a while". "Good idea, she agreed, with all of the recent events in our lives, I just need to be able to think clearly, and sleep may be the best remedy for now." I also needed time to read the letter again, and try to decide what course of action would be best for Robin to pursue. Uncle Harry had just about mastered the old fashioned typewriter, and thankfully, because his handwriting was so difficult to read, he had painstakingly set out the brief history of Robin's father's business life in type.

Robin's late father was a City 'High Flyer', who had an unequal knack for making money, wheeling and dealing in mega money transactions across the whole of the world, and his real speciality was buying and selling shares on the global stock market. He had a 'nose' and an uncanny way of finding A.I.M. companies with low share values in both technology and mining. He would buy up as many shares as he could for both himself and his clients just before a Company either made a significant discovery or were about to be declared bankrupt. Invariably the investors would break up the assets of these bankrupt companies, into smaller units and sell them for huge profits. The emerging companies would eventually grow into conglomerates, and the shares would be traded at the appropriate time, or if the company became successful would be sold as a going concern. He often quoted a well known economist who said that technology change and visionary entrepreneurs give birth to new things to obliterate old things, only to see those new things obliterated by the next generation. He never remained too long in any one deal, although some of his clients did. His success bought him beautiful homes in London, and Paris. He also had a penthouse apartment in New York as well as his own island in the Caribbean, which was his favourite place on earth. It was here that he found tranquillity, away from his hectic business life. Quite naturally, there were some deals that weren't at all good, and some of his clients, lost money, but overall, most of them took a view, and were very pleased with the way that Hugo Fraser & Partners had conducted business in a very professional way.

There was one case that seemed a huge risk, he recalled, when Hugo had been told that there was the perfect opportunity to make a killing in Hong Kong, in about 1995, two years ahead of the handover of sovereignty to mainland China. His local contact, Chung Li had told him that the new government would put a stop to private redevelopment on the island when the Chinese eventually took power, and the demand for private homes was growing daily. The time to buy land was perfect. Hugo set up a very powerful consortium, including investors from all over the world, and purchased the last waterside site for about two billion American dollars. In order to make the site viable, about 100 wooden shacks, the homes of local fishermen, whose families had been on that part of the site for centuries needed to be acquired, but having secured the vast majority of the site, they just refused to move. No amount of money in the world would change their minds. One night, a bulldozer destroyed all of the remaining shacks, killing 55 fishermen and their entire families. As you can imagine the blame was put firmly at Hugo's door, as the leader of the consortium. It almost caused diplomatic relations between Great Britain and China to be cut off. Hugo always strenuously denied his involvement in any part of the carnage, and instructed his solicitors to issue writs against anyone for defamation of character. The Hong Kong Governor gave explicit instructions to withdraw the planning application, and legally declared the site a memorial park, with no compensation to be paid to the speculators. An absolute fortune was lost, but most of the investors were large institutions that could afford to take a loss. They would just increase the premiums to their own customers next year to recoup their money. There was only one real dissenter, who was a relatively new client, which was later discovered to be the power behind The Human Heart Group, one of the largest gaming operations in Macau. Basically, they had gambled, and lost. It was not good to lose face, whilst 'Mr Teflon' as Hugo was known was relatively unscathed.

Hugo kept a low profile, whilst all the flack was flying around him, and escaped the publicity by taking an enforced break on his holiday island home. Whilst he was out of the Country, someone sent him a parcel bomb to his office, which was unfortunately opened by his secretary, who suffered severe shock as well as first degree burns on her arms and face. Her office was destroyed totally in the blaze that followed. She was lucky to escape with her life. Some months later, his car was hijacked, but fortunately for him, he had cancelled his appointment and was not in the car when the attack took place. His driver, ended up in hospital with delayed concussion, following a beating that he took to his head. Neither of these incidents were reported to the police, as he didn't want any undue publicity at that time. The next attempt to get at him was through his private bank account, as a clever computer hacker had managed to gain access to this account, and left 1 penny in it, just to show that there hadn't been a bank error. The theft was later fully reimbursed via the Bank's insurance policy.

It was at this time that Hugo confided in Harry, his partner, and said he suspected that because of the abortive Hong Kong deal, someone was in his words 'out to get him'. Hugo was a very clever and resourceful man, who had influential contacts at the highest level but as yet had not wanted to call them in. He devised a scheme to fake his own death, that would hopefully put an end to the matter, and with the help of his contacts at the police, put out a story that he was killed in a helicopter crash over the English Channel, and there were no remains. He went to great lengths to protect his identity through plastic surgery and booked into Clinic La Prairie, in Montreux. It was half term, so he decided to take the family to Gstaad, whilst he underwent the surgery. He was driving his Jaguar from Gstaad to the clinic, when the fatal collision occurred, and you know the rest of the story. The body of Robin's brother was flown home and buried at Wimbledon Cemetery. Hugo's body was never found, and the police assumed that it must have been thrown clear of the car into the very deep and inaccessible crevasse. Accidental death was declared by Dr Chen, the Swiss coroner.

I moved onto the next page, and there was a copy of the Will. It was short and sweet. Everything that Harry owned had been left to Robin, and the original will was lodged with his solicitor, Montagu Littlewood, of Walter, Johnson and Littlewood. It was now well past midnight when I had finished reading so I decided not to disturb Robin, as she was in a deep sleep. I climbed the stairs and flopped down on one of the beds in one of the 7 spare bedrooms, but I had a restless night, as my mind wouldn't switch off, as I kept thinking about the contents of Uncle Harry's letter.

We arranged to see the solicitor at the end of the week, and he told us that he would need to have a copy of the death certificate, in order for him to be able to inform all of the relevant parties. "Good morning, he greeted us, please come into my office." Montagu Littlewood was not at all how we had expected him to look. He was a junior partner of this recently formed practice, which was born out of the merger of three local progressive law firms. He was modern and thrusting, and his very manner gave us confidence that he would get things done quickly and efficiently, and not just use the files to sit on. He wore an open neck pink striped shirt with monogrammed initials on the shirt and the cuffs. Smart jeans and a pair of Timberland boots. "Please sit down, he said directing us to the bucket seats by the side of a coffee table, away from his desk. Can I offer you some refreshment"? "Tea would be fine, Robin said, for both of us". He picked up his phone and ordered the drinks. "I'm very sorry to learn of the death of your Uncle, it was such a shock, as I had seen him only a few days earlier to update his Will, and he seemed in fairly good health at that time. I certainly didn't think that I would be dealing with his estate so soon, he said. My sincerest condolences. May I call you Robin and Jeff, it makes it more comfortable, I believe, and you may call me Monty". I looked at Robin, and we both shook our heads in confirmation.

"The whole of Harry Vaughan's estate, which includes the properties in Somerset Road, his country house in Weybridge, the flat in Bournemouth, as well as his many commercial investments have all been left to you Robin. I need to go through all of his papers and files that I have here, as well as those that you have brought with you today. He also left with me full details of his bank accounts, and I can assure you, he said with a smile on his face, that you, young lady shall be very rich and wealthy, once I have proved the will". "Approximately, I asked, how long will that take"? "I don't really know, but I have to get valuations on all of the properties and investments, as well as the magnificent collection of paintings that he took great pleasure in showing me. I suspect that it could take at least 6 months to complete, if I am lucky. I've known large estates to take much longer to resolve, but in this case I hope not". " I don't really like to ask, as it is a sensitive matter, but is there any chance that we might be able to have some money now, as we are both in need of a break, and had hoped to go away somewhere abroad soon", Robin asked. "I know the Bank Manager, where Harry held his many accounts, and I can ask him to release something to you, providing that it is not a huge sum. About how much do you need, £20,000?". "My goodness , no, she said, we only need a small sum say £3,000, any more than that, we shall pay ourselves." "You are being very sensible, why don't you book somewhere and then let me know how much more you will need". "Thank you very much for being so helpful in these difficult times, I said. I can see why Harry chose you to act for him." The meeting lasted for a couple of hours, and Monty told us that he would keep in touch and update Robin when there was anything to report.

"Oh, just before you go, Robin, aren't you forgetting something else?, Monty said in a tantalising way. "No I don't think so", she replied looking somewhat confused. Monty picked up the phone "Please bring in the file on Hugo Fraser." Robin put her hands to her face in astonishment. "How could I forget my own father" she wailed. The file was put in front of Monty, who opened it and pointed to the sheet of paper that was stapled to the inside of it. There were lots of numbers in neat columns and at the bottom underlined in large numerals was a total. "Your late father left a will, when he died, initially leaving everything in equal shares to you and your brother, Monty read. Well, his estate will officially be yours, when you have reached the age of 25. I've been managing it on your behalf, on his instructions. I think that you had better sit down again, because the latest value of his estate is mind blowing". Robin, sat down and held my hand for moral support. "There are so many noughts in the total of assets that he left and has now grown to a staggering figure of...............................the lights blew out as a devastating explosion ripped through the building scattering glass, papers and people in all directions. Robin and I were tossed high in the air. I was unable to move as I crashed down to the floor on top of her. I listened to the roar of the flames all around me . The last thing that I remember was the beating of my heart, getting weaker and weaker, and my painful breathing becoming shallower, and then.......... nothing at all.

CHAPTER TWO

The debris spread across the road, whilst the blast destroyed some of the other properties in the street, killing 1 adult and injuring 6 other innocent people including 2 children, I was told when I eventually came out of my coma, several days later, and my first thought was for Robin. I was in a hospital room, wrapped up in acres of bandage around my head and body, but I could see and still talk. "Where is Robin, I asked, is she alright"? "She was extremely lucky, that your body shielded her from most of the serious blast that was caused by a faulty electrical circuit, and a spark from it ignited the gas supply to the building. She was released from hospital, last week, having recovered from mild concussion, and badly bruised arms and legs. She lost some hair in the fire, but that will grow back shortly. She's been at your bedside, night and day since her recovery, and she has only gone down the corridor to look in on Monty Littlewood to check his progress, which I am afraid is 'touch and go' as the blast had come from directly beneath his desk, and he took the full brunt of it." I forced myself to try to stay awake, as I desperately wanted to see Robin, but the strong pills took me away into the land of nod.

I floated in and out of consciousness during the next 48 hours, and could remember nothing at all during that time. I evidently managed to stay awake long enough to discover that I had only broken my left arm, as well as a few ribs. I had a series of third degree burns all over my body. The injuries were not life threatening, and I was alive. I was trussed up like a Christmas turkey. "When we got you here, Dr Heath told me, you were at death's door. Your heart had stopped for about 10 minutes, but thanks to the paramedics, they managed to get your heart started in the ambulance that brought you here to the Royal London Hospital, where our highly skilled team kept you alive with their expertise, that they had obtained from a similar incident that happened to Fabrice Muamba, the Bolton Wanderers footballer, last year. We have arranged that your burns be treated at your local hospital. You will need to go there on a daily basis to have your dressings changed".

Robin entered my room, and walked steadily over to me, and planted a soft kiss on my sore blistered lips, the only part of my face not enveloped in bandages. "Great to see you alive and well, perhaps not exactly kicking, but with my help, you'll soon be back on your feet" she grinned, or maybe, she said mischievously, you would prefer to be lying in your own bed. She gave me an enormous wink. The great news is that I think that my memory is starting to come back to me, and I have arranged to go to my specialist next week to see if that part of my brain is now functioning properly". I wanted to hug and kiss her, but my bandages restrained me. FANTASTIC, I mumbled, through thick dry lips, but don't you want to wait for me to get out of here to come with you?" "I'm a big girl now, and I think that I am quite capable of taking a taxi on my own. I won't get lost."

A day later I was discharged from the Heart Hospital, and I arranged to go back on a weekly basis to have my heart monitored. The burnt skin on my body had started to respond to treatment and was healing slowly. I was thankful that I wouldn't have to undergo skin grafts, as had first been envisaged. My arm was put into a softer plaster, and I no longer had to wear a sling. My ribs were still very painful, and it didn't help when I developed a dry cough.

I was unable to drive my car, and Robin had never had the opportunity to learn, so we went everywhere by public transport, or if we felt flush we would take a taxi. The enormity of her inheritance had not yet sunk in. "I'm going to go with you, I told Robin, when you go to see Mr Schneider, as I am just as anxious as you to hear his comments about your memory." "It's not Mr Schneider that I shall be seeing, said Robin, but my neurologist, Mrs Abbey, who incidentally has her consulting rooms in the same building as Mr Schneider. I tried to arrange an appointment with her this week, but was told that she is currently away on holiday, and I have made arrangements to see her at the end of next week."

In the meantime, we learnt that sadly, Monty never recovered from his injuries, and died. Naturally, we were very upset, and went to his funeral. After the service we were approached by Edmund Walker, the senior partner of the law practice. He was short in stature, and grossly overweight. His black Crombie overcoat struggled manfully to stay shut with the buttons fighting what looked like a losing battle as several of them had obviously popped off, leaving a shirt full of blubber trying to escape. His round face was a light shade of red, and the thin veins on his nose were very prominent. Under his bowler hat his head was almost bald. Wisps of grey hair grew out of his ears. "A very sad day", he said, as he put out his flabby hand for me to shake. I reluctantly gripped his hand. It felt like a wet slimy fish. "Monty was far too young to die, and he was going to take over from me, when I retired next year, but unfortunately it was not to be, he continued in mournful tones. I know that now is not the right time, but would you be good enough to come to our temporary offices soon, as we still have to resolve the matter of your late father", he told Robin. "I had assumed that all of the records were destroyed in the fire, I replied, so how can we continue without them?" "Fortunately, we always keep back up discs that are kept in a fireproof environment, off the premises, and can be accessed by us on line". "Very sensible. Please let me have details of your new address and phone number, and I shall arrange an appointment". He put his hand into his top pocket, and produced a business card, which had all of the details. The only thing that had changed was the address.

Robin duly kept her appointment with her neurologist. "It's far too early to completely analyse the state of your memory, Mrs Abbey said, but it does appear that the recent accident has helped that part of your brain to reopen, but it may take a very long time before you may, and I cautiously say may, regain your full memory. My advice is for you to go back to the place where you initially lost some of your memory, and see if somewhat familiar surroundings may just jog it back into place. It's a long shot, but I have used this method of recall on other patients of mine with varying degrees of success. What have you got to lose?" "I'm very reluctant to go back to the scene of my worst nightmare, Robin said soulfully, but if you really think that it will help, then with the support of Jeff, I'll do it." "Brave girl, I said, but with me by your side, there is nothing to fear, but fear itself."

"We need to go and see Edmund Walker, but he has taken a few weeks holiday to get over the tragic loss of Monty, and he also needs to recharge his batteries following the destruction of his offices. I have a great idea, I told Robin, why don't we take up Mrs Abbey's suggestion and go to Switzerland, and see if we can persuade the police to re-open their files." "Let's take the train, Robin said, it's more civilised than flying. I'll look up the schedule on the internet right now." Before I could reply, she had made a bee line for her I-pad, and within a few seconds announced, "The Eurostar can take us to Paris where we could stay overnight if we want to, for some retail therapy. We then take the new fast TGV Lyria service that goes to Lausanne, onto Montreux and finally arrive in Gstaad, a really lovely way to travel without hassle". I was all for it, as we would have time on the journey to plot a course of action. "Where shall we stay?", I asked Robin and without hesitation or thought she said "The Gstaad Palace, of course". "You know of it"? , I said, "yes, we always stayed there". Robin and I both stopped dead in our tracks. "Your memory, I shouted at her, it's back". We hugged and jigged up and down. We couldn't believe what Robin had just said. "I wonder whether the hotel will still remember your family visits? I said, , after all it is 13 years since they were last there". "I'll phone them right away and see if, yes I've remembered him also, Andre Scherz is still there. It was a family run business for years.

"Gstaad Palace Hotel, good afternoon, how may we help you"? the telephonist answered. "Is Andre Scherz there please?" "Who shall I say is calling?" He may not remember me, but tell him it's Robin Fraser, my father Hugo always brought us to your hotel to stay with you up to about 12 years ago." "Just connecting you". The line went quiet for a moment, and then the voice that she recognised came on. "Robin, of course I remember you, you were a little minx, always getting in trouble, how could I forget you? His voice went quiet and said how sorry he was when he heard about the loss of her family. "Well, I am now all grown up, and my fiancée and I would love to stay with you, if you have room, next week." "Let me check with my booking clerk, and I'll call you back soon. Please, what is the best number to reach you"? Robin gave him the land line and our two mobile telephone numbers, and then said goodbye. We had already booked our train tickets, as we were going, in any case, so it was only a matter of where we stayed.

The land line rang, and the display showed International Call, so we guessed it would be Andre calling back, and indeed it was. "We have just one De Luxe room that overlooks the beautiful gardens and has spectacular views of the Swiss Alps, and it is available from Monday next. How long would you like to stay?" Robin and I had thought that our initial stay should be for a minimum of 2 weeks, but as Edmund Walker was not going to be available for at least 3 weeks, we said we should take three weeks. "3 weeks please, said Robin". "Just perfect, I look forward to meeting the new you next week. What time will you be arriving at the station?" "The train arrives at 18.09 said Robin". "Fine, I'll send a car to meet you". "Thank you Andre, see you soon". "That's booked, now let's sort out the hotel in Paris".

"What about your hospital appointments ?", Robin asked. "No problem with either of them, but if I need any assistance whilst we are away, they had previously told me that they can make arrangements with the local hospital to see me if necessary. The ointment for the burns, is working well, and I'll take some extra tubes, just in case".

"Come on, slowcoach, we've got a train to catch", I yelled to Robin, who was still in the house, whilst I was waiting and chatting to our taxi driver. "Just coming" she shouted back, I'll only be a moment." "Women, I said, exasperated, give them a minute and they'll take ten" looking at the driver for confirmation of my feelings. His eyebrows shot up in agreement. I had already struggled with our bags. "What in heaven's name goes into them. We men can manage with just a small holdall, whilst they think that they are going to a third world country, and won't be able to buy their usual 'stuff' ". "Here she comes now, he said. I don't mean any offence, but she looks like a million dollars, well worth waiting for, if you ask me."

I locked up the house, and set the newly installed burglar alarm, jumped into the taxi and sped away to the station, to catch the train to Paris, and then on to the George Cinq Hotel in Paris for one night. We dropped off our cases and walked down Rue St-Honore, and mainly window shopped, but Robin was tempted and bought a huge soft cuddly white dog, with a red and black chequered beret on its head. We were due to visit The Louvre, and didn't have too much time to shop. We recognised many of the pictures in The Louvre and agreed that Uncle Harry's collection would not be out of place here. We were quite tired, and went back to the hotel to relax, before taking the Bateaux Mouche along the River Seine for a moonlight and romantic evening. The meal was excellent. We danced until we dropped. My skin was still raw, and just holding onto Robin was an effort.

The next morning, after a typical French breakfast, of hot chocolate with tartines, which are slices of baguette spread with jam, we boarded the TVG high speed train to Gstaad, and had about 6 hours to work out a plan of action for our stay in Switzerland. The train stopped in Lausanne, Montreux, and finally Gstaad, where a chauffeur driven limousine was waiting, to take us on the short journey to the hotel. Awaiting our arrival, in the Reception was Andre, and when he saw us, came forward and took Robin's hand and kissed it, before she planted a kiss on each of his cheeks in the French style. They were both beaming. "My, how you have grown, he said, you, if I may say so have grown into a most beautiful woman." "Thank you, she replied. Let me introduce my fiancée, Jeff." A firm handshake passed between the two of us. "I have your room ready for you, and your luggage has already been taken to it, so relax, and enjoy your stay with us". The porter took us to a most fabulous room, designed in a modern classic French style, with the centre piece being the four poster draped double bed, we assumed to be a replica of Louis XV1, only to be told that it was in fact a genuine antique, although the mattress was relatively new. We unpacked the cases, and took a long shower, before dressing and going to dinner.

CHAPTER THREE

Our first port of call, in the morning was to go to the offices of Gstaad Life, the local newspaper to read reports of the accident, some 13 years earlier. There was nothing in them that we didn't already know, which I suppose was unsurprising, but there may have just been something that the crash investigators had missed, but there wasn't. We had telephoned the Gendarmerie Nationale and requested a meeting, but there was no one available until tomorrow. We had the afternoon free, and so we decided to take a taxi to the scene of the accident, and see, if by just being there, it helped in the reconstruction of Robin's memory.

The road was now a dual carriageway, and a lay-by had been created, to take in the view of the Alps, right on the bend of the road where Robin thought that the accident had occurred. The taxi pulled over, we got out and just starred at the crevasse which must have been at least a mile deep. I held Robin's hand, as she was trembling, not with the cold, but obviously with the memory coming back to her of that fateful day. "This is the spot, she said, right here where the collision took place, but I have no recall of what happened once the other car had veered off after crashing into us. I can remember my father screaming that some idiot was on the wrong side of the road, as he tried to avoid the collision, but hard as he tried there was no escape." She was now almost in a trance, desperately trying, in her mind's eye, to remember the events that followed.

We sat down on the bench, in complete silence, the only movement we saw was the cigarette smoke that came from our driver that floated past us in the light wind. We must have sat for 10 minutes when she suddenly jumped up and in a very excited voice said, "I remember". Then she slumped down again onto the bench crying her eyes out. "What do you remember?, I gently asked her . "It was right there in the front of my memory and on the tip of my tongue, then it just disappeared, she sobbed. It was within touching distance." "That's enough for one day, I said, let's go back to the hotel, and we shall come here again tomorrow, after we have seen the Police". I led her back to the taxi, holding her as tight as my burns would allow, and returned to the hotel. It had been a very traumatic experience for her.

The Gendarme, Officer Leroux, called into our hotel as arranged, and went through all of the records, but there was absolutely nothing to point towards anything other than an accident, and no new evidence had surfaced in the intervening years. Once again, it was unsurprising. However, the policeman gave us a list of 19 people and their addresses who had been interviewed at the time of the incident, and we were welcome to see if any of them could help. We thanked him, and he left us with our thoughts. We had planned to telephone them, first, but decided not to, as we wanted to surprise them, leaving them no time to think of a reason not to see us. " Why don't I see if the concierge can help us plan a route, I said, as it will save us criss- crossing our route, and save time". I gave him the list of addresses, and he told me that two houses were no longer there, as they had been demolished to allow the new dual carriageway to be built. "I will check with the Mayor's office and see if they stayed in the area or have moved on to a different district ", he said. A little later, he advised the new addresses, and very efficiently had outlined the route in red on a map that he handed to us. The relevant houses were circled and numbered to correspond with the police list. "On a good day, the concierge said, it will probably take about two hours to drive to all of them, but if you manage to speak with any of the potential witnesses you should probably allow at least half an hour per visit, on top". Although there were 19 names on the list, there were only 4 properties that we needed to visit.

"Best to start tomorrow, I said to Robin, when I returned to our room, but I think that it would be a good idea if we go back to the scene of the accident, and hopefully, the name on the tip of your tongue will jump out". Our driver who was the same man as yesterday, collected us and drove slowly up the mountain, where he parked in the lay-by. "Robin, I said, if you are up to it, why don't we walk down the mountain road for say about half a mile to that bend in the road, I pointed out, and see if the walk can jog your memory. Let's go." We walked quite quickly down to the spot that I had pointed out, and then deliberately took our time walking back, step by step, pausing a few times on the way up the mountain. When we stopped, Robin stared across the lower hills and mountain, willing her memory to click into gear, but no such luck. "At least, we have had a nice walk, and taken in the fresh air and wonderful scenery, and perhaps, although not today, something will, hopefully release the block in your long term memory bank soon", I said encouragingly. "I hope that you are right, she replied, because right now, it still remains a complete blank. Maybe if and when we meet the people on the list.................." she left the rest of the sentence unspoken.

We went back to our room in the hotel, by which time she had cheered up a little. "How are your ribs healing?" she asked with a glint in her eyes. "They are improving daily, I said, but they are still quite sore, as are the burns on my body, but if you are thinking what I hope you are thinking, then I think that I am fit enough for some more indoor exercises", I grinned. "Using one of the first sayings that you said to me in similar circumstances, I'll be very gentle with you", she laughed, as she carefully wrestled me onto the bed. "I'm glad to see you laugh again, as I am sure that you, and I have been so pre-occupied with the crash, a little bit of 'Rumpy Pumpy won't go amiss". She carefully removed all of our clothes, and we made love very slowly and amorously. "The ointment for your burns, has really turned me on, she said, it's helped to smooth the way. We must use it again, even when the burns heal, she giggled from beneath the rumpled bed clothes. We stayed in bed the rest of the day, and called down for room service to deliver a meal, which we ate hurriedly, dressed only in the hotel bathrobes, which were soon discarded once the meal had been eaten, as we got back to the main business of devouring each other.

In the morning, the same taxi driver, who we discovered was called Claude, met us as arranged at 9.00, and armed with our route map took us to our first destination, where we had hoped to meet a potential witness. He pulled up outside a modern looking brick built chalet, and on the first ring of the door bell, the door was opened by an elderly man, who looked like an under nourished scarecrow, with his wild long hair going in all directions, as if he had been pulled through a haystack backwards. He spoke no English, and both Robin and I were very rusty in French, and German, let alone a strange Swiss dialect. Claude came to our rescue, and he acted as our translator. Claude found out that there were four other people who lived in the house, but none of them had anything further to add to the statements that they had given to the police, some time ago. I was not really satisfied that he was talking for the other people, and I made a note that if we didn't get any further from any of the other witnesses, I would re-visit, and speak to the other occupants of this house.

We thanked him, and made our way to the next property on our list.

"There it is", said Claude, pointing at a rather shabby looking house. We approached it via a grass pathway and knocked on the door. No one answered, so we knocked again. This time a voice called out, and we at least got the gist of it, asking us to wait a minute. An upstairs window swung open with a creek. "Who are you and what do you want?, an Asian looking lady called out in French. Rather than use our rusty language skills, Claude explained to her why we were there. She listened, and agreed to let us come in. I took a careful look at the building, and was amazed that a strong gust of wind hadn't blown it down. It was rickety and looked like it would topple over, if anyone moved too violently. I looked through the rear cracked picture window, and saw the full extent of the land that it was sitting on, with a superb vista towards the spectacular mountain behind it. The site was ideal for property developers to build a small estate of houses on it, I thought. She walked down the stairs dressed in a long black kaftan, with a hijab covering most of her face.

"Sorry, she said, I had assumed that you were yet another of those blasted property speculators, coming to offer me vast fortunes to move, but, how do you English say?, there isn't a snowball's chance in hell that I would sell, whilst I'm still alive, she said in no uncertain terms. "My family has lived here for nearly 40 years, and the only way that I shall leave this house will be in a long wooden box". Claude asked her the list of questions that we had prepared, but yet again, we learnt nothing new from her. "How about the rest of your family?", she was asked. "The only one that may be able to help you is my son Abdul Haq, who was out on the mountainside that day, tending to the herd. He told me that he thinks that he saw something, but the police didn't think that it was important, and they never even interviewed him." "Can we talk to him, ourselves"? "He'll be back here tomorrow, and if you think what he saw could be important, then I shall make certain that he is here to see you, at let's say mid-day". "That will be perfect", Claude replied on our behalf. When we returned to the taxi, we put a red circle around Abdul's name and wrote MID DAY TOMORROW next to it. "That makes 9 of the 19 names on the list, only 10 to go", I said. We stopped, en route to the third house, for a short break and grabbed a coffee with light snack.

The next house was down in the valley, but there was no one at home. The name on the post box outside the front gate was displayed as H. Petersen. "Maybe, although we didn't really want to contact him by phone, it would be prudent to see if he has a telephone number listed in the directory, and make an appointment to see him, I suggested. Let's check, when we get back to the hotel, although we could always try and find him, using your I-pad. Only one more place to visit today, let's hope that we strike gold there."

The last house on the list proved very hard to find, and we missed the narrow turn off twice, before eventually the taxi turned onto an unmade track, along which the taxi rumbled to a halt in front of it. It looked unoccupied, but I saw a curtain move, as we got out of the taxi. A young woman answered the door, and told us that she and her family had moved in the house about 3 years ago, and when Claude enquired about a forwarding address, she told him "Yes I do have one, but I'm not quite sure where I have put it, as they don't seem to get any mail these days. I'll try and locate it, but I don't have much time today, would you leave a contact number, and I will call you when I find it." I doubted very much that she would bother.

"Not a complete waste of a day, I said when we arrived back at the Hotel. One out of 15 is better than none out of fifteen. There is still an outside chance that Abdul may have something more to tell us". We found a telephone number for H. Petersen, and called it, but it went straight onto an answer service. There was no point in trying to leave a message, so I decided to call back later, which I did, and the phone was answered almost at once. "Helga Peterson". I didn't expect a woman's voice, as I had imagined that the H would be a man. "Hello, I said, do you speak English?" "Of course I do, how may I be of assistance?" I quickly related the story about the accident to her. "Ar zow, I remember it well, but I am sorry that I have no new evidence that can help you". "What about your family? I asked. "I'm afraid that I am the only one left, following the disaster with the avalanche some years ago, my whole family perished, and I was fortunate to get out with my life." I apologised and gave her our condolences, and said goodbye.

"The trail, looks like it ends here, I told Robin, when I got off the phone, and related my conversation. Our only real hope is Abdul". "Or the other people at the first house", Robin reminded me. "Let's go back to the first house, first thing in the morning, I suggested, as we may catch them totally unaware, I replied, and then onto what appears to be our last hope, Abdul". Neither of us slept well that night in hopeful anticipation of the revelations that we might discover tomorrow.

We took our usual taxi back to the first house, and as we suspected, arrived just in time, as four people were about to get into their car. Claude parked across the drive, slightly blocking them in, just in case they didn't want to speak to us. Claude went through the motions, and they knew why we were there, but they only confirmed what the old man had told us yesterday, that they had nothing new to add. We apologised for stopping them leaving the house, and moved the taxi aside to let them pass. "I've a feeling, I said, that they are not being completely truthful, and they are hiding something, although I'm not sure what it is". "I don't get those vibes, replied Robin, but if you have a hunch, why don't you speak to Officer Leroux?" "He'll just laugh at me without any concrete evidence. I shall reserve our position, until we speak to our one and only hope."

Claude suggested that as we had about 2 and a half hours to 'kill', he would take us up the mountain to the lovely little cafe where we could enjoy the views, as well as the wondrous hot chocolate, served in a conical mug. " The thick syrupy drink tastes like a liquid truffle , and is served with fresh croissants. I know it's not the really the start of the day, but it makes a perfect way to start the rest of the day, " he said almost salivating. He drove to Marta's, which was a great place to fully appreciate the stunning views of the skiers skilfully making their way down the slopes. With the sun shimmering off the snow, we had to put on our sun glasses to keep the glare away. We managed to get a table on the terrace, and for the first time in days, we started to unwind. We could have just sat there all day. "I've an idea, said Robin, you have got the telephone number of Abduls' mother, haven't you?" "Yes I have". "Why don't you phone her and suggest that we send Claude down to collect Abdul , and we can have the meeting here, and buy him lunch". "What a great idea, I'll call her now". It only took a few moments to organise and we sent Claude to collect him, while we continued to enjoy the views, and a second mug of hot chocolate.

Abdul joined us on the terrace about 20 minutes later. I put his age as being about the same as us. Bright intelligent eyes on a suntanned face, or was it his natural colour, it was hard to tell. He had thick, slicked down black hair. He wore a waterproof jacket and blue denim jeans. He was very businesslike, and I thought that he may still be at university. We made the usual introductions. He ordered omelette and chips. "I know why you want to talk to me, he said, as my mother has told me about your visit to her yesterday, and maybe I shall be able to help, but I'm not certain." "In your own time, I suggested, tell us what you know, but don't let you lunch get cold". "Well, he said, I do remember that particular day, as it was my turn to look after the sheep . I had started early, as it was my half day off from school. I didn't need to be in class until about 2pm. He wolfed down another mouthful of chips. It was sometime around 11.00. I recall checking my watch at that time, just to be certain that I still had plenty of time to get home and get to school, when I recovered two of the herd that had wandered off from the pack. I heard a terrific bang, and instinctively looked up to where I believe that the noise had come from. Another fork full of omelette was shovelled into his mouth. His table manners were not very good, but what the hell, he was giving us his story. He continued. I realised that there must have been a car crash on the dangerous bend in the road. I was far too far away to be able to help, but I used my mobile phone immediately to alert the police of what I had just heard. Abdul had cleared his plate of food in no time at all. "Want anything else?, I enquired". " Just some fresh fruit, and a mug of hot chocolate please", he said. He continued. It was then that I saw movement from the area of the accident, and it looked like a man tumbling down the mountain side into the crevasse. I never saw the figure again. I had assumed that anyone falling into that crevasse, would have no chance of survival. I heard a car start up, and drive away, and that is all that I know. I told the police, but nothing further happened, until you contacted us yesterday."

His fresh fruit and hot chocolate arrived, whilst we considered what he had said. "The person falling down the mountain, was it large or small? I asked. "Couldn't really tell, he said, as I was so far away, but if you want my opinion, it certainly looked like a well built man. "Were there any traces of clothing that may have snagged on the way down?" I asked. "I don't know, that is for the police investigation team to answer", he said. "Have you any idea what is at the bottom of the crevasse, and could it be accessible, now?" "The answer to your first question is that no one has ever been to the very bottom, and I believe that the only access would be via an experienced rock climber. Once again you should enquire whether the police ever sent anyone down there. If you need someone to go down there now, my tutor at University is part of the mountain rescue team, and I am sure that he would be willing to investigate on your behalf. Please let me know. " He scribbled his mobile number on a serviette. "Thanks for lunch, any chance of a lift back home"?

"Certainly, we are all leaving now, so it is no problem", I said.

"All of this detective work is making me very tired, and there is very little hope that we shall find anything meaningful", Robin resignedly told me. "Don't be so negative, it's not at all like you, I replied with more enthusiasm than I actually felt, I'm going to adopt Mr Macawber's optimism 'That something will turn up' . How about an early night, as I can tell that you are absolutely shattered?" "I'm not too shattered, that our regular little indoor games be postponed", she coyly replied. "You're just over sexed, I teased, as I tenderly pushed her onto the bed. This is one game that won't be abandoned."

"Officer Leroux", he announced as he picked up my call the next morning. "Good morning officer, this is Jeff Thorn, and I have Robin listening on loudspeaker. We met Abdul Haq yesterday, and he suggested that we ask you if anybody had been to the bottom of the crevasse, just after the accident happened". "Let me open the file, which I just happen to have in front of me, and check. Can you hold on?" A few minutes later after listening to the pages being turned over, he came back to the phone. "At the time of the accident there was a gale blowing and it was far too dangerous to ask any of the mountain rescue team to go down there as you know the crevasse is at least 1500 metres deep, and there was no way that we were going to risk it. The physical inspection was overlooked, as we could see that there was no way in this world that anyone would still be alive, and so we didn't bother. We just assumed that it was Hugo Fraser. The only living relative was an eight year old girl in a life threatening condition, and our main concern at the time was for her, and also to try to find the driver of the other car." "I know that at least 13 years have elapsed, but we would be happy to pay for someone to have a thorough inspection, I said." "The Red Tape from our end would take months to get through, he said, I would suggest that you arrange for someone to go down and see if there are any human remains, or indeed evidence of clothing. Should you find anything, then I am certain that the file could be reopened immediately".

I telephoned the mobile phone number for Abdul, and left a message asking him to call me back, when he was free, as I wanted to contact his tutor, to see if he would be willing to help a damsel in distress. He didn't call me back, but Pierre Gomez did, and introduced himself as Abdul's tutor, and he would be pleased to help, over the weekend, when the University had no lectures. We arranged to meet on Saturday at 9.00 and he brought with him, his team of mountaineers, and two of them slowly descended into the abyss below, taking care not to snag their ropes on any overhanging obstacles. He gave us a radio transmitter and receiver, so that we could listen to any progress that they made. It seemed like hours, but eventually the radio cracked into life. "We have found a collection of bones, and what looks

like part of a shirt attached to one of the bones, he said, but the interesting thing is that on the tattered material there was a gold cuff link." My heart started to race, but I didn't mention all of it to Robin, as at this stage there was nothing concrete about the discovery.
"They've found some bones, which may or may not be human, and some tattered cloth, that may belong to the bones, but until they have been verified, we don't have very much to go on, but it is something that the experts can deal with." The two climbers returned to the top of the crevasse, and handed us the bones and material, that they had wrapped in plastic bags. "We are most grateful for your help today, I said, how much do we owe you"? "Nothing, he said, as we used this as part of our training exercise". "But I must give you something, even a donation to the Mountain Rescue Team," I insisted. "Very well, I shall get a donation form dropped into you at the hotel."

We called Officer Leroux, and asked if he would be good enough to meet us back at the hotel, where we would be able to hand over some evidence. Whilst waiting for him, I looked at the cuff link, and sure enough the engraving on it was not AV or HY as first thought on the link found at the scene of the crash but HV. I told Robin of my discovery and she was shocked to think that I had thought of Uncle Harry, being the only HV that we knew . "Those bones most certainly are not Uncle Harry, as he had only just died, and the accident took place some 13 years ago" she scolded me. "Very strange, I thought, but of course there must be hundreds of people visiting Switzerland every year with the initials HV." "Only a DNA test will prove that it was not Uncle Harry, she said, but let's leave it up to the pathologists to find out."

"The only way that we can be certain that it is not your uncle, Officer Leroux told us, is for the Swiss Police to obtain permission from The British Ministry of Justice to exhume the body, and test match it against our findings here, It normally takes about 20 days to process and obtain consent, in conjunction with the Local Authority in which the grave is situated". "Must we disturb Uncle Harry, sobbed Robin, why don't we let him rest in peace"? "I know how difficult this is for you, but we are very close to solving the mystery, if indeed the DNA matches," I placated Robin. We subsequently found out that the bones were human, and the pathologists managed to obtain a DNA sample from the tattered cloth, and just to be certain they wanted to compare it with the DNA from Uncle Harry.

We returned to England, and made the necessary application to have the remains of Harry Vaughan exhumed, and subsequently received permission. Robin did not want to go to the graveside, so I went in her place and met a team of police pathologists, who had already erected a tent around it. The coffin was opened and a few samples were taken from the bones, and some hair follicles, and went to the laboratory for testing, against the DNA found on the tattered shirt found in Switzerland. "Unfortunately they were not a match, but it seemed rather a strange coincidence that cuff links with Harry's initials were found at both the scene of the crash, and also at the bottom of the crevasse," I said. "I told you that we should have let poor Uncle Harry rest in peace", Robin complained . There was no way that they would match, as it was my father's remains that we had hoped to find. "Maybe the evidence that was found in Switzerland should have been compared with your DNA, Robin, I suddenly realised. We've been barking up the wrong tree, being confused by the cuff links".

"I've got it" screamed Robin. My memory it's back she yelled. The man that I called Uncle Harry was not my real uncle, but my dad's business partner, and I remember him coming with us to Gstaad at my father's request, in order for him to be able to drive all of us back home, after dad's operation. I can see it clearly now, he drove a blue Mercedes, and I recall that he was coming to meet us, when his car went out of control, having hit an ice patch that was hard to see on the gunmetal coloured road. The two cars collided, and my dad jumped out of our car to help Harry, who was slumped over the steering wheel. I saw my dad pull Harry to the side of the road, shouting and screaming that Harry was dead. My dad, quickly pulled out of Harry's pockets various documents, and placed his own papers on the dead body, and I saw him push Harry into the crevasse. I then passed out, and I have had no recall of it since." She was crying her eyes out and her body was shaking uncontrollably in realisation of what her father had done at the scene of the crash.

I eventually managed to control her tears and near hysteria. "Your father was a very resourceful man, I said, and he must have thought that the crash was a perfect opportunity for him to swap documents, and hopefully change his identity, in one fell swoop to get away from his pursuers, as was written in the letter that 'UNCLE HARRY' had left for you." "I do remember, said a still tearful Robin, that some people confused the two of them, as they did look somewhat similar, but with my accident and loss of memory, it never really occurred to me until you mentioned it, just now. "Then who's the body in the grave of Uncle Harry?"

EPILOGUE

We arranged a meeting with Edmund Walker upon his return to England, about a month after the funeral. He confirmed to us that he had been fully aware of Hugo's change of identity, but using his Solicitor to Client confidentiality, could never disclose any details, as he was sworn to secrecy. Not even Edmund Walker's partners knew of the deception. Robin told him her version of the accident. However, he had no idea that Hugo had pushed the dead body of Harry into the crevasse, because if had known, he would have had to advise the authorities. The secret could only be revealed upon the death of the person known as................. HARRY VAUGHAN.

THE INTERVIEW

'The word SPY says it all. Covert surveillance, high speed car chases, exotic locations, beautiful women. Shoot outs in casinos. We all know what spies do, don't we?'

These were the enticing words in the newspaper advert that had attracted Phil Brown to see if he had the credentials to be the next James Bond. After all, he had just finished at Birmingham University with first class honours, and there was nothing on the job market that had appealed to his sense of adventure. He was resilient, and resourceful, and very intelligent. He had drive and imagination. He had studied Politics and spoke 6 foreign languages fluently. 6'7" tall, he had captained the successful university rugby team that had swept away all opposition before them. He was built, as the saying goes like a brick shit house. Wasps Rugby Club, had offered him a trial, last season, but a serious knee injury had put paid to that, and he didn't really want to be a professional rugby player for just a few years, as action NOW, was his real goal.

He sat in front of his laptop, and downloaded the application form from The Secret Intelligence Service, also known as MI 6. He looked at it with disdain. It would take at least 6 weeks to process, but he completed it nonetheless. I'm a doer, not a form filler. I'm going to take the bull by the horns and go directly to the Headquarters at Vauxhall Cross, and make myself known to them, he thought. He first of all checked his facts, of whom he should be meeting, and also who was the personal assistant to the boss. He carefully, mocked up a cleverly faked e-mail reply to his application, and printed it out.

He meticulously planned his journey from Derby to London, noting the times of trains and connections needed to arrive first thing in the morning, hoping to catch the MI 6 off guard, and bluff his way in to see someone that could fast track him. 'A good test for my cunning and ingenuity , he thought. If I can get in, it will be a real feather in my cap, that will go a long way to showing them how resourceful I am'.

Arriving in London on the 08.06 train, he took the underground to Vauxhall, crossed the extremely busy road by subway and arrived at MI 6 Headquarters at 9.00. "I've an appointment at 9.30 with Carew Faulks, the head of Intelligence", announced Phil, as he reached the reception desk, smiling sweetly at the bespectacled middle aged lady, whose name was Veronica, which was printed on the label attached to her breast pocket.   "Who did you say you are?", she enquired. "Phil Brown, I sent my application form to him last month and received an e-mail reply from Cindy Lovall, his PA advising that I should be here at 9.30, today, but I am a little bit early" he bluffed. "I've no record of this appointment, she said, looking up and down the long list of appointments scheduled for today, but you may be lucky, as the appointment due for 8.30 has yet to arrive. I'll see if I can slot you in." Veronica buzzed the intercom to Cindy. "I've a Phil Brown in reception, saying that he has an appointment with Mr Faulks at 9.30, but I have no record of it on my computer." "Neither have I", Cindy replied. "The appointment that is on my list for 8.30 has not turned up, could we put in Mr Brown instead?, Veronica asked. You know how impatient and grumpy old Carew is, when he has a busy schedule, I'm sure that he won't mind". "Let me ask him, and I'll get right back to you".

"What is the normal procedure for the interview", he asked. "What happens is that at your appointed time, Cindy will see you first, and take down all of your personal details, that are not on the application form, and hand them on to Mr Faulks. You will then see him", replied Veronica. "Approximately how long shall I be with him?" "That depends on him. I've known some to be as short as 10 minutes and others longer than an hour."

"We're just checking if Mr Faulks can fit you in just now. Have you got your application form with you?" "Naturally, he replied, I always keep a hard copy of anything that is important". The intercom on the reception desk rang. "Veronica speaking". "This is most unusual, said Cindy, but we just can't find any application form from a Mr Brown, does he have a copy of it with him? "Not only does he have a copy of it, he has also a copy of a reply from your office, confirming the appointment". "Mr Faulks is not at all happy, but if you send it up to me, I will get security to do a quick check, and if everything is above board, we shall see him at 9.30. Please tell him to wait".

"Very unusual, but security are doing a basic background check on you, and if they are happy, you will be seen at about 9.30 this morning. Take a seat, and I shall call you when the check has been finalised. You can get a drink, if you wish from the dispenser, over there", she said pointing at the machine, hidden in the corner. Phil took advantage, and after reading the very complicated instructions, selected the button marked TEA, placed the plastic cup under the spout, and inserted a pound coin into the slot. It immediately rattled through the machine and dropped with a clunk into the rejected coin compartment. He tried again, with the same result. He found a different pound coin in his pocket, and tried again, and was successful this time as the hot steaming brown liquid dribbled and spluttered into the cup.

About 20 minutes later, the door of lift number 3 slid open with a soft hiss, and a very attractive, long legged young lady stepped out and strode towards Phil. She was wearing a black pencil skirt, and a white blouse with three buttons undone. Liquid eyes, and a shy smile. " I'm not trying to embarrass you, but I can't seem to see your name tag on your chest, he said, that's why I keep staring at you". "I'm Cindy," she said, turning a deep shade of red, and blushing. "I really can't understand what has happened to our system, this morning, as not only has our internal computers not recognised your application form, but our security division has no record of you whatsoever. Unfortunately, until security has cleared you, we can't allow you access into the building ."

Feigning shock, Phil replied "I gave my application to Veronica at reception, together with a reply from your office confirming my appointment, surely that has to be good enough, doesn't it?" " I'm afraid not, and unless security give you clearance, you can't come in." She turned sharply, heading back for the lift. "Please, he pleaded, I can wait here all day if necessary, whilst more checks on me are carried out. Cindy chose to ignore his pleas, and entered the lift. Phil watched the light panel above it indicating the lift's progress to the second floor, where it stopped, before returning empty to the ground floor. He had no option, but to leave the building, but before doing so, asked Veronica, if she would be good enough to photocopy his application form, and place the original in front of the right person for normal clearance. She agreed to do this. 'Not a complete waste of £65 that I paid for the open ended return train journey, he said to himself, thank goodness that I can still use my student rail card for a few more weeks yet.' He looked towards, Big Ben, and saw that it was not quite 10.00 and despite all of his bravado, he just could not get into the building.

His first thoughts were not to waste the day, as he had originally planned to leave London late in the afternoon. He scrolled though his list of contacts on his phone and punched in Bob's number. "Phil !, Bob , answered the phone, how the devil are you"? "Even better now that I hear those dulcet tones, said Phil. I'm in London today, and am at a bit of a loose end, are you free?" Not during the day, as I've got a part time job at Harrods. Don't finish till 5.00. I'm meeting some of the gang from Uni later today over a pint or three at the Elephant and Castle, why don't you join us"? "What time"? "We are thinking of meeting at about 7.30, and then going on to a club, up West." "Let me cogitate on that, and I'll call you back." No need to, you'll either be there or not" said Bob, in his usual cheerful way.

Phil picked up a copy of the free Metro newspaper, and saw that the new James Bond film, how appropriate he thought, Skyfall, was showing at The Odeon, Leicester Square, and made an instant decision, to go to the Cinema after a tour of the State Rooms at Buckingham Palace, as he had missed the tour the last time that he was here. If his mood was good, he would meet the gang later, and try to cadge a bed for the night from one of them. Apart from the early morning hiccup, he was determined to enjoy his unexpected extra time in London.

"I had a great time today, he told Bob, John, Russ, and Dan, over a pint of beer, when they all met up later that evening, at The Elephant and Castle by Vauxhall Cross. Nearly didn't make it, as there was a delay on the underground, and we were all evacuated from the station at Leicester Square, due to a fire, and had to wait in a long line to get three buses to get here, but you know me, once I have a bee in my bonnet, nothing will stop me." "What did you do this morning, asked Russ?" "I went for a job interview, only it never happened, but one of the pre-requisites is that I am sworn to secrecy and I must not discuss it with anyone yet." "Sounds a bit cloak and dagger if you ask me, chuckled Dan, are you applying for 'M's job"? "Don't be daft, a) I'm not old enough, and b) I'm no lady!" Phil realised just how close they were to hitting upon the truth.

"We're going on from here to Stringfellows in Covent Garden and have a table booked for 10.30, said Bob. Phil, are you joining us?" " I will if I can doss down with one of you tonight, unless I get lucky and pull", he answered. "I've got space on my floor, if that's OK with you, said Russ, and I'm quite close to Euston, which should suit you. Here's the address and my phone number, should you need it." "Thanks pal, let's go and party". They all clambered into a taxi, and whilst the driver told them that he was not licensed to take more than 4 passengers, he would turn off the 'FOR HIRE' sign, and the meter, just in case he was stopped by the police, but would charge them £35 straight fee. They accepted happily, if slightly drunk, after all it was only seven quid each. A bargain.

"I've just come from here, announced Phil, in a loud slurry voice, looking towards Leicester Square. I saw that James Bond film wasn't it exciting?" "Boring, boring chorused the group, we're from London, don't you know, and most of you local yokels ain't gonna see it just yet", they laughed. You were lucky to get tickets." They tumbled out of the cab and gave the driver 2 crisp £20 notes. "Keep the change, you bandit", one of them shouted. On slightly unsteady legs, they went past the doorman outside the club, and were directed to their table, by their hostess. "I've got you a great table, she said, right at the front of the dance floor, and if there is anything, legal, that you want,... then don't ask me. Oh I almost forgot, she said, we have a few Hen Parties coming in later", she smiled in that knowing way.

"Let's set up a tab, behind the bar, and we can settle up later" said Bob. "I've got a better idea said Phil, why don't we put £200 behind the bar now, whilst we are still fairly sober, and sort it out later?" "£200 won't get us very far at these prices said Dan, I suggest that £400 would be more appropriate". They all fished into their wallets, put £80 cash each into the kitty, and hoped that would be enough money to cover the cost of their evening's entertainment.

It wasn't too long before a cackling, screeching crowd of girls descended into the basement area, where the dance floor and bar were situated, and the noise was a raucous babble of laughter, music and screaming. Conversation, could only be made, either outside, or when the slow smoochy music was being played.

Everyone was having a ball, letting their hair down and gyrating to some fantastic sexy music.

Through the dark misty haze, Phil squinted across the floor and was sure that the girl in the long figure hugging diaphanous blue dress was someone he knew. The curvaceous body was emphasised by the tightly fitted dress that didn't leave much to the imagination. Her elegant walk, in her diamonte stiletto high heels made her look like an Egyptian goddess the way she glided across the floor towards him. She had long flowing jet black hair that just about covered the ample cleavage peeping out provocatively from the satin dress. "Don't I know you? he spluttered, taken aback by her beauty, I know that you will think that this is a 'come on' line, but haven't we met somewhere before, perhaps in another life?" She wafted on by him, towards the bar, completely ignoring him. Phil staggered to his feet, regretting the amount of liquor that he had already drunk. "I'm sorry, but I'm sure that I know you from somewhere, he began, a lovely creature like you would never ever be forgotten. Let me buy you a drink". "No thank you, I've just about had my limit for tonight, and anyway I'm with that party over there, pointing at the unruly mob of girls, totally legless. I'm here on a Hen Night, and I wouldn't wish to upset the bride to be". "At least, let me ask your name, and if you would be willing to meet me for a quiet drink sometime, I would be very happy to be your host." "I'm sorry, she said, but I don't usually agree to go out with just anyone, especially, a total stranger. For all I know you could be related to Jack the Ripper."

She turned away from him, but he was determined not to let her out of his sight. "Did you see her, he said to his mates, with his tongue hanging out, what a stunner. Have any of you seen her before"? "I think that I might have, said Russ. I'm not meant to say this, but I am sure that she is the same person that I met when I went for an interview recently".

The penny suddenly dropped. Of course, Phil realised, 'I knew that I knew her'. He strode confidently over to her. "You're Cindy, aren't you? Sorry but I didn't recognize you......... without your clothes on. "She smacked him hard on his face, and with a huge grin said, "Well, I suppose that was an unusual way to break the ice. "You're Phil, quite a chancer aren't you"? "Guilty as charged" he replied.

"My girl friends just can't hold their drink. Just look at them cavorting around like a bunch of wild animals. I'm going upstairs to arrange taxis for them. I'll be back. Don't you dare go away." "I'm not leaving your side, said Phil, now that I have found you, there is no way that I'm going to let you out of my sight."

It took about 15 minutes to bundle the girls, loaded with drink, balloons, and presents, into the waiting taxis. "Shall we stay here, or would you prefer to go somewhere quieter? Phil asked, as it would be such a shame to waste what could turn out to be a fantastic evening." "What do you have in mind?" "I know a little place, just off the Kings Road, much quieter, that stays open late on a Friday night, and is very discrete. We could go there if you like", Phil said. "Is it Embargo 59"? Cindy asked. "Yes it is, how do you know it?" "It's one of my favourite places, and I know the owner very well, and she will get us a quiet table on the roof terrace. "I'll call her now and tell her that we will be with them in about 20 minutes".

"Let's get going. Do you have a wrap, or something to keep you warm?" "No, I don't have a wrap, but I suspect that I do have someone that will make sure that I don't feel any chill", she teased. They managed to hail a cab, jumped in and made their way to Chelsea.

"Cindy, how lovely to see you again so soon, effused Arabella, when she greeted them at the Club, and who may I ask is this G O R G E O U S hunk of a man,?" eyeing Phil's physique with envy. "Oh, just someone that I picked up earlier this evening at Stringfellows. He was at a loose end, so he told me, and poor man, has nowhere to stay tonight. If he behaves himself, she winked, he could end up on my floor". "You do like your stray cats, don't you", smiled Arabella. "You jest, of course, you know that I don't pick up any Tom, Harry or that other fellow, what's his name"? "Oh, you mean Dick, Arabella said smuttily. I have a table for you on the Terrace, follow me".

Under the Patio Heater, they cuddled closer together, to keep out the early morning chill, and chatted about themselves, kissed and canoodled, until Cindy announced that it was time for her beauty sleep. "You can come home with me to my new little flat, if you like, but you must promise me that there will be no hanky panky, not on our first sort of date. It's only a bed sitter, one level up, but you are welcome to sleep on the floor, if you wish." "I shall promise, with most of my heart, you have taken the rest of it, he said holding his hands together in mock prayer, that I shall be a good boy and do as instructed. Where do you live?" "In Burnaby Street, not five minutes gentle walk from here".

As they left the Club, the heavens opened. Thunder roared and forked lightening lit up the sky. Phil scooped Cindy up into his muscular arms, and ran the quarter of a mile to the flat in world record time. The torrential downpour soaked them completely, by the time that they had reached the flat. Cindy, still in Phil's arms fumbled for the keypad, punched in her code, but nothing happened. The storm had caused a power failure. Dripping from head to toe, Phil saw that there was a window open above the porch. "Where does that lead to, he said pointing upwards at the opening". "Goes straight into my kitchen. You're not thinking what I'm thinking are you"? "I don't know what you are thinking, but I'm going to shin up this pipe and climb in and release the front door latch." "You're crazy, she squealed, you could kill yourself if you fall". I've had worse things happen to me on a rugby field, don't worry".

In clothes, not designed for 'house breaking', Phil struggled to keep a hold on the slippery pipe, and after several attempts, he finally reached the comparative safety of the roof of the porch, and prised open the small kitchen window. At that moment, the power was restored and the loud siren of the burglar alarm sent screeching sounds through his already quivering body. Fortunately, for him, Cindy had managed to open the front door, and deactivate the alarm. Shivering in the kitchen sink, where he had fallen head first into it from the window, he groggily freed himself from his stainless steel cage, and was now sitting, huddled up on the floor when Cindy got into her flat.

"What a sight, we are, you on the floor, and me in clothes, not designed for the English summer, we had better get out of these things right now before we catch our death of cold." "That's the best suggestion that I have heard all night, or is it morning?" he said. Giggling like big kids, they helped each other strip off their wet clothes with gay abandon. Phil, with trembling hands, managed to locate the zip at the back of her dress, and in one swift movement, the dress slid off her shoulders onto the floor. She was completely naked. "You're beautiful", he gasped in a whispered hoarse voice. Cindy unbuckled his wet trousers, and they joined her dress in a heap on the floor, at the foot of her bed.

"Wow, you're not too bad, either, she said breathlessly. Don't forget your promise, Cindy retorted in a stern but cheeky voice." .... "What promise, I hit my head so hard on the kitchen sink that I can't remember any promise, he grinned. This was going to be a dream interview.

"OOHAH, groaned Phil, where am I?, my head feels like I've got the whole of the Salvation Army playing inside it." He tried to roll over on the hard floor, but not only did his head ache, but so did his arms, neck and back. 'Must have been all of the exercise last night' he inwardly smiled. He gently prised one eye open, blearily looking for the lovely vision that he had spent the night with. "Sleeping Beauty awakes. You've had a rough night." "W..W..W....what, where am I?" "You spent the night in my flat,........................... after you passed out at Stringfellows, having slipped on the wet floor, you hit your head on the bar, and collapsed like a sack of potatoes, when Cindy smacked you", said Russ.

THE RUNAWAYS

CHAPTER ONE

After yet another backbreaking day, Hymie called out to his younger brother, who was not yet old enough to do the hard labour in the small repair workshop, that was attached to their tiny Shtetl on the outskirts of Nikel, in Northern Russia, "Shmul, please go and tell mama that I shall be ready for something to eat soon. Is there anything more nourishing than the thin soup that we have been eating all week?"

The thick, newly fallen snow, lay across the whole of the village that they liked to call home, and like all of the other buildings that surrounded it, twelve in all, their family had occupied the ramshackle wooden structure for more years than either of the boys could remember, and Hymie, now 10 years old had had to help his mother in the workshop, as unfortunately, their father had recently died, leaving no alternative, if they were going to survive the harsh Russian winters, or the very unfair, in Hymies' opinion, directives from the Tzar , penalising the Jews, for being just that, Jews.

Shmul was nearly 7 years old, and looked up to his older brother in awe, and dreamt, that one day he would also be able to help. "Sorry, it's the same as yesterday, and the day before, but mama has managed to make a fresh loaf of bread " he replied.

At least, thought Hymie," I won't have to break my teeth on the very hard and stale bread that the rats and mice seemed to enjoy so much, judging from the tiny holes in it".

The days were very long, albeit it was now in the middle of winter, and the light faded very quickly at this time of year, and without enough wood to kindle the fire, they would have frozen to death, but this is where Shmul had managed to help, by rummaging daily in the woods, and ditches for suitable firewood.

The three of them sat by the fire, to try to keep the biting wind out of their bones, and over the food, Mama told them the bad news that she had heard today, from her friend .

"Sarah, who as you know, seems to know and hear everything that is going on in the area, as she has befriended the Prefect of the District, told me that unfortunately, he is going to have to collect more taxes, starting next year. With what we can just about scrape together now, it is going to be impossible for us to stay here" she said in hushed tones, as she didn't want to alert any of her close neighbours, of her worries.

"What do you mean" the boys responded in unison, are you suggesting that we run away, but where would we go?"

"Yes, said Mama, but we are going to have to plan it very carefully, so that no one knows of our plans". " You know that Uncle Joseph now lives in America, and we could always go to stay with him for a short while until we find somewhere for us to live"

"It sounds a good idea, said Hymie, but how will we be able to take all of our belongings with us, and get past the guards at the crossing"?

"We won't be able to take anything with us, as it will only weigh us down, and slow our progress, and I shall have to think of a way of getting us out of the country unseen, but not another word until I have found a solution to the problem".

Mama knew that the border with Norway was only 4 miles away, and on foot, even in these harsh conditions, it would not take many hours to get there. She could not think of a plan, but she could not stay here, anyway, so she made her decision.

The following day, Mama crept into wake the boys " we're going to make a break for the border this evening after dark" she whispered. Get your sturdy shoes, and wrap up in layers to keep the sub zero temperatures out, and take only something to drink".

"Can't we say goodbye to our friends? wailed the children, we may never see them again " " I wish that you could, but no, you'll just have to contact them when we get to America, Mama sternly replied. No more tears".

The day dragged on so slowly whilst the boys were anxiously waiting for Mama to tell them that it was time to go.

It had been cloudy and there had been no sun at all that day, and so as soon as it was dark, Mama, Hymie and Shmul, quietly left their home for the last time and quickly made their way across the well worn tracks into the forest. "Be as quiet as mice whispered Mama, her breath freezing into a small white cloud above her mouth, we don't want anyone to know that we are here . Only speak when I say".

The thick forest was mostly Siberian Pines that stretched way up into the sky, and for the moment gave them complete shelter from the blizzard that had just started. What Mama had not told the boys was that there were many wolves and other predators that roamed the forest, so she had be very careful where they walked. They had not walked for very long, when she suddenly stopped and waved the boys to the floor of the forest, as she had seen a faint light glowing in the distance. "We are very close, now, that must be the crossing point". Mama said.

Carefully, they approached the crossing, and saw about 10 metres away, a hole in the fence. " This blizzard is a godsend, said Mama, if we make our way through the fence, we shall not be seen, as the snowfall is getting thicker and thicker all the time".

They climbed through the hole in the fence, and started to walk away when "who goes there" was shouted directly at them in Norwegian, and they knew that they were safely out of Russia, and on their way to the New World.

CHAPTER TWO

Mama, Hymie and Shmul, looked back from where they had just come, and lighting the night sky they saw huge flames flickering in the distance. The roar from the inferno could clearly be heard in the eerily silent night, although they were nearly four miles distant . Mama started to cry. "What's the matter?, said Hymie. She was sobbing, uncontrollably. Though very emotional Mama managed to choke out a few words "It looks like we've got out just in time. Wiping her tear filled eyes, "They are burning our Village, and I just hope that all of our friends are safe . We have all heard of the atrocities that have befallen other villages in Russia, but I didn't think that it would happen to us so soon".

Her wailing could be heard by the border patrols, nothing new to them, and a friendly giant of a man, dressed in a fur hat , coat and boots approached them. "Don't be afraid, he said, you are the ninth family to cross here in the last few days, and fully understand your anguish. Come with me into our warm and cosy hut, and you can have shelter here ". They followed him, and were welcomed by two other patrolmen, warming themselves around a blazing hot fire. "What are your names? asked Hymie. "Call me Henrik" said the main man. " I'm Petr, and I'm Olaf", the other two said.

"The Russians are just pigs, spat out Henrik, not a human feeling amongst them, I hope that they rot in Hell". "Please don't use that language in front of the children. I know how angry you are, and we as a family have more regrets than you will ever know", said Mama. "What shall we call you? He said. I'm Sarah, this is Hymie, and the little one is Shmul". "Don't call me little, Mama, I'm seven years old, said Shmul, standing on tip toes, stretching himself to his full height.

"Where should we go from here? enquired Mama the following morning. We don't have any papers or passports, and I think that Russia is the only Country so far to issue them. Do you know if anyone else has yet followed their example? We had better be on our way". "In that regard, said Henrik, you are lucky, as far as I know, no other Country has yet issued them." "The other families have made their way into Lofoten, a fishing village, and they are expected to take the first boat away from Norway, to where ever it lands, not a great plan, but as far away as possible from Russia," explained Petr. "Our uncle Josef lives in America, said Hymie, and our plan is to go to him there". "I've heard that America is a huge Country, a little bit like Russia, do you know where in America that he lives"? "The last letter we have from him says New York City".

Huddled up in the only clothes that they possessed, they thanked the three guards. "You see that road down there? pointed out Petr, just follow it for about 6 miles, and you will tread the same path as the other evacuees , and will eventually arrive in Lofoten, where I am sure that you will meet up with some of your compatriots. I am aware that a small lodge has been made available for travellers, such as your family, to rest and plan your onward journey. Good luck, and God speed". "Thank you so very much for your kind help. It's unlikely that we shall ever be back here . Good luck to you, also". Mama said, as they waved goodbye and started the next stage of their perilous journey.

They walked, trudged, and slid their way through the thick snow, stopping every hour, to rest, and drink some of the delicious Borscht that they had carried with them from their home. "Let's play a game", said Mama, desperately trying to keep up the spirit of the boys. "Must we, they said, we're tired, can't we sit down?" "You must keep moving, or we will freeze to death, and we don't want that do we?" She tried to sound encouraging, but deep down she knew that she was fighting a losing battle. Just then, they saw smoke and heard voices. "Hide said Mama, it may be the Prefect and his men, looking for us". The boys, slithered down behind a hedge, whilst Mama quietly crept forward. She saw a group of fishermen, cooking some of their catch on an open brazier, and the smell wafted into her nostrils. She envisaged the good Shabos night meals that she had enjoyed with her family only a few years ago. She was salivating, or hallucinating, she couldn't decide which, when a voice called out to her to come and join them around the fire. "Boys, boys, she called, it's alright, come out from your hiding place".

The three of them were greeted by yet more friendly people, and after initial introductions, were told that they were now in Lofoten, and that they could have shelter for the night at the small lodge, just around the bend. With renewed heart, and more optimism than they had any right to expect after their difficult journey, they arrived at the Lodge. Exhausted. They flopped down on the floor, covered themselves with a thin blanket, and fell into a deep, deep sleep.

"Wake up", Mama felt a gentle shake of her shoulders. "Where am I? She asked. "Safe, and sheltered, is all that you need to know just now. Wake up your boys, they have slept like logs, and get something to eat. I'm sorry it's not much, but it is at least fresh". "Who are you?" Mama enquired. They call me Helga, and your name is? "Sarah, and this is Hymie and little Shmul" she replied. " I'm not little, shouted an indignant Shmul, stop calling me that!".

Breakfast consisted of herring, and some bread, and they washed it down with a mug of steaming black tea. To them it was a banquet.

"What plans do you have now? asked Helga, as people who arrive here usually want to go to America or Europe fairly quickly". "We have relatives in America, Sarah said, and we hope to work our passage there". "We are living in very difficult times, just now, and the best that I can suggest is that you take the boat tomorrow morning to Germany, and try to board another one, that is heading across the Atlantic to America" Helga replied. "What time should we be ready? It leaves on the high tide, at about mid day. I shall let them know that you are coming".

The sea was very rough, but buoyed by the thoughts of starting a new life in America, eased the discomfort for Sarah, but both Hymie and Shmul were as sick as dogs, like so many of the boat's occupants. The stench was horrible, and thank goodness that a quick rain shower, washed most of the vomit away. They journeyed on for two days through ever increasingly heavy seas, before, almost like Jonah's whale, the ship spewed them up on shore at Hamburg in Germany. Hundreds and hundreds of drenched, wretched souls were thankfully on dry land at last.

They got a congregation together, and for the first time in many days, all prayed , thanking the Lord for their deliverance. The service was led by Elijah, a young good looking man in his late 20's, with long sideburns, and a distinctive fluffy beard, all under a wide brimmed black hat, whom Sarah and family had met once before, when he came as a guest Rabbi to their Stebl. "Thank you for restoring our faith", said Sarah, pushing her way to the front of the crowd. "Don't I know you? He asked. "Yes, she rather embarrassedly said, do you remember my boys, Hymie and Shmul, they played a wicked trick on you when you visited our Stebl late last year." "Oh yes, he replied, stroking his beard, I DO remember, and in the fullness of time, I MAY forgive them he said cheekily. Where are you heading for?"

Hymie, perked up , " America, my uncle lives in New York City", he beamed. "What a coincidence, that's where I'm going as well. Perhaps we could all travel together", he replied. "That would be nice", she coyly answered, enjoying the company of such an attractive man would be most welcome, she thought.

The boatload of passengers were taken to a large warehouse, which was to be their base for the next day, until the steamship SS Deutscland, was ready to cross the Atlantic.

Just like Noah, the following day, everyone and everything was loaded, two by two, and they found some space on the upper deck, where they stored their meagre belongings. There were so many languages being spoken, it must have sounded like the Tower of Babel, with many different tongues and accents, from all over Europe. Everyone decided that the common tongue was Yiddish, and most knew enough to get by. The crossing took weeks, and during that time, Sarah and Elijah seemed to be getting closer and closer, and they related their entire background and history to each other, whilst the boys slept. They had a lot in common, both had been married, and both through tragic circumstances had lost their lifelong partners to tuberculosis. They had come from large families, with seven or eight brothers or sisters each, that had all now left home, to get married and start their own families. Between them they had nearly one hundred cousins, scattered all over the World. Their love was blossoming quickly and they decided to ask the Captain to marry them, under a hastily constructed canopy, in the middle of the Atlantic, so that they could start their new lives as a family.

Apart from the violent seas, the crossing meandered on, until on a bright but cold spring day, the sight of land excitedly alerted everyone that they were nearly in America. The rush to the gunnels on the ship was like a stampede, with nearly six thousand immigrants, clamouring for a view of the promised land, America. The ship moored at Ellis Island, where immigration took forever, and when asked their names, an interpreter was present to translate.

"What's your name, please said the chubby faced official, and where are you from?" Using the interpreter, she said that her name was Sarah, and she came from Russia ."What is your surname? He enquired. Sarah looked blank. What's a surname?" she asked. "Never mind he said, from now on you will be known as Sarah Fishman and your boys' names please.

"Hymie and Shmul". "Those aren't American names, let's call them Harry and Simon". Sarah, not quite understanding what had just happened, signed the document in front of her, and made her way through the inspection hall to the exit. She had arranged to meet Elijah, at the gateway. "Have you also got a new name", she asked. "Yes", he said, I am now Rabbi Ellis Fishman. Oy Vey!!

As a married couple with two boys, they were told to go to Cherry Street, on the Lower East Side, where accommodation would be available. It was a two room apartment in the basement of a rundown tenement building, with no hot water or heating. The only running water, was down the walls. The mice and rats were constant companions, as well as the army of cockroaches. The constant buzzing of the flies, nearly drove them mad. "This is supposed to be the Promised land? queried Ellis, now getting used to his name. I shall try to find work in the synagogue, he said." I'll try the hospital, I'm sure that they need midwifes' ", Sarah replied. They needed money badly, and Harry became a newspaper boy, hawking The Evening Journal, for a few pennies a day. Simon, got a job as a helper in a bakery. The pittance they earned was given to Sarah, every evening when they came home. Life for them and other immigrants was very very tough, but here at least they could make their own decisions, without too much fuss.

They tried to find Uncle Josef, but the community was now so large, with over two and a half million people, that despite extensive enquiries, he could not be traced.

The family was just about keeping their heads above water, when one day, a few years later, Harry, the enterprising one, told them that he was about to quit his job, and be a newspaper man. "Whatever do you mean, a newspaper man", asked his family.

"I've seen the future, he announced, and people want to read about what is going on, every day, and not wait until Shabos to gather the news, and gossip from title tattle that they heard at the synagogue. "And how, may I ask are you going to get started asked Ellis, with shirt buttons I suppose". " No, retorted Harry, I'm going to work in a bar at night, and with that money, I shall go to the Bank and ask for a loan". "You're crazy, said his mother, have you any idea how much money is needed to start a business?". "I've already thought about that, and I have spoken with my friend Bill Hearst, who has said that we could be partners in a new enterprise here in New York City, and whatever he puts into the venture, he is willing to let me buy 25% of the paper over the next 20 years". Absolutely flabbergasted by this statement, Ellis enquired. "Who in the world is Bill Hearst?" "His father owns the San Francisco Examiner, and has great plans for our future. If I don't try now, I never will".

The rest, as they say is history, as William Randolph Hearst created the largest newspaper and magazine business in the World, with Harry, hanging onto his coat tails as he was swept along in the torrent. He went from strength to strength.

Sarah and Ellis had four more children, and with ever increasing prosperity, mainly due to the support from Harry and Simon they lived to a ripe old age in relative comfort. Little Shmul, Simon, worked for pennies in a bakers shop, before he thought that the idea of serving deli food to the masses was brilliant, and with his friend Willy Katz, opened the now renowned Katz Delicatessen, which at the last count sold weekly 10,000 pounds of pastrami, 5,000 pounds of Salt Beef; 12,000 hot dogs, and 2000 pounds of salami.

HISTORICAL NOTE: The characters in this story are fictitious, with the notable exception of William Randolph Hearst and Willy Katz.

FACE AT THE WINDOW

I had needed to find a retreat away from the City, as I just could not concentrate amidst the hustle and bustle of my daily family life, and when my wife suggested that I go to a haven in the Country, I jumped at her idea with glee. " I just need to get away, and think, I told her, probably for about three weeks or so".

"When we were in lake Windermere, last year, she reminded me, there were several cottages available for short lets, advertised in the local press, and even at the Hotel, the proprietor, recognising me from publicity in respect of my current best seller, 'The Secret Olympic Diaries of Games Maker, Stephen Sharp', had recommended 'Bluff Cottage', where other writers had often stayed".

"Great Idea, I'll phone him now"

"Good morning, Linthwaite House Hotel, how may we help you" the friendly voice on the telephone said. " Good morning to you, this is Stephen Sharp. May I speak to John the manager, sorry I have forgotten his surname". "It's John Campbell, i'll put you through".

"John Campbell". "Hello John, it's Stephen, Stephen Sharp, do you remember, that we stayed with you last year ?" "Of course I do, how are you"? "Very well thank you, I have a favour to ask you, I said". "Ask away, I am always pleased to help if I can, said John."

"I desperately need some quiet time, and location, to try to finish my book, 'Do vampires live in Transylvania', that my publisher's are pushing me very hard, as they need it in the shops in time for the Christmas market. You mentioned to my wife 'Bluff Cottage', could you find out for me, please, if it might be available for say 3 weeks or so, right now."

"Let me check, said John, leave your contact number, and I shall call you back once I have managed to contact the owner".

I left my mobile number with him, and reported the conversation to my wife.

"I shall be glad to get rid of you, you have been nothing but a grumbling old man for the past few weeks," she said. I hope that the cottage is available, as I don't want you getting under my feet, right now. I should also like some peace and quiet myself".

John called back almost immediately. "Hello, Stephen, you're in luck. The Summer season is over, and the cottage is readily available, with the normal rate being £200 per week, but as he needs to get the place rewired, because of constant power failures, he will let you have a three week let for £500 all in, and he will leave the key with me for you to collect".

"Wonderful, I replied, I shall be with you, tomorrow, arriving on the 8.30 train from London. Would it be possible for you to arrange a taxi for me please".

"Certainly, said John, it will be the Albany Taxi Service, who are very reliable, and Dan will be there to meet you off the train".

"Thanks again, what do I owe you for organising this for me?"

"Nothing, said John, but I would like a personally signed copy of the book as a thank you".

"You are already on my list, and it won't be a problem, I replied. See you tomorrow".

I packed my case, laptop, and spare batteries, just in case the power went off, together with plenty of 'nibbles', that I always chomped on, when in a creative frame of mind, and took the underground train to Euston Main line station, to catch the 8.30 to Windermere, which necessitated changing trains at Lancaster. British Rail was surprisingly on time, and I duly arrived at 11.39, where Dan met me, under clear blue Autumnal skies, and took me straight to the cottage, as he had been told by John that he needed to collect the keys from him, prior to collecting me.

"Looks a bit worse for wear," said Dan, as we approached the unmade pathway from the tarmac road. He got out of the taxi, and using the set of keys, unlocked the 5 bar gate, which had dropped off its' hinge on one side, making it difficult to manoeuvre, and with my help, managed to open it wide enough to drive through. "Wow, that was difficult, I could have damaged my back," Dan said. "Too right, I replied, puffing and panting from my exertions, whilst clambering back into the taxi. How far to go"?

"The path winds its' way down to the cottage for about half a mile, and then we shall have to walk the final 250 yards, as there is no way that the taxi will be able to deal with all of the deep rain filled potholes", said Dan.

The location of the cottage, was just how I remembered it, and it was sitting in the most idyllic hidden undulating countryside, in about 15 unspoilt acres, with fantastic views, and gentle hills, meandering down to the lake. "Just stop a minute, whilst I take this in, I told Dan, I had not seen this side of the cottage before, and wanted to imprint it on my memory. With views like this the image will last forever".

"Do you know the weather forecast for the next few days", I asked. "The Lake District has a micro climate of its' own, replied Dan, and I think that we could be in for a storm tonight". "That's a pity, I wanted to stretch my legs, after the train journey, and refresh my taste buds with the superb beer at the local pub, later" . Not to worry, I shall have plenty of time for that whilst I am staying here".

We eventually walked on to the cottage, and upon entering was delighted to see that all of the lovely fittings enhanced the appeal of the place. "Everything in order?" asked Dan. "Just perfect, I replied. I shall be here certainly for 3 weeks, please leave me your contact telephone number, and I shall call you, giving you plenty of notice, as to the date of my return". "There is no network coverage here, I am afraid, you will have to go to the main road to get a decent signal, said Dan. "OK, I am not afraid of a gentle walk up the hill, I shall be fully relaxed by then", I replied.

Dan gave me the contact telephone number, and I watched him bump along the unmade road, until I saw in the distance his indicators blinking, and brake lights, shining in the twilight, which confirmed to me that he had reached the tarmac road. I had told him, that as the gate was very difficult to move, to just leave it open, until his return trip.

The cottage, under a thatched roof with its' distinctive bottle style windows was perfect with a chintzy style lounge, having a huge inglenook fireplace, complete with its' fireside set of poker, tongs and brush. Neatly chopped logs, spilling over the wicker basket next to it. The quaint country style wooden fitted kitchen was directly off the lounge. Upstairs via a concealed staircase, were two spacious bedrooms, together with a bathroom, in the middle of which stood a fantastic roll top bath, standing on four clawed feet, big enough to bathe more than one person. Pure unabashed indulgence awaited me.

I opened the windows, as the musty smell needed to dissipate, unpacked my luggage, and settled down in the lounge, where I set up my temporary writing station, utilising the spectacular tranquil views, over the sun dappled landscape, and started to think about my book.

The sunlight was fading quickly, and I stopped for a break, and something to eat. "It seems to me that the clock moves at a much slower pace, here" I thought to myself.

With the temperature dropping, I went around the cottage and closed all of the windows that I had opened about an hour ago, arranged some logs on the hearth, went into the kitchen, found the matches, and with some gentle persuasion from the bellows, managed to ignite the fire, which sparked ,crackled, and spat initially, as some of the logs were still wet.

My wife had given me some pre-frozen meals to take with me, along with a selection of fresh fruit, and decided that tonight I would microwave the pasta as I was now hungry, having not eaten since breakfast.

I devoured my pasta penne, and fresh fruit for dessert, and by the time that I had washed up, and cleared everything away, it was now late at night. I looked through the window, and it was pitch black outside, with hurricane force winds and torrential rain, hammering on the glass, and everything that was not securely tied down, was being hurled across the lonely landscape of my hillside retreat. Metal dustbin lids went cascading around the brick walled enclosed formal gardens , clunking and clanging with enough noise to raise the dead. The young, recently planted saplings, were being bent double in the sudden ferocious storm, that had come out of a clear blue sky, only hours ago. "I'm glad that I am inside" I said to myself , but I could not even to begin to contemplate writing, as the noise was so intense.

The lights started flickering, " Oh no, I thought, where did I see the candles"? I hope that the roof is secure, and that it doesn't leak.

The lights went off for a few seconds, then came back into life again , and then went off again, this time for about a minute, before the power was restored. I rummaged around the kitchen and found some candles and lit them, just in time as the power failed again, and the candles and the flames from the fire were now casting eerie, leaping dancing shadows on the walls, playing havoc with my imagination. I have heard of people being found mutilated in lonely spots, just like this. Maybe this was not the right time to be writing about ghosts and ghouls. My mind was racing faster and faster with all sorts of unimaginable disasters that might befall me. It was sending me loopy. I grabbed my mobile phone, but to no avail, as I had forgotten Dan's earlier conversation, advising that there was no service from the cottage. "Great, what a night to be stranded," I mouthed, but no words came out. Tap tap tap, the window shook and rattled, in its' wooden frame. Tap,

tap, tap. " Was it just the leaves and branches making the noise, or was there someone out there?", I sincerely hope not. Maybe it's a stray animal looking for shelter. I've never been worried about the dark before, but now all sorts of horrific images were flashing through my mind.

I was not sure how the sounds were being made, but I was not going to take any chances, so I slid across the wooden floor, under eye level, collected several splinters for my trouble, and even managed to bump my head on the coffee table. I put my hand through my hair, and rubbed my head, trying to discover whether I had drawn blood, but luckily I had not, and fumbled around the fireplace, until my hand shakily gripped the poker. I stood up to my full height, and smashed my head again on the low beamed ceiling, letting out an involuntary yell. I groggily stumbled over to the window, I looked like an ancient swordsman. Brandishing the poker in my hand, I bravely swept the curtains aside,   hoping that there was no one there. No such luck, as I was stunned into a quivering wreck, my heart leaping out of my chest, and my legs turning to jelly, when I peered out of the window, to see the scraggy haired lunatic grinning and starring maliciously at me.

I waved the poker threateningly at him, and ducked down, and at the same time, so did he. I jumped up quickly, and blimey, so did he. What was going on? I ducked down again, trying to trick his actions. I snuck down again, and rapidly approached the window from the left, and so did he. This man was mimicking my every move........ and then it hit me..................the lunatic outside was.... ME, and I was being scared shitless by my own distorted reflections from the bottle glass window.

Slightly regaining my composure, with trembling hands, I somehow managed to pour myself a large stiff whiskey. I slumped down into the armchair, and called myself all the names under the sun for being such a wimp, but it had given me an idea for a future book.

LIVING IN THE PAST

Pat Ward, 92, was found dead at home, alone. The Harrow Observer reported on its front page last week. But why the front page. Obituaries usually appeared towards the back of the newspaper, but this story was the Headline leader.

I had met Pat Ward, a couple of years ago, when my boss, Peter Parker, of Parker Removals, asked if I could do a little favour for him on my way home to Uxbridge. "I've just had a call from my uncle, who is thinking of moving out of his house in Paines Lane, in Pinner, and he would like someone to give him an estimate of the cost". "Let me have a note of his telephone number, I replied, and I shall arrange to see him". "Sorry, he doesn't have a telephone, he called me from a public phone box". "How do I make contact with him?" I enquired. "You can either write to him, or drop by on your way home, and take a chance that he is in". He is , oh I don't really know his age, but he is probably in his eighties, and I suspect that he is mainly house bound now". "Alright, I said, please give me his address and I shall try to call in one evening this week". "On second thoughts, said my boss, although I haven't seen him for years, I do remember him being rather grumpy, and it is probably best if you write to him in the first instance. Here is his address."

I took the details from him, and dictated a short letter to Mr Ward, introducing myself, and decided to drop it in to his house that evening.

Putting the letter in my backpack, I left my office, put on my helmet and cycled the short distance to Pinner, through Hatch End Broadway, with its multitude of restaurants, thinking to myself, how does an area as small as Hatch End, manage to support so many eating establishments, especially in a recession.

I turned down Paines Lane, and cycled up and down the lane twice, looking for the house, that had no number, but was known as 'The Elms'. I could not find it. I got off my bike, and walked the complete length of the very long road, but still could not find hide nor hare of it. Must be a mistake, maybe its Paines Close, so off I went again searching for the so far non existent house. I was now getting more and more anxious, had I taken the address from my boss, and incorrectly addressed it?

Just as I was about to give up, I saw a pedestrian walking towards me. "Do you know of a house called, 'The Elms, I asked". "Is it the rather run down property?" she replied. "I don't know, except it is occupied by an elderly gentleman; Mr Ward, do you know him?" I said. "Of course everybody in the Village knows him, he's quite a well known local character, but I didn't know the name of his house. It's over there, she said pointing at a small unmade pathway, mainly hidden by overgrown bushes and unkempt trees. See it?" she said. "No wonder I couldn't spot it, it's basically hidden from the road". Thank you very much. I could have been here for hours without ever seeing it" I replied.

I pushed my way past the undergrowth, along a well worn stony footpath, and there in front of me was 'The Elms', a timber built house, probably built in the late 16th Century. A diamond shaped chimney stack, protruding from a well worn thatched roof, the Oak front door being, in my estimation only about 5' high, with no visible letter box, bell or door knocker. After all of my effort to find the house I had no way of delivering the letter.

I stood in front of the house thinking 'should I just go to the nearest post box, and leave it up to the Post Office to deliver it, or just rap hard on the door with my hand, and hope that he was in'. I saw smoke rising in thin wisps towards the evening sky, from the chimney and thought that there must be someone at home.

Bearing in mind what my boss had said about him, it was with some trepidation that I approached the door. "What was the worst thing that could happen to me, I thought, he's an old man, I'm in no danger". I rapped loudly on the door, but there was no reply. I knocked louder, and longer, but still no reply, and decided that there was no one in, so I would, after all have to use the services of the Post Office to deliver the letter. It would probably take several days to reach him!

I started to walk with my bicycle back to the road, when I heard a shout from behind me. "What the hell do you want?" I turned to see a well built, scruffily dressed elderly looking man, with long strands of thinning hair, holding a pistol in his hand, pointing it steadily at my head. "Get off my land, you have no business here with me. This gun is loaded, and I am not afraid to use it, if you don't leave right now," he threatened loudly. You're from the Government, aren't you?"

"N....No. I' .....ve only come to deliver this letter to you sir , you are Mr Ward, aren't you? I quivered, it's from your nephew Peter". "Peter? Peter who" he was now yelling. "Peter Parker, from the removal Company" I said. " Say again, he said, I'm a bit mutton ". "Peter Parker, from the removal company I shouted back".

The penny had dropped, and he showed some recognition in his crumpled face, and with that he lowered the gun, stepped slowly forward towards me, apologising profusely for his threatening behaviour "I don't usually get any visitors, and I like to keep myself to myself. Sorry. Give me the letter please". I handed it to him . "Not really necessary to read it, I replied, as all that I wanted to do was to make an appointment to see you to give you an estimate for your removal". "Removal, what removal? He queried. I'm not going anywhere, my stupid nephew must have misheard me when I telephoned him. It was a very crackly line. "I told him that I needed taking to a reunion".

His demeanour had changed dramatically, and he asked " would you like to come in for a cup of tea, especially, as you have made the effort to find me, and what with me frightening you, I think that is the least that I can do". I looked at my watch, and It was now nearly 8 pm and I needed to be at the squash club by 9.00, so I declined politely, and suggested another time. "What about 6.pm tomorrow? He said. "That's fine with me, I answered, I now know where you live, and how to find you. I would be delighted to join you for a cuppa. Till tomorrow".

I said goodbye, got onto my bike, and had lots of thoughts bouncing around my mind during my short journey home. I suspected that he must be lonely, and just wanted someone new to talk with.

"The old boy has lost his marbles, said my boss, when I related my story of the previous night to him, he most certainly told me that he wanted to move. Never mind, at least you are doing me a favour, keeping him occupied for a little while yet, as I understand that the doctors have told him that he has only a few months left to live. He really should be in a home, but refuses to go". " I can't really blame him, I said, as he seems more than capable of looking after himself, even in his current state of health".

I had left plenty of time to get to Pat's house, as the High Road, was clogged up with cars caused by road works and traffic controls, yet again, and was glad that my bike was able to weave past most of the jams. Arriving just before the clock of the 14th Century Parish Church of St John the Baptist struck 6, I made my way down the path and knocked on the door and waited,... and waited,.... and waited. Could he have forgotten that I was coming? I put my ear to the door, and heard shuffling feet, and realised that Pat was no longer able to get about quickly.

"Hello, young man. He greeted me with a warm and very firm handshake, that I had not expected from him. Mind your head, this door was made in the 14th Century, when people weren't so tall, and the rest of the house was built out of ships timbers, that's why no floor or wall is even," he chuckled. "Come through to the kitchen, the kettle is on the stove". The hall was wide and had no ceiling, and I glanced upwards to see a charred roof lining above me. "Did you have a fire here at one time", I enquired. "No, this house, when it was built didn't have a first floor, that only came in the late 16th Century, and this hall, with its' open hearth, used to be the passage to the parlour, where the cows were milked. If you look carefully at the roof area, you will see several very large hooks, and a smoke bay, that did formerly have a small hole in the roof. The farmers used to hang the dead animals and using a fire down here would smoke them ". "Fascinating, I said, you seem to know a lot about your house. May I ask what else you know about it?"

We sat in the kitchen, and the furniture looked as if it belonged to a time gone by, the table and chairs, shiny from years of use. As we sat down, I swept the crumbs off my seat, and I could see the clouds of dust rising, reflecting in the sunlight that beamed through the original glass and leaded casement window. Pat went to the dresser, took out two cups. I noticed that the Butler stone sink was full of un washed dishes. He removed the fluff from the cracked cups with his fingers, and enquired how did I take my tea. "Black, please, no sugar, thank you". "Just like me" he replied. He took the tea from a caddy and hoped that I wouldn't mind if he made it directly in the tea strainer, "Saves washing up" he giggled. He poured the hot water from a retro Swan kettle . The tea was just awful, but I was not going to say so, it tasted like boiled twigs. It probably was.

"You were asking me what else I know about the house, he said. Well let me ask you what do you know about Pinner?" "Not a lot, I replied, as I was born the other side of the river, and only moved to North London when I was a boy. The area is fairly new to me". " Pinner he announced is mentioned in the Doomsday Book, although it was known then as Pinnora, and this house was one of the first built in the settlement". He took me to a side wall and uncovered a mural, of a hunting scene, which has a Preservation Order on it as the only remaining example in the Greater London area. "This property was one of only four in the area allowed to hold non conformist meetings at the cottage, in the 17th Century. He was in his element now. "Do you want to see the rest of the house". "Yes please ", I answered happily.

He drew back a curtain, dust flew everywhere. Cobwebs were evident in the corners of the room and I doubted if it been cleaned in the past 10 years! It appeared that we were now in his living room. Dark, low ceilings, tiled fireplace, totally out of character with this Period house, and a single bulb hanging precariously from a threadbare flex. The small window, letting limited light into the room which overlooked the vast garden. The wood stained panelled walls with a picture rail where there were several dusty photographs that had probably hung there for many, many years without so much as a glance, or a duster. "What is this one?, I asked, walking over to a group of men in army uniform, looks like there might be a story or two from this". He put on his glasses, took them off again, and fishing a dirty crumpled handkerchief from his trouser pocket, spat on the glasses, and rubbed them vigorously . "That's better, I can see clearly now". He looked at the front row. "Jonny Jonson, he said, what a voice, kept us entertained for hours. Left to join the Opera, soon after this was taken, but I have lost touch. "Don't know if he is still alive", he said mournfully. Then, pointing to the man in the front row," that's what's his name, oh dear, my memory. Yes, yes , got it, it's Bonzo, Bonzo Harris, never knew his real name, but I now remember he went on to teach, somewhere in Willesden. Probably dead too. That's me at the back, third one from the right, handsome bugger, if I don't mind saying so myself". " Oh so many stories, too many to recall. War is a terrible time, but if you survive, well"................he left it unsaid.

I didn't want to ask too many questions, but there was one on my lips that I was dying to know. "What did you do in the war, Pat?", I tentatively asked. He went very quiet, and shrank a little into himself. "It's something that I would rather not talk about if you don't mind". He sat for a couple of minutes in an uneasy silence, his eyes glazed over, as if recalling something very painful to him, then he perked up.

"Would you like to see the rest of the house, now" he asked, changing the subject rapidly. "Righto, lead the way". We went from the living room into the back room, sparsely furnished, and as a centre piece, sitting on the sideboard was a wireless, which was a large contraption in a polished wooden box. It had a speaker covered in a sort of rough fabric and three knobs. It was also covered in dust. Surrounding it were more photographs, but none showing any family. There was no television to be seen, only a pre war Edison Fireside gramophone in the corner, covered with yet another thick layer of dust on the golden trumpet, together with carefully packed boxes, full of 78" records, un played for generations, I guessed. Upstairs were two minute bedrooms, both with wardrobe cupboards bearing the Utility stamp CC41. Loose threadbare carpets, the pattern long faded, that must have been a hazard, but I didn't wish to upset my host again by pointing it out. The bathroom, had an old fashioned bath with a Ewarts Vivo geyser water heater with a swivel arm that also served the wash hand basin. The toilet looked as if it were an original Thomas Crapper, although contrary to widespread misconceptions, Crapper did not invent the flush toilet. "Blimely O'Reilly, I thought", he is living in a time warp. No modern inventions for him. Maybe not a bad thing with credit cards, knife crime, sex and violence, reality shows, bad language, and insolence, mobile phones, computers, i-pads etc

Pat's mood suddenly changed. The tour of the house ended abruptly, as I am sure that I had hit a very sensitive nerve with him, when I had enquired about his army life. "It's getting late, said Pat, I think that you had better leave now". With that he showed me off the premises. I was never to return there again.

It had worried me, to such an extent, that I reported my meeting to my boss the following day. "All I asked him was what he did in the war, I said, and he just clammed up". "No one really knows, said Peter, but we do know that it was top secret, and he spent a great deal of time undercover". "The latter day James Bond," I quipped. "Maybe, but we shall never know."

A year or so later, I spotted a bill board at the newsagents that displayed PAT WARD DIES- SECRET REVEALED . Could this be the answer to the question that had remained in the back my mind since meeting him? Curiosity got the better of me, and I rushed into the shop, handed over my 70p and bought the Harrow Observer. Here it was, at last I would know his secret . The face staring out of the newspaper at me was not the person that I had met on that evening at 'The Elms', but a photograph of a lady of the same name. I quickly read the article................   'The long lost documentation has been found in the home of Pat Ward 92, who died last week, confirming her to be the illegitimate granddaughter of Lord Nelson and Lady Hamilton, sometime residents of Pinner' .

The Pat Ward that I knew, coincidentally, also died last week.   His war secret had gone to the grave with him.

ITS ONLY A GAME

"Today was the day that it would all come together", thought Sam Fleming, as he stood on the first tee at the golf club. The sun was blazing down on the superbly manicured course, not a wisp of cloud in the azure blue sky, nor was there any tricky wind to contend with. Sam ,looked resplendent in his tailored blue and black check trousers, white shirt with the club emblem embroidered on it above his left breast, and a natty check flat cap that matched the trousers perfectly. His new white golf shoes fitted so well and comfortably that he thought that he was wearing slippers. Together with a brand new set of golf clubs, that the golf professional had recommended to him, he felt on top of the world. He had practised hard with the new clubs, and he had the notion, borrowed from Gary Player, the South African super star, that the more you practise the luckier you get. However, in Sam's case, this was not at all true, as try as he might, he could never get to grips with the game. His handicap was a generous 28, the highest that a man can have.

Sam was now in his early 70's and had been playing golf on a regular basis, sometimes three or four times a week, since he took early retirement from business some ten years ago, and he had arranged to play in his usual four ball today. The other three men, all about the same age as Sam, were David Brown; Roly Watson and Chris Smith. All three of them were much better golfers than Sam, but with their handicaps, it made for good competition. As usual they all put their marked golf balls into a hat and drew for partners. Sam got Roly as his partner. "What shall we play for today, said Chris, the usual?". "That's fine with me", answered both Roly and David, simultaneously. "How about you Sam, you have that certain glint in your eyes, what do you say?" "I'm feeling on top of the world today, and I feel that we should up the stakes, because I am sure that with these new clubs, I can, with the help of Roly, give you a damn good game. Let's play winner take all £20. The other three looked shocked at this, not because of the money, but the audacity of Sam to expect to win. Frankly, he was hopeless, and he only remained a playing member, due to his generous donation to the Club, when they may have gone out of business four years ago, and for that he received life membership. Anyone drawn with Sam, knew before they teed off that it would be a losing cause. Nonetheless, they enjoyed his company.

Sam watched with envy as all three of them teed off and effortlessly hit their balls straight down the middle. "No pressure then "said David "None at all, I'll show you", replied Sam. He stepped up to the tee, clutching his new driver. He unwrapped a brand new ball, and set it up on the tee. He went through his usual routine. He took two practise swings, wiggled his hips and addressed the ball. "You're going straight down the middle. Keep your head still, left arm straight, steady. Nice and smooth, and don't forget to transfer your weight", he kept saying to himself. Whoosh, the club raced through the air. It just about made contact with the top of the ball, and it dribbled about twenty five yards, not even past the ladies tee. "Bollocks", he shouted. "Not exactly a golf term" teased his partner, Roly. "Who's bloody side are you on glared Sam, you're supposed to be my partner. A little encouragement would have been more useful" Sam stormed over to his golf trolley and thumped his driver into the golf bag so hard that it bounced back and hit him on the head. He was really pissed off, this was going to be his best round ever, and what a stupid way to start. Roly walked with him to the ball. "It's only one shot, he tried to be encouraging, it's just like missing a little putt, it doesn't matter if it goes 250 yards or 3 feet , it still only counts as one". "Good advice, replied a slightly happier Sam, I'll try to take that on board for my next shot." He still had nearly 500 yards to get to the green, so he took out his 3 wood. He went through his pre shot routine, and struck the little dimpled ball so well, that wiped the smile off all of their faces. It travelled about 250 yards. "That's the way do it", he mimicked the puppet Mr Punch. He kissed his 3 wood, and replaced the cover, and gently put it back into his bag. "That's more like it", maybe this really would be his day after all.

Sam had never managed to score well, and it was his burning ambition that someday soon his score for the entire round would match his age. He had worked out that he needed to get his score down below his best ever of 100, but he reckoned that even if the good Lord was kind to him, his body would never stand up to a round of golf at the age of 100, so he had ambitions in the next ten years to get his score down to 82, some 18 shots better. Not impossible, as he only had to improve by one shot a hole over the whole round. Easy peasy.

The first hole was 490 yards, par five, and having walked to where the ball lay, he thought, that the ball was almost winking at him from its slightly elevated position, saying "go on big man, hit me again, like you just did, and you'll be on the green in 3 shots, with a chance for a birdie". With adrenalin pumping, Sam took out the three wood again, went through his routine, and smacked the ball. It was the most horrendous slice that took the ball deep into the woods. He hacked it out and miserably trudged toward the green, having taken 7 more bad shots to get there. The hole was lost. His mood had turned sour. "Why does this always happen to me? " he lamented, as the group made their way to the next tee.

If the first hole was bad, the next three were even worse. He lost his ball in the field that was out of bounds on the second; deposited a ball into the deep bunker at the next and couldn't get out, made worse by Bill quoting that his golf was like Hitler. "What do you mean, like Hitler? asked Sam. "Two shots in the bunker", Bill laughed. They were already 3 holes down, when Sam, having regained some of his composure came to his nemesis, the forth. Never in all the time that he played here, had he managed to get onto the short green from the tee. He watched the others play. It was then his turn. The water in front of the hole was glistening calmly in the sunshine. He would not take a new ball at this hole as he had nearly always splashed into the water hazard. He put down an old ball. He heard a voice from above, "Put down a new ball, be confident". He looked around him and the only people that he saw were his playing group. "It must be an omen", he thought. Then he heard the voice again. "Take a practice swing". Sam knew that divine intervention was at hand. As usual he practised with two swings of the club. He was just about ready to hit the ball, when the voice said "Sam, put down the old ball". That could mean only one thing, that was that the ball would go straight into the water. Undeterred, he stepped up to the new ball, swung gently, and missed it altogether. "Was that a shot?, enquired Chris. "No, it was just another practise swing", lied Sam. He hit the ball perfectly, and it soared into the blue yonder in a parabolic arc, climbing higher and higher, until it dropped onto the green, and started rolling straight towards the hole. The excitement was unbearable, as Sam had only ever dreamt of a hole in one, but this looked perfect. At that moment a large blackbird swooped down on the ball and picked it up in its' mouth and flew over the water and dropped it in to the pond. Sam went apoplectic. "That was a sure hole in one", he screamed. "No one can be certain that the ball would have gone in the hole, said Bill, I think that rule 19-1 applies here and you'll have to play it where the ball lies." "Don't be daft said Chris, I think this would be under rule 18-1 where you have to replace the ball from where it was taken". A long and heated argument followed, and because no one was certain of the rules, Chris and Bill said that Sam may have the hole with a 2 rather than a hole in one, but just to be sure, we'll check it out later. "Not fair, not fair, ranted Sam, who had never been this close to a hole in one. "Well, it's up to you, but you could always go back to the tee and try again with a penalty". "This is meant to be a friendly game, let's keep it that way" said Roly. " I agree" said both Bill and Chris, but Sam would not be denied his hole in one, and stormed off to the next tee.

They reached the next green, which was adjacent to Melanie Scott's Spanish looking bungalow . In the garden was a heart shaped swimming pool with the deep azure blue water looking very inviting on such a hot day. Scattered around the water that glistened in the sparkling sun light were several sun loungers, upon one of which, a young Melanie, completely naked, had draped herself, soaking up the hot sun and improving her ever deepening Mediterranean all over tan. The men all scrambled over to the hedge, jostling for a better view, and ogled her lovely figure. The golf game was completely forgotten for several minutes, and when it resumed, none of them could concentrate properly, and 4 or 5 putts was not unexpected. Still, it made for an enjoyable interlude from the match.

Sam's round went from bad to worse to disastrous. The hole that he thought that he had won, was, according to the rules, lost, as he should have played his ball from where it laid, and as it was in the water hazard, he should have taken a penalty stroke and played it from behind the water . He was furious, but there was nothing that he could do. Rule are rules. The match was over shortly after the 11th hole and £20 had gone down the Swanee River. They agreed to finish the round, and coming up the long 18th hole, Sam hit a screamer of a drive. "I know that I can play the game, he said, but how can I get any better if I can't string together 2 decent shots. The golfing gods always let me play well on the last hole to encourage me to come back again". Sam stood over his next shot, and inwardly prayed that he make a good connection that would send the ball over the large lake. He pulled out his 3 wood, eyed the ball and smacked it straight into the middle of the water. P E R L O P. He charged up to the lake, undid his bag from his trolley, and with all of his might threw the bags and clubs into the centre of it. "Good riddance to bad rubbish" he chuckled.

They went back to the clubhouse. Sam anxiously patted his trouser pockets. "What are you looking for"? "My keys, replied Sam"..........................and then he realised that they were in the pocket of his golf bag, at the bottom of the deep lake.

LOTTERY WIN

George married Judy, his childhood sweetheart, who he had met in the third year of their secondary school in Stratford, in East London. They had come from totally different social backgrounds, and at first, everything in the garden was rosy, but Georges' lack of self belief had nagged away at Judy, as she had always thought of herself as Middle class, but he was definitely working class, she had hoped, in time to change him. It had taken several years of courtship before her Parents would consent to the marriage, as they had demanded that he obtain his City and Guilds qualification.

Having qualified, as a master craftsman, he gradually blossomed and was taken on by her fathers' successful construction Company. The first step on the ladder, to taking over one day, hoped Judy. Within a few years, Georges' father in law, retired and handed over the reins of the Company to him. Judy was delighted. She could now become a woman of leisure, lunching with friends, and enjoying her life, rather than struggling on, in her words, a pittance.

With bold and new ideas, George invested in new equipment, vehicles, and a National advertising campaign. However, in the early 1990's the bank interest rates had soared to a massive 18% and despite taking out further loans the Company went bankrupt. The rows between them became more and more heated and vindictive. George blamed her, and she blamed him, and when the financial situation became untenable, she was ready to leave him; but not just yet as she was pregnant, and she would review her marital state once the baby was born.

She gave birth to a sturdy bouncing baby boy, that she named Henry. Not Georges' ideal choice, but as long as Judy was happy, and the baby was healthy, then so be it. The years rolled by and there was an uneasy cessation of hostilities between them, and by the time that Henry had reached secondary school, she divorced George, and won custody of Henry, with maintenance being paid by George. Love had gone out of the window, and she was like a woman scorned as she had been denied what she believed was her rightful inheritance from her fathers' business. Women and elephants never forget. George's confidence had taken a battering, and he had no real ambition now, and all he had wanted was a quiet life....until he met Mary. It was love at first sight, for both of them, they were completely besotted with each other, and he married for a second time. 20 years had passed since his disastrous first marriage.

George and Mary lived in a nice part of the town in a rented flat above the chippie, and no matter how hard they worked they just could not made the ends meet. They were both employed by The London Borough of Newham, during the day with his job in the maintenance division, which he had held down for the past four years, and also used his decorating skills 'moonlighting' for his 'beer money'. Mary worked as a dinner lady at the local comprehensive school, and really enjoyed the daily banter with the children. Secretly longing for a family of her own soon, but no chance just yet, as it was hard enough to feed just the two of them.

"Wouldn't it be fantastic if we could pay back the £500 loan to Mum and Dad", said Mary, fondly remembering the great East End 'knees up' to celebrate their recent wedding, only a few months ago. "We could always win the Lottery" joked George, in one of his more upbeat moods, as he normally was so pessimistic about life in general.   A trait that he felt that he had inherited from his rather morose dad. "Money doesn't always buy happiness replied Mary, but it won't 'arf help if we had a few quid of our own in the Bank."

"I've heard that The King's Head are looking for a new bar maid, George told Mary, and it pays good money. I know Fred, the landlord, do you want me to put in a good word for you?" "I dunno, I've heard that he's a bit of a letch, and I suspect that is why he has to change his staff so often" replied Mary. Just look at him, he is like a great big bloated porpoise, and has a reputation for 'wandering hands'. Who in their right minds would want to be on that side of his bar"? "I wouldn't go that far, snapped George, we are so short of money right now, that as Tesco says 'every little helps'. Please consider it, but if things get out of hand, literally, I'll sort it". "OK, let me sleep on it, and I'll let you know in the morning", said Mary.

Sitting in the cramped front room, with the stale smell of fried fish and chips wafting up into the flat, and clinging like super glue to everything, they were desperate to find somewhere else to live, but in their current financial predicament, it seemed hopeless. "Trying to get enough money to find a better flat is like pushing a pea uphill with your nose, I just don't how we will ever be able to afford to move from here", moaned, Mary. "With the opportunity of overtime at the Council, I reckon that by the end of the Summer I would be able to have saved enough money to at least be able to find something better, George replied, and if you took the job at the King's Head, we certainly would". "As I said before, let me sleep on it".

"I'm going up the 'frog and toad' to buy my fags, announced George, Do you need anything from the corner shop"? "No I don't think so, off you go, and don't be long, as dinner is in the oven, warned Mary.

George closed the front door, and heard Mary shouting to him "Don't forget to but the Lottery tickets". "OK, I will, he called back, how many lines do you want?" Mary threw open the window, and told him "get a fivers worth", I feel lucky, punk", a line that she often misquoted, that she had got from 'Dirty Harry' a film starring her current favourite actor, Clint Eastwood. "Usual numbers?" enquired George. "Yes, said Mary, do you know them, without me having to write them down for you?" "Of course I do, I've been buying the tickets every week, so I should jolly well know them off by heart", fumed George.

They always referred to Tesco as the corner shop, it was their little joke, although technically, it was. Situated at the junction of Eastern Avenue, in Romford, it was not in the colloquial sense, a little shop, but a vast Superstore. Gallows Corner was a far cry from its' origins, when it was a lonely country crossroads, famous for its' Gallows, and highwaymen. George thought that with the high prices of goods in the store, nothing much had changed in the last 200 years!!!

George bought his usual brand of cigarettes, went to the Lottery counter, marked the form with the same six numbers that had been chosen between them, being the birthdates of both of them, and various other memorable numbers. George crossed his fingers, as he did every time, mirroring the lottery logo, hoping that it would bring them 'The Big One' , went to the checkout and paid.

He returned home, and Mary had made a tray supper for them, whilst they spent Saturday night in front of the television, and the Lottery show with Dale Winton was eagerly anticipated. "What would you do with the money if we won tonight, George"? "I dunno, 'spose it depends on how much", said George, a tenner wont go very far". "It's better that a slap in the face with a wet wombat. Don't be so negative, we could just be lucky and win something big" enthused Mary. The show started, and they both enjoyed the quiz that preceded the actual draw, shouting out the answers to the contestants. "Cor blimey, they aint arf thick, how do some of these people get on the show, and with little or no knowledge, win thousands of pounds every week" moaned George. "If you're so clever, why don't you apply"? said Mary. "I think I will, where do I have to apply?" "They give the address at the end of the show, make a note of it then".

The lottery draw took place, and the balls fell into the slots, and as usual, not one of the balls matched their selection. "Oh well, it's back to work for us next week", sighed George, as the prize money this week of £2.1 million pounds was announced.

On Sunday morning, they walked to the pub, and on the way posted Georges' application form for tickets to the Lottery show. "Have you thought any more about the job at the Pub," asked George. "Yes, I am going to 'bite the bullet' and apply," said Mary. "Excellent, said George, and gave her a quick peck on the cheek.

Fred, stood at the bar of the pub, his bald head shining, and crooked nose, spread across his face, showing signs of his previous life as a professional boxer. His huge belly escaping from his tightly fitted clothes, resting on the bar. "Morning folks, what can I get you bellowed the landlord, the usual? Yes please, they both answered . "Have you got a minute? asked Mary, as I believe that you have a vacancy for a bar maid". "I've always got time for a young attractive lady, like you, let's go to my office, where we can chat in private".

"I would prefer to chat over the bar, if possible, as you don't appear to have your usual Sunday rush, just now" said Mary, fully aware of his reputation, and certainly did not wish to be left alone with him. Looking around the pub, Fred could see no reason why they couldn't have a brief chat about the job, and said "OK".

They talked for about 5 minutes, discussed the working hours and pay, and Fred told her "the jobs yours if you want it". "Let me mull it over with George, as I would like some time to consider it, I will let you know my decision, later today". Mary took George into the corner of the Pub, and related her conversation with Fred. " On the face of it, it looks like a decent offer, and I know that I can do the job, but there is something that is bothering me", said Mary. "You know that we are in dire straights' financially said George, what's the problem "? "He wants me to always wear a low cut top, and lean over provocatively, exposing my tits when I serve the male customers, and whilst I am no prude, I feel uncomfortable".

"Why don't you, at least give it a try, you could always quit if you don't like the job . Tell him you would like to take it, but why not have a trial of say a week, to see if you both are compatible", suggested George. "Good idea, I shall tell him now". "Excellent exclaimed, Fred, when can you start". "Tomorrow evening , at say 5.30 said Mary. See you then".

Three weeks later, George came rushing up the stairs of the flat, excitedly waving an envelope in his hand. "Mary, Mary, I've got a letter inviting me to appear on the lottery show in October, the 28th to be exact, screamed George, it also says that I can bring a partner, will you be free?" " I will have to check with Fred, but I suspect that he can spare me for a few hours, as I have been working my little butt off since I started, with no breaks, said Mary. I'll ask him when I go in later".

"It's not really convenient, as we have a 50th birthday party in on that night, but I suppose, that you deserve a rest. Custom has certainly increased since you started, he said, staring at her very low top and ogling her in his leery way. Go on then". "Thanks, and don't forget to record it, so that you can see how George, 'The Brain of Britain', gets on," she said cheekily.

The next few weeks flew by, and despite all of his bravado, George was really nervous, and his temper was fraying very badly, snapping at everybody. "You had better get out of that mood, warned Mary, or once you get on the show, the audience will give you hell, if you are not seen as being a 'nice' person". I'll be alright on the night, it's just so nerve wracking appearing before millions of people at prime time on tele." "I know, but keep calm, and just be yourself", encouraged Mary.

Arriving at the BBC studios in Shepherd's Bush, George was introduced to Dale Winton, along with the other contestants, and then briefed on how the show worked, which he already knew. "We shall be going live at 7.00, and good luck to everyone, said the producer, and try not to look to nervous. You've got three hours till kick off"

"Can I leave the Studios", asked George. " Yes, but make sure that you are back in Make Up by no later than 6.00".

George, wandered along and found himself in the Westfield Shopping Centre, and suddenly realised that in the excitement of the day he had forgotten to fill in the lottery ticket for tonight, found a booth took a ticket, but unexpectedly his mind had gone blank, and he could not remember his numbers. "Mary, will kill me, if I don't do it", thought George, and I won't lie to her, so I had better put my thinking cap on.

He walked into a Starbucks, coffee shop, and thought that the caffeine kick, would clear his brain. "A double espresso, please, George asked the barista, and a chocolate chip muffin. How much is that?" "£4.50 please." George fumbled in his jacket pocket, but he was all fingers and thumbs, and it took him quite a few minutes to locate the loose change. "Are you alright, sir, enquired the barista, you look quite unwell". "Yes, I'm OK, just a little off kilter right now, but it will pass."

He sat down, drank his coffee, and devoured the muffin, but no matter how hard he tried he could not remember the numbers. " Was it my birthday, Mary's birthday, our telephone number, an anniversary, our flat number, Oh blimey, what an idiot I am".

Looking at the clock on the wall, he had sat there for nearly 2 hours, and he was due back in 15 minutes. "Blast and damn it, i'll just have to randomly enter six numbers and hope for the best", he said out aloud. He gave the completed ticket back to the lottery booth, paid cash, and miserably made his way back to the studio to prepare for the show.

"Break a leg" Mary said, when she met him at the studio, "What's that supposed to mean"? he grumpily answered. "It's a show biz expression that people say before a show, I think that it means, good luck", do your very best, replied Mary.

The show started, and it was not too long before he heard Dale Winton say "George Mathews, join the Winners Row". The caffeine was now making him hyper, and he literally bounced along to take his seat. "Good evening George, tell us a little about yourself". Well, I'm 48 years old, married to my lovely wife, Mary for four months, and work for the local Council as a painter". "Another Rolf Harris, I suppose," Dale quipped, which brought a huge roar of laughter from the audience, "sorry George, I was only joking."

"Are you ready for your first question?" "Certainly, ask away, replied George, more nervous than he looked. Questions followed, and George answered them all correctly, until there were only two contestants left on winners row, including himself and an elderly lady from Huddersfield. "Tonight's jackpot stands at £15,000" announced Dale, "WOOOOOOOOOO" exclaimed the audience. "You must remember, that it's winner take all, and one of you will unfortunately be going home with nothing". "Not to worry said the lady from Huddersfield, I've had a great day. Good luck to you George, and the same to you, replied George". £15,000 would be a god send, if I manage to win, thought George. He glanced up at the audience, and spotted Mary, who blew him a kiss, and mouthed GOOD LUCK.

"There are three questions to be answered, and the first contestant to get 2 right will walk away with the jackpot. Are you both ready?" They both answered yes. The first question was answered quickly and correctly by George, who smiled inwardly. I've got this in the bag, he thought. The second question was tricky, and George thought that he knew the answer, but wasn't sure, and his hesitation seemed to give his opponent renewed confidence, and she asked "Is it Peru? Dale". "It most certainly is my love. It's one all now".

The final question was asked in hushed silence, and at the end of the question, they both pushed their buttons in front of them almost simultaneously, but George was a fraction of a second late. "What's your answer, please". "144" she said. "Absolutely correct, very well done, but hard luck George, I know that you knew the answer, but your finger was not quite fast enough. So sorry to be losing a great contestant". The audience went wild, they were certainly on the side of the pensioner from 'oop North'.

George was devastated, the money was in his grasp, but she had snatched it from him. No words of consolation could placate him. He had a face that looked as sour as a shrivelled crab apple, with the colour of a ripe fig.

"What a letdown, I knew it was 144, but the fickle finger of fate has beaten me again" moaned George, when he had reached the sanctuary of his changing room. Mary tried to be positive, "what we never had, we never lost; anyway, there is still the Lottery draw to take place. Let's put on the TV, and watch the Draw". She switched on the television, and saw Myleene Klass who announced "The Lottery stands at £5.1million. Tonight's celebrity is, Gary Barlow, Gary, please push the button".

"The first ball out is number ....The television suddenly went off, " must be a bad connection", said George. Immediately a voice on the television announced "Sorry for the interruption to this programme, there is a technical fault, and we are doing everything possible to restore the programme to you". "Bloody idiots, don't they know that this is the most widely viewed show all week, and the imbeciles have probably forgotten to put a shilling in the meter!! Whatever next, we're meant to be a first world Country, but some days, it makes me wonder", ranted George. "Don't get yourself all worked up, it's not that bad, as we can go to the studio and catch the end of the draw live," Mary suggested. Let's go, hurry, we don't want to be late".

Winding their way through the narrow corridors and up several flights of stairs, they arrived just in time to hear that there had been only one winner this week, who lives in London. "Could be us, hoped Mary. How can we find out?" They rushed up to the floor manager, and they were told that tonight's winning numbers for the Lotto draw were posted on the notice board in the centre of the studio . They almost fell over each other in the rush to look at the board, and there in six foot high letters were the numbers. "Well at least we've got £10. Let's hope for better luck next time."

" I've got Monday off work, said Mary, let me have the ticket and I will redeem it then". George put his hand in his right hand trouser pocket; not there, put his hand in his left hand trouser pocket; not there. "Try your back pocket you fool." Not there either. "Where could you have put it? Think man, think".

"The only other place I can think of, said a now profusely sweating George, is in my sock, where I sometimes put small items, so that I don't lose them". "Get them off, now, before I throttle you, you silly sod". George kicked off his shoes, and almost ripped the socks off his feet, and there sitting gently on the floor was the missing ticket. "Are you sure that this is the right ticket, as these are not our usual numbers, only numbers 1: 40: and 45 are ours said Mary. " I was confused when I went to buy the ticket earlier today, and my mind went a complete blank, although I thought that I had put the crosses in the correct boxes, but obviously not, I don't know what to say"...................

"Well it's, not a total disaster, we're lucky enough to get 3 numbers, so it's £10 " replied Mary. " Well it is in my book, grumbled George, have you forgotten already that I nearly won Fifteen grand". "As I said before, said Mary, we never had the money so we didn't lose it. Cheer up it's not the end of the world". With that, she put the ticket into her purse.

She couldn't shake George out of his miserable depressed state, and was moaning and groaning about life's little disasters that always seemed to befall him, all the way home on the train . He was totally disenchanted with life in general, only to be compounded by the ever present smell of decades old grease in their flat. " When will life ever throw me a decent bit of luck"? "Let's have a few drinks and forget about it," coaxed Mary.

His bad luck got worse on Monday, when his boss called him into his office. "George, he said, I don't really know how to say this, as you have been one of my better workers in the time that you have been here, but I have received instructions from my bosses, that due to the economic slowdown, we are having to make redundancies, and am sorry to say that your name is included in the 200 people that I am having to sack". "I've been a very hard worker, and loyal during my time with you, surely there must be a mistake", pleaded George. "No, there is not, look at this written directive, your name is on the list, there is no mistake. Please collect your personal belongings and go". "What about my redundancy money?" "It's all in hand, and Personnel have instructed the wages department to pay the money straight into your Bank Account, at the end of the week". "What am I to do now". "Don't know, said his sympathetic, now ex boss, you could always 'sign on' at the Employment office. You're young and fit, and maybe some Private companies are looking for good workers like you. I am happy to give you a reference. Good luck, and goodbye".

His miserable day continued, when he arrived home at mid-day. "What are you doing here at this time of day", demanded Mary. "I could ask you the same question", said George. " You first, Mary instructed, but I think that I can guess from the look on your face". "I've been made redundant by the Council, not enough work, so me and 199 other guys have all been laid off". "What about you", George queried. "That Fred is an effing pervert, cried Mary, I was in the cellar, helping him bring up some bottles, when he made a grab for me. I just managed to avoid his lunge, picked up a broom and smashed him in the goolies, at the same time as telling him to go to hell. I'm never going back into that pub again. Naturally, I also lost my job".

"I'm going to collect the Lotto winnings, Mary said. I'll call into the newsagents, by the bus stop at the school, and at least there will be a Tenner for us". "Suit yourself" shrugged George. I'm off to the Labour exchange, or whatever fancy name they call it now days, to sign on". There were no jobs available, as no one was hiring anyone at the moment. The property market was as flat as a pancake, and D I Y was the only industry that was making money. . At least there was Marys' money, small, but money, all the same.

Mary took the bus, and was walking towards the school, when she remembered that the Lottery ticket was still in her purse, made a quick U turn, towards Martin's newsagent, and a little tinkling bell alerted the shopkeeper, that there was a customer in the shop.

"You're new here, aren't you?" Mary asked, when she was greeted by someone that she had not seen in the shop, previously. "Yes, this is one of the Group's training shops, where new recruits learn 'the ropes', before being moved on to larger stores in the organisation, he said. How may I help you?" "I've only come in this morning to claim my £10 winnings on this ticket, it is OK to claim it here, isn't it? said Mary, although it was bought at Westfield in Shepherd's Bush" . "Of course, let me have the ticket please". Mary handed him the crumpled ticket, and apologised for its' condition. He looked at it, and handed her a crisp new £10 note, from the shop till. " Thanks ", said Mary, and then made her way to school.

As soon as she was out of the shop, the man in Martins', locked the front door, and hastily put a 'Temporary Closed' sign on the front window, put the ticket into the Lottery Machine, looked at the list of winning numbers again , just to be certain that the 6 crosses matched, collected all of his personal belongings, to make his way to the Lottery Office, to claim £5.1m. Before embarking on his journey to Watford with the ticket, Henry, telephoned his mother. "Judy Mathews" the voice answered. "Hello Mum".

MISSING

It was just another ordinary day, if one could call life ordinary, but in my case it certainly started off that way.

The gentle buzzing of my alarm clock woke me as usual at 4.30, and I reluctantly got out of my bed, fumbled in the dark for my slippers, that I had carelessly kicked off last night. Scrabbling on the floor I discovered one had landed in the waste bin, whilst I couldn't find the other one, so I limped into the bathroom, dragging one foot behind me. I switched on the lights, which appeared so bright that I had to shield my eyes from the glare. The shower, that until recently had been playing up, with the thermostat deciding what temperature the water would be, that was going to be inflicted on my body . Some days hot and some days cold. I usually braced myself, playing 'cat and mouse' with it and gingerly put my hand under the dribble that I had expected, only for the water from the shower head to cascade down like a waterfall, making me involuntarily pull my hand back so quickly that I smashed it into the door. It was, unexpectedly the perfect temperature.

I finished in the bathroom, and went downstairs to the kitchen and made my usual breakfast of a glass of orange juice, followed by a bowl of cereal. Today it was corn flakes, and at the same time popped two slices of wholemeal bread into the toaster. The electric kettle was whistling and so I poured myself a quick cup of instant coffee, that I would take through into the newsagents shop that I managed on the High Street, right next to the Station. The shop blinds were still drawn, when the first bundle of newspapers thudded onto the pavement, by the front door, and I quickly retrieved them to save them from getting soaked in the pouring rain and sleet that was hammering on the windows.

My brother, Billy, was due to arrive at 5.00, as usual, before setting off to his full time job at ICI, to help me get the papers sorted in order for the paperboy to deliver them, but he still had not shown up by 5.30. This was very unusual, as he was always so punctual, that I could set my watch by him. Was he unwell? If he was, and never in the time that I ran the shop was he absent, surely he would have telephoned me? I checked both the land line and my mobile phone to see if there had been any missed calls or messages, whilst I was in the bathroom, but there were none. I phoned him, but there was no answer from either of his phones so I left messages for him . Very strange. Not like him at all.

Billy was in his mid thirties, seemingly fit and healthy, who lived a bachelor's life, for some time now, since his Columbian wife, Maria, had died in suspicious circumstances. He had met her whilst he was travelling in South America, during his gap year, after gaining a first class degree with honours in chemistry and physics. They had a whirlwind romance and married within six months of meeting, much to the chagrin of her very strict parents, who had already 'earmarked' a very suitable Columbian for her. Billy had left home in Brighton a single carefree young man, but he had met Maria and they had initially settled in her hometown of Bogota, before his return home, single again some 2 years later. The job market in the United Kingdom was nonexistent in the late nineteen eighties. Despite numerous applications and interviews there were nothing available for such a highly qualified person.

Back in 1990 he told me that he was going to America . He had read an advert in 'The Times', that had seduced him, with the opportunity to make his fortune in the big wide country that welcomed all qualified people with open arms.   He had ants in his pants, and just couldn't sit still. Silicon Valley in California, was his destination at the cutting edge of technology and research.   He told me that If that didn't work out, he still had got some contacts in Cartagena near Bogota, and not to worry about him. He confidently assured me that he would be alright. We kept in constant touch by telephone. Billy had many jobs in America, none of which he suited or they didn't suit him, and even after a brief visit to Columbia, he landed back in England after seven years, and with some of the money that he had earned, had enough to put a small deposit on a flat, just up the road from my shop.

"Now that you are home, what are you going to do?" I enquired, when he telephoned me, last month. "I've landed on my feet, he said, and I shall start with ICI next month, in Millbank, in London." "That's great, when can you come round for a get together?, I'd like to catch up with all of your time in America." "I don't know about all of it, it would take too long, but am very happy to come to yours, anytime in the next few days". "Let's pencil it in for Wednesday, at say 7.00 after I have closed the shop." "Excellent. See you in a couple of days."

I was slightly shocked, when Billy arrived at my door, as he had lost a considerable amount of weight, and he walked with a slight limp, that he had not had previously. Otherwise it was the same old Billy, but a little more careworn. We sat around the glowing open fire, that threw off a serious amount of heat, so much so, even though the outside temperature was near freezing, I opened the window to get some fresher air into the room. The curtains billowed in the wind, and the traffic noise came in as well.

BANG, BANG, BANG loud cracks echoed around the room, . I looked across the room to see Billy instinctively duck behind the settee, as if avoiding a gun shot. "What the hell are you doing ? , I shouted at him, it's only a car back firing". "Sorry, he said, as he heaved himself up from his prone position on the floor, I suppose you ought to know a little bit more about my time abroad." "Let's get a couple of beers, I suggested, and I have the whole evening to listen to your story."

"I'm not certain where to begin", he said, as we sat ourselves down in the lounge, by the fire. "Why not start at the beginning, that's as good a place as any", I joked. Taking a long swig on the beer bottle and wiping his mouth with the back of his hand, he started.

"When I left university, you recall that I went travelling in my gap year to South America, where I had imagined a perfect way for me to unwind. I saw myself chatting up tourists and selling trinkets on the beaches and clubbing with the locals. It was at Cafe del Mar on the waterfront, where all the locals hang out, that I met Maria Garcia Gomez. Incidentally the Columbians don't have one but two surnames, taking them from their respective parents. Anyway, I digress. She was the most beautiful woman that I had ever set my eyes on, and I think you would agree, from the photographs that I sent you. She radiated an aura that lit up a room. She was a lightly dark skinned stunner, about 6' tall with long legs that stretched right up to her slim waist. Her jet black hair hung loosely down her back and had a magnificent sheen. Her deep brown eyes were like pools of crystal clear water, that gleamed and sparkled. The sensuous mouth and perfect teeth always had a lovely smile. Her fabulous body was to die for. An absolute goddess. She had also just graduated from university, and was modelling on a part time basis. Everything about her was just perfect, except at the time, I didn't realise that she had a South American temper. It was love at first sight as far as I was concerned, and I would do anything that she asked, as I was totally besotted by her."

She lived in her family's house which was originally constructed in the late 1500's and harkened back to a time gone by. Hidden behind a large wooden door with brass door furniture that included the most intricate circular brass knocker. The door opened onto a colourfully paved courtyard, that blended perfectly with tropical fruit trees that surrounded a central fountain, splashing gently into the pond.

"I know that I am no David Beckham, but she saw something, that attracted her to me, almost instantly. We were inseparable. Just like a strong glue . Life was just perfect. We spent our days, lazing on the beach, at Bocagrande; taking a boat to Islas del Rosario, an archipelago of 25 small coral islands, which had an amazing array of marine life. It was ideal for scuba diving. I met lots of her friends, both male and female who made me feel most welcome. Groups of us would ride horses on the vast open lands, like the renowned Pampas in Argentina, where temperatures hovered near 100 degrees. And by night, sneaking away from the crowd, and, well, I don't need to be more explicit. Let your imagination run wild, and then some. I was in heaven. The only 'fly in the ointment' were her very religious parents, who didn't like me very much, as they had already agreed with another family that their son would marry Maria. I discussed this at length with Maria, who was very strong willed, and it didn't matter what her parents had agreed, she would do whatever she wanted to do, and made it very clear to me that she would defy her parents. She was going to be my perfect partner."

Opening a second bottle of beer, Billy went on with the story.

"Maria's parents' were upset, as we announced that we were to be married. Family loyalty and obedience is very important to Columbians, and any marriage agreements that were broken were deemed to be an insult to the offended family, and dishonour for her parents. We told them that the ceremony would take place in the little local Catholic church just outside Cartagena, but despite all of the persuasion under the sun, they refused to attend. As far as they were concerned Maria had been tempted away from them by a Gringo, and she would no longer be part of their life. It's such a shame that our parents are no longer alive, as they would have most certainly have loved Maria, and they missed the most wonderful day of my life. The wedding, as you know from the video that I sent you, could not have been better. The party that followed, was unbelievable. Our friends had done us proud. The party went on for a week. Those Columbians certainly know how to enjoy themselves."

We finished our beers, and made some sandwiches for us to eat, while Billy continued.

"We now had to decide whether to stay in Cartagena or move to Bogota, where there was more chance of me finding work, whilst Maria, using her contacts could always find work as a model in a big city. I applied for a couple of jobs, but because my Spanish was not yet good enough, nothing was available, although Maria was always in constant demand, and basically for the first few months I was a kept man, living off her wages, in a tiny flat on the outskirts of Bogota. Fernandez, one of our friends, knew of my plight, and suggested that we meet, as he heard of something that would interest me. He told me that his company, which was a member of the National Association of Columbia, had heard that there was an opening at the headquarters in Bogota, that could be right up my street. He knew the managing director, on a personal basis, and could 'open a few doors' if I was interested. I was, and he arranged for me to meet one of their Presidents Carlos Villegas. I, as you know, got the job in their research and development department. It was very 'hush hush' as I was working on a Government project to try ways to stop the illegal drug trafficking. I was just a member of a small elite team, and had to sign many documents, the equivalent to our Secrecy Act. We were making a good life for ourselves, before tragedy hit me."

"Maria and I had been invited to a fancy dress party, in Cartagena one weekend, and we thought that it would be a good idea if we were to go as Laurel and Hardy. I found a costume outfitter, who specialised in hiring costumes and arranged to go to his warehouse with Maria in the week preceding the party. We tried on several, before finally finding the right sizes, and were in stitches when we put on those silly bowler hats. Mine was too small, and Maria's fell down over her eyes. The assistant padded out her hat, and said it would be just fine. I thought that a small hat for me was also good. We took the train to her hometown and booked into a small hotel for two nights. On the Saturday night, the night of the party we went to our room, pulled down the flimsy blinds and made unbridled passionate love on the creaky bed. Our lovemaking just got better and better, discovering new and exotic ways. Neither of us were in any hurry to go to the party. We showered, each other, slowly, dried off, and before getting dressed in our outfits, ordered a taxi to take us to and collect us later from the party. "

"That's when all hell broke loose," he choked back the emotion that was welling up in his eyes as he recounted the terrible events that were to follow. "Do you want another beer, or soft drink"? I offered, seeing the state that he was in. "No thanks, just give me a moment to compose myself."

"The gunshots rang out with such a noise, at first I didn't comprehend what was happening, until I looked across the room and saw Maria lying face down on the floor with blood pouring out of her neck. I rushed over to her, whilst keeping my body close to the floor, as a hail of bullets ripped into the room from the open window. One of the shots hit me in the leg and another shattered the ceiling light. The bedside lamp cast an eerie shadow across the room. I crawled over to her, clutching my leg, and I could see that she wasn't moving, and the deep red pool of her blood got larger and larger. She was dead. I'm no hero, but foolishly I threw the bullet ridden curtain open to see if I could see anything that might be the shooter or getaway car, but no luck. Within minutes pandemonium broke out at the hotel, with guests and staff running hither and thither, in total chaos. I shouted for someone, anyone, to get the police and ambulance, as I was losing consciousness due to the bullet hole in my leg. I must have passed out, for the next thing that I can remember was the bumpy ride in the back of the ambulance. I kept fading in and out of what was happening."

Billy paused for a good minute or so to try and regain his composure, but I could see that he was in no fit state to carry on. I rushed quickly to the drinks cabinet and poured him a huge brandy, which he swallowed in one swift movement. He sat for a while and let the warming glow of the drink calm him down sufficiently for him to continue with the story. Pulling himself upright from his slumped posture he said " By the time I had regained my mind, as the drugs that the doctor had given to me had knocked me sideways, a week had elapsed. The State had buried Maria. Captain Manuel Ortiz Diaz from Police Region 1 in Bogota, had been sent by The National Police of Columbia to interview me, as it seemed that I was the only one left that could possibly help them, as the only three other guests at the hotel had also died in the attack."

"There was nothing more that I could add to their very limited account of the events, and whilst he sympathised with me, I could tell that there was nothing else that he could do to help catch the killer. He told me that the shooting had probably been associated with a drug cartel, and we were just unfortunate to be in the wrong place at the wrong time, so much for justice."

"I was released from the hospital and had to learn to walk on crutches, but my first port of call would have to be to my in- laws, a visit that I was dreading. I telephoned them, but they refused to take my call. I telephoned one of Marias' close friends and told her of the events that had shattered my life, and asked if she would be good enough to speak with my in- laws, and request that I needed to see them urgently about Maria. She told me that as far as they were concerned, Maria had died the day that she married me, and didn't want any contact with either of us ever again. I wasn't going to just leave Marias' death unsolved, and spent the next 18 months, following up every lead that I could. The hotel had CCTV, and I studied and studied the tape for hours on end, trying to identify anything, however insignificant, to try to lead me to her killer. A big fat zero. Depressed, and heartbroken, I came home, and you know the rest of my story."

That was three days ago, and now Billy had gone on the missing list, as far as I was concerned, and concerned I was. There was something in his story that I felt that he was not telling me, but for the life of me I couldn't put my finger on it just yet. I carried on as usual, without Billy this morning, and telephoned my head office to ask if I could take some compassionate leave. They were very understanding, and allowed me 2 weeks off.

I drove to Billy's flat, and let myself in with the spare set of keys that he had given me. Nothing out of place at first glance, but I did notice that some of his clothes were strewn over the floor, as if he had been looking for something. Nothing odd about that either as he was always the untidy one when we lived together at home. I looked in the wardrobe and saw a space on the floor, where he usually kept his travel holdall. I went to the bathroom, and the medicine cabinet was empty. He had obviously gone on a short trip somewhere, but hadn't advised me. After all I was not my brother's keeper. Just to be on the safe side, I called into the local police station on my way back home, to advise that Billy had not been seen or heard since last Wednesday, and told them that it was probably nothing, but for them to keep an eye open for him. I gave them a description and old photograph of him, together with details of his Ford Ka.

I received a call later in the day from the Police, who told me that Billy had left England on a Lufthansa flight to Bogota which left London Heathrow at 11.05 this morning and has one stop over and will arrive at 23.35. I thanked them, put the receiver down, and wondered why he hadn't told me of his plans. What should I do now. Wait, or be decisive, and try to get to him in Colombia, as I was now sure that Billy must have stumbled upon some new evidence that may help solve Maria's murder. I made my decision. I would try to find him in Colombia.

I took a taxi to Heathrow, and boarded a non-stop flight to Bogota, which arrived 10 minutes before the Lufthansa flight was due to arrive, and with luck, I would get there before him. My plane touched down at 23.12, due to the tail wind that had sped up our flight, and as I was coming through the arrival hall I noticed that the Lufthansa flight had also landed. I waited for the passengers from his flight to disembark, and confronted him in the hall. "What the hell are you doing here?" he exclaimed when I approached him. "Just making sure that we stick together, this time, as 4 eyes and ears are better than two." "What are you talking about?" he said in mock surprise, I'm here on a relaxing short holiday before I get stuck in to my new job". "Pull the other one, I said, I wasn't born yesterday. I know that you're up to something, which I suspect has more than an element of danger attached to it, so here I am, on my white charger to help you in whatever quest you have. Blood is thicker than water, and if there is anything to be discovered, two heads are better than one." It took some time to convince him, but he relented, and told me that indeed, something had come up, and he would be very glad of my help.

We checked through immigration and passport control, which was run by the Colombian Police, and after extensive questioning, we picked up a taxi outside of the airport and made for a hotel that Billy knew from his previous visits. He told me, before we entered the taxi, not to speak to each other, as the DAS, the Colombian Secret Police, had eyes and ears everywhere, as do some of the taxi drivers who could be connected with criminal gangs. When we got to the hotel, he signalled for me to say nothing. We checked in to a small, but clean, family run hotel, unpacked our few belongings and went to Bolivar Square in the centre of Bogota. Hundreds of people filled the square and the noise of the traffic made our conversation almost perfect as it drowned out what we were saying. "Fernandez and I have been in constant touch since I left here, and through his network of friends and contacts has been able to find someone willing to talk to me, Billy said, and I have a contact number to set up a meeting. I have purchased two mobile phones on a pay as you go basis, and they will never be traced to us, as we shall destroy them, once we are in a 'go' situation." "Spies, spies and more spies, sounds like a scene from 007, and no doubt a web of lies and deception is what I suspect we shall encounter", I mocked back at him. "Not forgetting the most important part are you? he said. "And what's that? I replied." "Our guns of course. I haven't used one since I was in the Territorial Army, years ago but it was Corp de rigueur, when I was last here, and I was pretty handy then. Bogota's reputation as a dangerous City is not entirely undeserved." "The only time that I have handled a gun, was when I won a Teddy Bear at the fun fair I said. Where can you get the guns from?" "I can pick them up from one of my friends later", he answered.

Early next morning, Billy phoned the number that Fernandez had given him, but no name was attached to the number, as the contact wished to remain anonymous . "We are here in Bogota, Billy said when the phone was answered. "Who are WE, the heavily accented voice replied, I was told that it would only be one person". "It's OK, it's me and my sister". "Let me think about it, and call me back on a different phone number in 30 minutes". The contact gave Billy a new phone number, and swiftly ended the call. "What did the contact say, I asked, you've gone as white as a sheet". "There is a query about you being here, and has gone away to think about it. I bloody well hope that you haven't ballsed it up for me ",he said angrily. He stomped off in a huff, towards the statue of Simon Bolivar.

The clock on the Palace of Justice struck, and Billy, now huddled over his phone, called the contact as arranged. "OK, the voice said, I've done some quick checks, and you've been cleared. Meet me at The Zona Rosa, on the Andes mountain road up to La Calera at 11.00 tonight."

"How will I recognise you?, Billy queried. "Don't worry, foreigners stand out, and I shall recognise you." The phone went dead. "The meet has been set up for tonight, so let's get back to the hotel and rest up. I'm sure that you are suffering from jet lag, as I am, and it takes it out of you, being at this altitude, some 8,500 feet above sea level," Billy said in a far better mood. "You're right, I'm absolutely cream crackered", I yawned at him.

Before returning to the hotel, we checked with the Tourist Information office, and discovered that The Zona Rosa was about a 20 minute drive, North East of the City on a well lit road, that made it easy to find, and not trusting local taxis', arranged to hire a small car from Avis, and drive there ourselves. Billy's Colombian driving licence was still valid, so no problems there.

We set an alarm call, and were woken from a very deep sleep at 8.00, enough time for us to pick up the car, and drive to the rendezvous. We wanted to get there early, but not too early so as not to attract unwanted attention. The night was clear, and a bright full moon helped to illuminate the tarmac road, that climbed steadily up the mountain. There were many restaurants and night clubs along this road, and we drove slowly as we didn't wish to over shoot our destination. "There it is, I said, pointing at the gaily decorated barn on the right hand side of the road, pull in here". The parking area was made up of crushed rocks, that threw up dust everywhere, as we looked for a suitable spot. "Make sure that you reverse in, and leave plenty of space, just in case we need to get out of here in a hurry," I said. "Good thinking Batman, it's good to have Robin on my side" , he laughed.

We climbed the few wooden steps upto the entrance, and were greeted by a blast of music, as we went in. "Bienvenido, a large ruddy faced manager said, as he doffed his sombrero to us. Make yourself at home, and enjoy your evening." He showed us to a table by the window that had spectacular views of the City of Bogota, with its' twinkling lights shining in the distance. "Dos beers, per favour" ordered Billy as the waiter asked what we were drinking. We sat for about half an hour, and had another two beers. The waiter put the beers on the table and handed Billy a note. We thought that it was the bill, and ignored it as we drank. A gust of wind from the window, blew it onto the floor, and I picked it up. It wasn't the bill, but a note in poor English asking us to leave the club now. I showed it to Billy. "Christ, he exclaimed, that was 5 minutes ago. Let's pay the bill and vamoose". I put 30 Pesos' on the table and hurried after Billy into the car park, where we were met by a tall willowy man, who said nothing, and indicated that he wanted us to get into his car, which we did. He put two sets of hooded blindfolds over our heads quite forcibly. He tied our hands behind us and removed our guns. The drive was over very bumpy land, which I assumed was not a road or even a track, and imagined that we were going down the side of a mountain. He drove for about an hour, and then stopped. He tugged off our hoods, and bundled us out of the car. We saw that we were deep into a forest, with no visible natural light anywhere, the only light coming from a roaring open fire. We were in some form of camp. Armed men surrounded us.

A dark swarthy man stepped out of the shadows. He had a shaved head, and wore a well trimmed goatee beard on his chin. He was smoking a small cigar. There was a tiny crescent shaped scar next to his right eye, on his weather beaten face. If he had a wooden leg and a parrot on his shoulder, I thought that he would look like Long John Silver. He walked slowly towards us, looking carefully at us with eyes that seemed to bore into us. Remarkably he spoke with a beautiful clipped accent that he had obviously learnt at Cambridge or some other English institution. He smiled. "Sorry to put you through the rough treatment, but I can't be too sure who is coming to this camp. Luis, untie our guests, and return their guns to them." Luis stepped forward, and did as instructed. "I'm,...well you don't have to know who I am, and the less you know the greater are our chances of remaining undetected, he said. We have formed this group of trusted people to fight the corruption, extortion, drug trafficking and murders that go on daily. The vast sums of money being made from these illegal operations often tempts people to change sides, so be very careful, and only speak to us. No one else. Understand?" "Understood, loud and clear", we replied.

"Without naming names, Billy said, I was told that you could help me, he turned towards me, - us, find the murderer of my wife, Maria Garcia Gomez, who as I am sure you know was shot dead some years ago, and the culprit remains at large. Can you help, as all of the investigations that I have made so far has led me to dead ends."? "Information has been obtained, don't ask me how, but be aware that it comes from an un-impeachable source, that you and your wife just happened to be in the wrong place at the wrong time. We believe, although we are not entirely certain, that it wasn't you and your wife that the gunman was after, but the couple staying in the room next to yours in the hotel, who worked under cover for us, and they were eliminated by gunmen from the Norte del Valle cartel, who as you probably know are amongst the largest drug dealers in the world."

"Well, at least I know why she died, but I want revenge, and I mean to get it, with or without your help", said a fuming Billy. "Calm down, I said, let's hear what more he has to say, pointing at the leader of the gang. "It's not as easy as that, he said, the cartel are all powerful, and they are well protected by the Secret Police, and as you know have many soldiers in their organisation who they pay very well, and breaking into them is virtually impossible." "That, I understand, but there must be a way to get close to them. You did it once, as you admit, so why can't we try again. I've lost everything, apart from my sister, and that means that I am prepared to risk my life so that at least my Maria can rest in peace." There is no need to risk your lives, if the plan that I have works. If not we shall just creep back into hiding and carry on our work here". "I don't want you or your group involved, said Billy, we can handle this ourselves, just point us in the right direction, and we shall take our chances."

"If you're sure, then I won't stop you, the leader said, but you have to be very careful not to expose my group, it would have International repercussions". "What group, we haven't seen any group", I laughed. It's no laughing matter, because if you are caught they will torture you, and I am afraid that you will crack, and jeopardise my operation, which I can't allow". "Can't we have cyanide pills, or whatever is today's equivalent," I said. "These are not stable, and I wouldn't want you to die unnecessarily because you accidentally bit down on one, he replied. The best and only way that I could allow this operation to take place, is by sending Luis with you, and he will know what to do if things go wrong".

Billy and I had a hasty conflab, and after much toing and froing , we agreed that I could be included in the operation, and Luis could be along to help if necessary. "We have a deal, I announced, when can we get started"? "You need to have a plan, and I think that I know a way that you can carry it out, and escape without putting yourselves in any danger, the leader told us. Let's go into my house, and I shall explain it to you". We were all ears, and the excitement was coursing through us, as he described, in his view, a good way for Billy to get to the Drug Lord.

Using the route that one of his men had used before to take us near the headquarters of the cartel, we took almost a week to get there, by being ultra cautious, and covering our tracks on the way. We slept, rough in the open, under the stars, and one of us was always on guard. Some nights we were alerted to strange sounds coming out of the forest, but although we were primed and ready, nothing untoward happened. We reached a spot about a mile from our objective and went over the plan of action one last time. We had it worked out with military precision.

Helicopters flew overhead, patrolling the perimeter of the huge estate that was the headquarters of Norte Valle, as did gun toting speedboats that sat in the water which surrounded the Island where a magnificent Colonial house stood in hundreds of hectares. The only road access being across a long wooden bridge, guarded at both ends, and a permanently fixed boat, moored underneath it. A railway track and loading area ran behind the house. The Colombian flag flew over the wrought iron gates that led to the house. This was a fortress that no one could hope to get into without an invitation.

"You can't possibly go in there on your own, I told Billy, it would be suicide." "I haven't come this far, just to look at the scenery, he replied. I've come to get revenge for the murder of Maria, and the way I feel right now, nothing in this world will stop me." "With that attitude, you will be in the next world very soon, I said, holding him back from making a reckless foray into the open, where he would meet his certain death. These guys are just animals, and killing one or two more people won't mean a thing to them". Luis helped me to restrain him, and after a fierce struggle, we managed to get him to calm down. "We need another plan, said Luis, as our first one is now hopeless".

A train was coming down the line, and heading for the loading area. "Did you see that"? I said, there doesn't appear to be any checks being carried out, as the train just travelled past the guards". The train stopped and turned 180 degrees on the revolving turntable. A group of men loaded crates into it, and when it was full, started on its' journey out of the estate. "I bet those crates are full of illegal drugs, said Billy. No doubt heavily guarded by the henchmen. Any chance that we could use the train for us to get entry?" " Not a snowballs chance in Hell, we would be shot to pieces if we tried. Put that idea out of your mind," Luis said.

"We just can't abandon this mission, sulked Billy, thrusting his hands deep into his pockets. Let's think on it overnight, and we shall make a final decision in the morning." We bedded down in a damp hollow, but I couldn't sleep very well as it looked like our long dangerous mission was about to be aborted. The nights were getting very cold in the mountains, and our thin blankets gave almost no warmth at all. I slept fitfully, and in the dawn light saw our one and only opportunity to get onto the estate . A thick fog had descended overnight, and you couldn't see your hand in front of your face. I looked around me and Billy's sleeping pack was empty. I couldn't see Luis either, but I assumed that he was in the bushes somewhere on guard duty.

I looked under Billy's blanket, and saw a scrawled note that was pinned to it. "Sorry guys, I couldn't sleep, and the thought of abandoning this mission was just too much for me to contemplate. I saw the fog, and I've gone to try and seek my revenge. If I don't make it, thanks for all of your help. It was signed 'Billy'. "What an idiot, I said , he'll not only get himself killed, but us as well".

At that moment I heard gunshots, and shouting, but had no idea where they were coming from, as the fog distorted my sense of direction, but I assumed that the shots were coming from the estate. A crashing noise was followed by more gunshots, and I saw a black SUV come hurtling through the wrought iron gates that had been ripped off by the vehicle. Bullets were pinging off the SUV. I realised that it must be bullet proof. A grinning Billy was at the wheel driving like a Formula one racing driver, tossing the vehicle this way and that, down an unmade path through the forest. Luis was hanging out of the passenger window returning fire. A posse of cars burst through the gap where the gates had been, but due to the thick fog, couldn't accurately follow the SUV.

I heard a most tremendous explosion, and the sky lit up. I grabbed my few things, and ran like a demented thing roughly in the direction of the car. I stumbled and tripped several times down the very slippery slope, with the overhanging branches tearing into my fragile body, until I fell headlong into a ditch. I was too exhausted to get out. Fortunately, I was covered in fallen leaves, so any pursuer would have difficulty in finding me. I lay shivering in the ditch for some time. My arms and legs were covered in cuts, scratches and my whole body ached. I could see large bruises forming on my legs.

I heard footsteps crunching on the ground nearby. I instantly froze and held my breath. I was about to be captured. I fumbled in my pocket for my gun. It wasn't there. It must have fallen out of my pocket when I made my hasty retreat. Bollocks. I was almost helpless, apart from a sturdy branch that I picked up off the bottom of the ditch. I awaited my fate. The footsteps got closer and closer. I had to breathe or I would suffocate. I let out a small gasp, followed by other small gasps, and hoped that I wouldn't be heard. I took another deep breath, and waited, and waited and waited. I could still hear footsteps, but they were getting fainter, so I bravely put my head up through the leaves and saw the backs of two men that I recognised. They were Billy and Luis. " Help, I whispered , help". They hadn't heard me. I didn't want to shout as it may alert my pursuers. With my last ounce of strength, I managed to claw my way out of the ditch, to where I thought that the boys were. I cautiously crawled on the forest floor, and saw them, hands tied behind them, being led by a lone man, pulling them by a rope.

They were being used as bait to catch me, I realised. The man tethered them to a tree, whilst he unzipped his trousers, to have a pee. His back was to me, and I sprang up and with all my might smashed the branch into his head, almost decapitating him. He went down, like a ton of bricks, fly still open and had to jump clear of the spray. "Great shot, Billy laughed through cracked and swollen lips. He's got a knife in his belt". I got the knife, and freed the boys. "That's the best forehand that I've ever seen you hit. What a winner", you should think about entering the Ladies singles at Wimbledon next year.".

Luis took the knife from me, and in one swift movement slit the throat of his captor. Blood spurted everywhere. "What did you do that for?", I tried to scream, as Billy put his hand over my mouth to prevent me from possibly revealing our location. "Had to do it, Luis replied, because he had a fate worse than death waiting for us, when he got us back to his base." "How did you get here? I thought that you would have escaped and be halfway back to Bogota by now". We couldn't just leave you, so we stopped in what we thought was a safe place, but 'Jonny' here, he said pointing to the dead man, was waiting for us, and he overpowered us quickly. He knew that there were three of us, and he had orders to take all of us alive. Let's get out of here."

We walked about 15 minutes and found the SUV, and drove back to Luis' camp. "You did a great job, the leader said, when we had been de briefed. How did you manage to explode the drug factory?" Billy spoke. "We go on to the unguarded train, that was standing next to the factory, and found a gas line that served the building. From my days as a Territorial Army member, I remembered how to set an explosion, giving us enough time to escape. I cut some holes into the gas pipe. I hotwired the SUV and we drove very slowly, at first under the cover of the fog, until someone saw us. At that point it was shit or bust, and Luis shot at the gas line and it ignited almost immediately. The rest you know". "You managed to destroy the whole factory, and I've had unconfirmed reports that most of the gang were killed, although Daniel Barrera, known as Crazy Barrera is on the run, heading for Venezuela. However, the organisation will probably re-form though under a new leader soon."

"I know that we did a good job, Billy said as we waited at Cartagena to board the helicopter, that would take us back to Bogota, but I feel that I have not really avenged Marias' death, and feel empty." "You managed to wipe out one of the biggest drug cartels' in the world, and you may have killed her murderer in the process", I tried to placate him. "I know, he replied, but I still feel that something is still missing ." A well dressed man approached us. "Are you Billy Wood?" he said in English. "Yes I am". The man handed Billy an envelope bearing the crest of the British Governor in Colombia. He tore it open an read the contents.

Thank you for your unofficial help in destroying one of the major drug factories. I understand that you are seeking clarification on the death of your wife, Maria Garcia Gomez, and can advise that she was killed by mistake by her jilted boyfriend, Jose, who was part of the drug cartel, in a small way. Jose has admitted that he followed you and Maria to the hotel, and thought that he was going to kill you, but the rifle jammed and shot haphazardly into your room, killing her and three bystanders. He has since been executed. I'm so sorry for your loss. It was signed Sir Thomas Duggin, Her Majesty's Ambassador to Colombia. Floods of tears flowed from Billy, and I hugged him tightly, trying to stop him from shaking. Not the news that he had wanted to hear.

We walked up the steps to the helicopter, strapped ourselves in for the short journey to the airport. The helicopter lifted gently into the blue skies over Colombia, and then exploded into a fireball that crashed into the sea. There were no survivors. .... The new drug lord, smiled as he watched the carnage, and gently fingered the small crescent shaped scar by his right eye.

NO TURNING BACK

Neil, standing at the corner of the pub in Temple Bar, looked at his watch , put it to his ear, just to see if it was working. "That's the third time that you've checked your watch in the past few minutes, said John, I don't know why you put it to your ear, modern watches don't tick". "Where the hell is David, it's nearly 8.00 and he is never late".

Neil Hutchins, John Stevens and David Peterson, always met after work on a Friday night, and had been doing so , since they had all graduated from Leeds University, some 10 years ago. They had chosen this pub, being equidistant from their places of work in the City of London. It was a little gem, built sometime in the Middle Ages, and used as a staging post between London and Manchester, before the advent of the motor car. The little street still retained the original cobbled stones, in this tiny enclave just behind St Pauls Cathedral. Unless you knew it, you would never stumble across it by mistake, and they liked it because it served their favourite brew, Old Peculiar. A very strong creamy Yorkshire beer, that is World renowned and known locally as the 'Lunatic's Broth'. A beer that they discovered whilst they were undergraduates.

The pub, was run by Graham, ably assisted by 25 year old Julie, another very good reason in the boys eyes, why they should frequent it so regularly. She was very attractive. A typical dumb blonde bombshell, 'she had often heard the 'boys' say. She had an hour glass figure, that made all of the male customers very flirtatious , whenever she served them. Neil, John and David, were no exception, and all had been out with her, separately, at one time, not for her brain, but her fabulous body. She was only working there because she was unable to break into the fashion industry as a model, just yet. She hoped that one day, one of her customers would spot her potential and sign her up on a lucrative photographic contract.

The pay was not great, but both she and Graham had supplemented their income, playing the Stock Market, by listening carefully to some of the conversations that their loud mouthed drunken customers often inadvertently gave them.

They were all single, and fast approaching 30, and still thought of themselves as 'The three Amigos'; lads about Town, who liked to 'play the field' before settling down. John, who saw himself as leader of the pack, ran the office of an up market Private Chauffeur service, that provided personal protection, and discrete anonymity to his clients. Neil, was a follower, and despite gaining the best results at University, had somehow, got left behind on the job front, and he was now employed at The Temple Court Hotel, as the principal concierge. David had a job in the offices of an International Bank, where he was 'a market maker', and whilst it paid a fair salary, there was no way that he could call himself a 'high flyer', and he had seen, lesser qualified people join the firm, and go past him in the pecking order, to earn, in his words 'immoral money'. Jealous?, of course he was.

"Here he comes now, announced Neil, as David, in a very flushed state, burst his huge frame through the saloon style swing doors. It's past 8.00 and we are already on our 2nd pint." "What a day, I've had, get me a pint please, said David, I'm absolutely knackered." He took off his Burberry raincoat and unwound his matching scarf, letting it fall onto the sawdust covered floor. He was sweating profusely and took a napkin from the bar to swab the moisture off his rotund freckled face, that peered out from beneath his shock of Boris Johnson style red hair.

"Sit over there, said Neil, pointing at the table at the back of the Saloon Bar, you'll get a cool draught from the back door, and you'll soon be back to normal." John brought over three frothing pints of beer, put them down, and no sooner done, than David had gulped his pint down in one swift movement. "Didn't even touch the sides, said David, wow, that's hit the spot". "Calm down, David, why all the drama?" enquired Neil. " Just let me get my breath back, properly, and I can reveal all," panted David. "I'll get the next round, said a much calmer David. Three more pints please Julie", David called out .

Neil and John, sat down, careful not to put their sleeves of their almost matching Armarni suits onto the beer that had slopped over onto the table. "What do you think has put David in such a spin?, I've never ever seen him like this before", said John. "Beat's me, we'll just have to wait and see" Neil replied.

David, now completely calm and under control looked at his friends and a smile slowly formed on his lips. "How would you two like to get rich, he said, seriously rich?

"What are you talking about? You know that we have always hankered after the good life, it must be the beer talking, that's affected his brain", joked Neil. "No it's not the beer talking, I'm perfectly, well almost perfectly sober, although I must say that perhaps I shouldn't have quaffed the beer so quickly. Do you or don't you want to hear my story?" Looking at David with a serious expression on his sun tanned face, Neil was totally convinced that his pal was far worse for wear than he would admit, and that David had 'come off the rails'. "OK, big shot, let's hear it". Taking a deep breath, and hoisting himself up into a more comfortable position David begun to relate his story.

"I was in your hotel earlier this afternoon, just after 2pm, you remember, don't you, Neil?, waiting in the lobby to meet Mr Umar Alfredi, a new and extremely wealthy Pakistani client". "Yes, it was only a few hours ago, idiot, at least my memory is in fine working order", chided Neil. David continued. "Well, whilst waiting for him to arrive, I heard a message being paged 'Mr

Alfredi, telephone call'. I went to the desk, and advised that he was not yet here, and I could take a message. I was directed to the phone booth, where I picked up the phone. "Don't speak, just listen, a gruff sounding slightly accented voice said. Go directly to Westminster Abbey, at about 4.30, just before it closes, and buy an entry ticket. A letter will be waiting for you in the third row of the central seating area, under seat number 65. Just follow the instructions".

"The line went dead. I was shaking quite a lot, as I have never, in all of my life had a call like this. I then realised that the call was not meant for me but for Mr Alfredi, my client. I would relay the message to him when he arrived."

I went back to my seat in the lobby, and waited for another hour, until about 3.30, but there was still no sign of him. I had tried his mobile phone, but it just kept ringing and going onto his answerphone. Somewhat pissed off, I left him a message asking him to call me to rearrange the meeting. You know it happens sometimes, a new client makes an arrangement, and then changes his mind. This was not the first time that this has happened to me, nor do I suspect that it will be the last.

David was in full flow now, and Neil and John were captivated by the events so far. "More beer? Suggested John, you need to whet your whistle, I think". "OK. Three more beers arrived, and David took a sip, and continued. "Just as I was leaving the hotel, I noticed the television in the Reception area with a bold notice emblazoned across the screen, announcing BREAKING NEWS. I stopped and went closer to the screen. "A terrorist car bomb exploded at 2.30 this afternoon, in Central London's Regent Street with many casualties expected . It would appear that the suicide bomber has died in the explosion. Survivors are being rushed to Charring Cross Hospital. We understand that 70 year old Pakistani, Umar Alfredi , in London for Peace talks in the Middle East, is amongst the injured. No further news on his condition yet. More news when we get it".

I Googled Umar Alfredi on my I-Pad and there was not a great deal of information about him, save to say that he was listed as a philanthropist, and an expert negotiator within The United Nations. He had made his living in textiles . He was a widower with no children.

"What did you do next?" Neil and John excitedly said, almost in unison.

"Well, what would you have done?" said David. Neither of them could come up with a sensible answer. "Get on with your story, David."

David, took another mouthful of beer, and let it slowly trickle down his throat, savouring the delightful taste. "In this world there are some life defining moments, and I made an instant decision that this was it. "Julie, three more beers please, and some salt and vinegar crisps". They drained their quarter full glasses in front of them. Julie served them with a new set of drinks.

"What decision did you make, slurped John, who had taken too much beer in his mouth and splattered some of it over his friends. "Sorry, said John, let me clear it up". He quickly cleaned the table, and patted down the wet areas, on everyone's clothes, and the story continued.

"I hailed a cab, and went to Westminster Abbey- YOU DID WHAT? Exclaimed an incredulous Neil. "You heard me. I bought a ticket, for £16, went to row three, lifted up seat 65 and pocketed the letter, looking carefully around me to check that no one was watching me. The Abbey was almost deserted as it was nearly closing time, and no, I did not see anyone or anything out of the ordinary. I thought that just in case there was , I would not open it until I had reached the safety of my home.

"I have read loads of spy stories and so I would try to be as clever as these fictitious people, and throw off any potential pursuer by taking a bus to Victoria Station, and mingle with the crowd of homeward bound commuters. I purchased a ticket to Brighton, that stopped at East Croydon, where I got off the train. Still saw no one that looked suspicious, made my way across the station, and boarded the London bound train back to Victoria. Real cloak and dagger stuff! Convinced that I was not being followed, took a taxi to

Connaught Square, and then walked the half mile or so to my flat in Bayswater Road, casting furtive glances over my shoulder every few minutes.

"I literally flew up the stairs, two at a time, to the second floor, where my bedsitter is situated. Put the key in the lock, and opened the door. A dim triangle of light formed on the floor as I quickly entered the flat. I carefully locked the door behind me. Threw my coat onto the settee, opened the fridge, and popped a can of beer. Sitting down, I fished the slightly crumpled envelope from my pocket, and using my Swiss Army knife, slit it open.

"Don't keep us in suspense, spill the beans"

"The envelope was not addressed to anyone, and I pulled out two sheets of paper, upon which were instructions, written in bold capital letters from words cut out of a newspaper . I have brought it with me. David dug deep into his jacket pocket and produced the sheets.

"Read it to us, said John, not too loud," as the pub was surprisingly quiet for a Friday night. The City types, were obviously working late, tonight.

David spread the sheets of paper in front of him, holding them close to his chest, as he did not want anyone peering over his shoulder. He read

MAKE SURE THAT THE PEACE TALKS FAIL. TWENTY MILLION POUNDS STERLING IS YOUR REWARD. A CASH SUM OF FIVE MILLION POUNDS STERLING NOW. BALANCE PAYABLE ON FAVOURABLE OUTCOME. David paused for effect.

On the second sheet, a small key was attached to the corner, and further instructions read

USING THE ATTACHED KEY AND THE SAME NUMERALS AS AT THE ABBEY (I assumed 365, said David), GO TO THE BROMPTON SAFE DEPOSIT IN KNIGHTSBRIGDE FOR YOUR INITIAL PAYMENT

Somewhat aghast by the contents of the letter, and very sceptical, "What are you going to do?" queried Neil, and was repeated , parrot fashion by John. "What are you going to do?"

Grinning from ear to ear, David excitedly said " I'm going to take the cash".

"WHAT???????????? YOU CAN NOT BE SERIOUS, using that well known John McEnroe phrase, that has now entered the daily vocabulary, the money is not yours".

"Oh yes it is- possession is 9/10th of the law".

"You will have broken the law, by stealing something that is clearly not meant for you. You have no legal right to the money, Kosher or otherwise", said John.

"Who says so?" "We do", they now sounded like a well rehearsed duo, speaking both at the same time. "It's not legal" said Nigel. "Why not?" "Because it's not, that's why."

The banter was going backwards and forwards, and David, slightly light headed from the booze, tried to reason with them once again.

"Listen guys, old Mr Alfredi is unlikely, so I understand from the news bulletins, to survive his injuries, and no one is going to go to the Police saying that the 'Hush Money' is theirs, are they?" " I suppose not". "So this is where you two can come in, if you want to. £1m each for you, and £3m for me. All we have to do is collect it, and you can watch my back, so to speak".

Nigel stood up from the table, they had been sitting there for over an hour, stretched his legs, and announced "I'm going for a 'Jimmy'. My bladder is full to bursting." With that he hurried to the loo.

"Let's wait until Nigel returns, and we shall then have a really meaningful discussion to decide whether you want any part of the money" David, coolly said.

When Nigel returned, David asked "Are you in or out, I'm not really sure that you are 100% with me? This is a once in a lifetime opportunity. If you take it, there's no turning back".

"Give us a few moments longer please, want any more to drink?" asked John. "No thanks, said David, I'm so full now, that another of those will make me a bit ' Brahms', I'm going to take a leak."

Nigel and John huddled over the beer in their glasses, and quickly downed the contents. "Ugh, it's gone flat. No surprise, We haven't touched it for ages. Another one?" enquired Nigel. "No thanks, I think that we have all had enough right now, and we still have to get home, somehow," replied John. What do you really think, about David's offer, It certainly sounds tempting, doesn't it?"

"I'm not so sure, said Nigel. The organisation behind this are obviously ruthless, having already arranged a car bomb, and are offering vast sums of money for the Peacekeeper to favour them. They certainly won't want to part with £5m knowing that the intended recipient is in hospital, on the danger list with his condition being 'touch and go'. They wouldn't be so foolish to lose sight of their money, would they? Maybe the bomb and message were activated by a well paid sympathiser, and the real terrorists are still at large in the Middle East".

John, listening intently, thought about what Nigel had just said. "Could be that as the bomber blew himself up in the atrocity, and with a news blackout, the real perpetrators may not be fully aware of how Mr Alfredi is, or is not progressing".

"John, I've got a reasonable job, paying reasonable money, and no real worries. I could never, ever be part of a scheme, however tempting, to accept 'Blood money'". "I agree with you, replied John. The more that I think about it, the more unattractive it seems. I certainly don't want to spend any time in jail, nor become a target for the terrorists. Let's tell David, when he gets back from the toilet."

They sat around, for another 15 minutes or so, and talked about the Arsenal versus Spurs football match that they had tickets to see, this weekend. David had not yet reappeared. "Do you think that he has had too much to drink, and has passed out in the loo? Let me go and check," said John.

John walked, on slightly wobbly legs to the door marked 'Fella's', pushed it open, and there was no immediate sign of David. He went to the first cubicle, it was empty. So was the next one. He pushed the door of the last one. It was stuck. He pushed again, he could just about open it, and he could see David sprawled on the floor. "Silly fool, he could never hold his drink", and obviously here was just another example of David's drinking capacity. John needed help to get him out of the cubicle, as it was almost impossible for one person to move a dead weight of some 18 stones.

He went back to the table, and told John the situation. "No worries, we'll get him out somehow. Julie, will you please phone for a taxi, David has passed out in the toilet, and we need to get him home", Neil shouted across a now crowded pub. "OK, it should be here in about 10 minutes", Julie replied.

John and Neil returned to the toilet, and somehow dragged David's limp groaning body into the open area of the washroom, when the restroom door burst open. "Pfoot, Pfoot, Pfoot, the silencer on the gun spat out the bullets softly, making neat holes in the centre of their heads.. Julie picked up the crumpled letter and key, "Who's a dumb blonde now?" she laughed , and quickly made her escape through the open window, taking the waiting taxi to the 24 hour safety depository in Knightsbridge.

THE WRONG SUITCASE

Sitting in his very plush first floor Mayfair office in this period building, watching the wispy clouds chasing each other across the sky, and the Autumn shadows lengthening, in that hidden treasure that is Mount Street Gardens, the intercom startled him out of his reverie.

"Jeffrey, his PA said, Manuel Ortiz is on the phone, shall I put him through?"

Manuel Ortiz, Manuel Ortiz, who is he? Jeffrey tossed the name around in his head. Oh yes I remember, he is the agent in Spain, that I used last year on that abortive transaction, yes put him through, Sonia".

After the usual opening greetings, Jeffrey asked what the call was about.

"This is your last opportunity" Manuel said, " to secure this fantastic re-development site, right on the beach front. It has eight hectares, and with my connections at the Mayors' office, I am certain that we can get planning permission to build a fabulous upmarket and infinitely superior Estate that would make Calahonda, seem second class, but this is on the other side of the A-7 Highway , and all of the units will have sea views. I know that your Client is familiar with the site, having visited it last year and expressed serious interest".

" How good are your contacts in the Mayors' office" Jeffrey replied, as I would not want to waste my Clients' time, nor expenses in trying to get the permission.

"My contact is 'as good as gold' and I know exactly what it will take to get the permission, and I recently concluded a deal that went, how you say in English, 'as sweet as a nut' "enthused Manuel. Jeffrey was very sceptical, as he had never been involved in any overseas development previously, but he had a small knowledge of the area, having spent several years holidaying in Spain. However, as a well established and trusted London Development agent, he knew his way around the British planning system, but not the laws that govern development in Spain.

"I've heard of these things from England, and it normally involves a 'sweetener' so I understand, said Jeffrey, am I correct?"

"It's not referred to as a sweetener in Spain, but as an 'enhancement' into the Mayors' coffers for use locally, advised Manuel. "Pull the other one, that money will go straight into his pocket won't it? , I wasn't born yesterday!"

"No, it really does go to the local government, and the last deal that I did, a new roundabout was built from the 'enhancement', Manuel said, and next time you are here I will show you".

"OK, you have me partly convinced, let's get to the bottom line, how much is required to ensure that planning is granted,"? Jeffrey asked.

"On a Major development, like this, the money is required up front, and it is normal that a percentage of the agreed 'enhancement' should be paid when we meet the Mayor, which incidentally needs to be CASH".

"I'm not sure that my Client will go for this, and I am certain that he would not wish to fall foul of the exchequer both here and in Spain, which probably has a jail sentence attached, if caught. Surely a bankers draft, all legal and above board, would suffice, it's like having cash, but only safer", Jeffrey replied.

"The only way that the Mayor will meet you, and guarantee planning permission would be for a minimum payment of 350,000 Euros, and then there is my finders' fee on top of that of a further 150,000 Euros, which as you can work out for yourself is a nice round figure of half a million Euros. That's the price, take it or leave it" Manuel said more forcibly than before.

"I'll have to take instructions from my Client, as I can not commit him to something that he feels may be illegal, but he knows the site, and was keen, as you know from last year, to progress with a purchase on a subject to planning basis. I'll get back to you later today".

"You had better be quick, as I have other development Companies that I can speak with right now, and I have a very wealthy Russian Oligarch, constantly chasing me about this site, and knowing him, as I do, he won't be put off much longer"

Jeffrey hated to be put under pressure, as all of his working life he was quietly efficient, and did not like to be told what to do, but he said goodbye to Manuel and then immediately telephoned his client.

"Charles, it's Jeffrey. You remember the site on Marbella beach front that you saw last year? Well it can now be bought, subject to planning permission for 25million Euros, are you still interested"?

"Yes I am. You know full well that I would give my eye teeth to buy it, and the price seems a bargain, even in the current market conditions. I had my architect draw up a scheme, last year, and I think that we can get in excess of fifteen hundred units on the site and the profit will be enormous. How can we secure it now?"

"You know of my contact in Spain, Manuel; well he has the ear of the Mayor, and providing that you can pay him 350,000 Euros in cash, he will make sure that planning is granted, but he needs it up front and now, and on top of that the greasy little Spaniard wants to line his own pocket as well , to the tune of 150,000 Euros, also in cash. I have told him that you will probably not wish to comply with the request as it most probably is illegal, but I told him that I would take your instructions first"

"Don't be a wus all your life, Jeffrey, if you don't take chances you'll never get rich. I take chances every day; all life involves risks, that's why I feature every year in the Sunday Times top 100 Rich List. Let's do it".

"When can you be ready"?

I'll instruct my bank in Spain to have the cash available for me on demand, and we can go as soon as they are ready. Let's close the deal before someone else tries to snatch it from under our noses.

Immediately the phone call had ended, Jeffrey phoned Manuel and relayed the news.

"That's great, when can you get here" asked Manuel.

"You name the time and the place for a meeting with the Mayor, and we shall be there."

Five or so minutes elapsed before Manuel called back, "the Mayor is available all day tomorrow, so name the time, and we shall all meet in my office for the transfer of money. How are you going to bring the cash?"

"I'd rather not say on an open line, but rest assured that it will all be there tomorrow, at say 3pm your time, in your back office, away from prying eyes. See you then"

"It's all systems go for the meeting at Manuel's office for three O'clock local time tomorrow, Charles".

"Great. I'll get my chauffer, Peter, to collect you at 6.30 from your home in the morning and we shall take my private jet to Malaga, where I shall arrange for my housekeeper Pepe, to pick us up in the Mercedes to go to my bank to collect the money. Incidentally, could you bring something with you, ideal to put the money into when we collect it from the bank"

"No problem, my wife and I have almost identical cases when we travel light, and I shall bring hers with me. See you in the morning"

Hurriedly, Jeffrey packed his suitcase, and placed his wife's slightly smaller empty suitcase, inside his, and put them on the floor by the front door, and went to bed.

A restless night ensued, as at the back of his mind, Jeffrey was uneasy about being party to breaking the law, more so in a foreign country, but surely they would be governed by the same money laws as the UK, as they were part of the European Community, weren't they? He had heard horrific stories about the conditions inside the Spanish jails, and most certainly did not want to end up incarcerated in one of them.

Ding Dong, Ding Dong, Peter stood at the front door, dressed in his immaculate grey chauffer's uniform, and peak cap, with his usual cheery face greeting Jeffrey with a very warm "Good Morning, Sir, nice to see you again" Are you ready to go?

"Yes, it's only this suitcase. "Let's get the show on the road ". Peter drove them to the private airfield at Elstree, where sun tanned Charles, with his long blonde hair swept back off his face revealing the wrap around pilot's sun glasses, beautifully attired in his Burberry jacket, and suede loafers, was already waiting.

The flight took less than two hours, and being a Private plane there were no customs checks on the way out. Pepe met them at Malaga Airport, and on instructions from Charles drove them to the bank.

"Buenos dias, senor Charles , had a good trip? smiled the Bank Manager. Shall we go into my office to conclude the transfer?"

"Really good flight, thank you, lead on and we will follow you."

"The money has been put into bundles of 50,000 Euros each, with 10 in total, equating to 500,000 Euros, and as requested the notes are all in 500's. Please sign here, pointing to the line on the document, in Spanish," to allow the money to be released to you".

Charles, having a good grasp of the Spanish language, and also a fully qualified solicitor, prior to becoming an entrepreneur, studied the document carefully, and satisfied, signed, where indicated.

"There is rather a lot of cash here, said the bank manager, how are you going to take it?"

"We have already thought of this. Jeffrey, please go to the car and bring in the suitcase, and let's see if it fits, instructed Charles". Jeffrey did as requested, and emptied the larger suitcase, and brought the smaller one into the bank managers office. The money fitted perfectly into the case, and Charles took the case with him.

"Muchas gracias" senor Javeir. It's a pleasure, as always doing business with you. See you again, soon."

Charles put the suitcase into the boot of the car, and locked it into a hidden compartment. They now had a couple of hours to 'kill' before meeting with the Mayor, and Manuel, so they decided to have lunch in a little seaside restaurant on the edge of the waterfront, very popular with tourists at this time of the year. There was nowhere to park, so Charles asked Pepe to collect them in about an hour and a half, allowing plenty of time to be at the meeting.

"Isn't it rather risky, leaving the money in the boot of the car," queried Jeffrey, as anything could happen, and you wouldn't want to lose it, would you". "Pepe has been with me man and boy, said Charles, and I trust him implicitly". " If you're happy, then that's OK with me".

Tactics for the deal were discussed in detail over a beautifully presented Paella accompanied by a magnificent bottle of Rosado, a chilled Spanish rose, whilst taking in the breathtaking palm tree lined promenade with vibrant coloured flower beds, a tranquil setting, away from the noisy main highway, from which they had just come.

Precisely at 14.30, Pepe arrived at the restaurant and Jeffrey and Charles got in to the car and were driven to the meeting.

Arriving at the offices of Manuel, the suitcase was taken out of the boot by Pepe, and was handed to Charles. " Please pick us up in about 2 hours from now, as we have some business to discus, and hopefully, if all goes well, we shall need you tonight, to take us to Robbie's restaurant in Estepona, where I have a table booked for 7.30 this evening, and we shall also need you to collect us late tonight"

"Si, el jefe, no hay problema (yes boss, no problem)".

The meeting started and after much 'horse trading' a deal for the site was eventually struck, almost three hours after the start, and in order to facilitate the transaction, a side letter was signed by Charles, the Mayor and Manuel, outlining the payment of the 'enhancement' money to both parties.

In very good English, the Mayor said "once I have the money, I shall start the process of securing the planning for you, which I expect to obtain a grant of planning in about a month"

"Excellent, to celebrate the deal, I have booked a restaurant for us tonight, and Pepe will be at our service all night" said Charles, but where is he, he should have been here about an hour ago?"

"Probably caught up in the traffic jam on the Highway, which seem to occur with more and more regularity lately, interjected Manuel, but in the meantime let's check that all of the money is here".

"I'll get the suitcase, said an excited Jeffrey, who could already see his very large commission looming up in his eyes, let me fetch it". With suitcase in hand he passed it to Charles, who with a large grin on his face, flicked the lock, and almost had a heart attack when it opened up to reveal only the overnight bag, and change of clothes that Jeffrey had packed the night before.

"What the hell is going on here, that stupid idiot Pepe, has given me the wrong suitcase, I'll read him the riot act him in the morning. He is pretty useless anyway, and I have only kept him on, as a favour to his late father, so if I have to fire him, it's no great loss. I'll contact him on his mobile phone and get him back here with the correct suitcase". Taking out his mobile phone, Charles carefully punched in Pepe's number only to hear the message in Spanish "The mobile phone that you require is not in service, nor does it allow you access. Please contact customer service by pressing 611". He tried again and again, and again, with the same response, becoming more and more angry, turning his sun tanned face into a red bloated one, as the situation became more obvious. "The Spanish dago has fleeced me, just wait till I get my hands on him.. Get me the police" bellowed Charles.

"Just hold on a minute, Charles, involving the police may cause more problems, as they will want to know how the money was going to be used". "It's none of their damn business roared Charles, it's my money, and i'll choose how I spend it" . "Calm down, take a deep breath, and think before you do something that you may regret.

"You're right , of course", I have my own sources, and rest assured we shall catch that little beggar, and he won't know what day of the week it is"

On leaving Charles and Jeffrey at 3 o'clock, Pepe collected his wife, who worked at the Bank, and had told him yesterday about the money transfer. They went directly to the railway station, booked two, one-way tickets, paid cash, therefore leaving no obvious trail. He had previously picked the lock on the secret compartment, in the boot of the car and switched the suitcase with half a million Euros in it. They took it aboard the Spanish National rail Renfe Train heading across the border to the very safe, and secretive Tax haven in Andorra, some 550 miles north .

The high speed train left on time, and soon reached its' maximum cruising speed of 350kph (220 mph). Pepe had calculated that by the time the switch of suitcases had been discovered they would be safely out of the Country, where they would be safe, and looking forward to a better life. Only a few miles from the border, the speeding train went out of control and crashed headlong into a nuclear waste tanker, straddling the railway track at an unmanned crossing, and immediately exploded into a spectacular fireball, creating a large mushroom cloud, that when dissolved left devastation and destruction of everything in its' path within a quarter mile radius . Complete and utter devastation...............

.............However, the train from Malaga to Andorra was not non stop, and with the formalities of completing official entry documents, at the border, which would have given any following investigators a clue to their whereabouts, they slipped, un -noticed off the train at Barcelona, and disappeared into the labyrinth of narrow sleazy streets just off the Ramblas and were never seen again.

HURRICANES

They were all gathered around listening to the Test Match at the Oval Cricket Ground in 1976, between England and the invincible West Indies. "The bowler's Holding the batsman's Willey". The witty deep brown chirpy voice of Test Match Special's Brian Johnston boomed out from the radio in the changing rooms of The Hurricane Cricket Club. "Did I hear him correctly" laughed Michael Carson, the new young captain. "You heard him all right, you've got a mind like a cesspit growled Colonel Peter Proctor, the ex –captain. You know full well that he is referring to Michael Holding, the West Indies strike bowler, and Peter Willey, the England all-rounder."

The Club, had been established exactly 175 years ago, by Peters' great, great, great grandfather on the land in front of the magnificent Georgian Manor House, set in some 500 acres, in a small village in the middle of Hertfordshire. Peters' family had been the owners for at least 300 years. Over the years, the club had grown in stature, and now played very competitive semi professional cricket in the first division of the National Club League. Over the years, the idea of a friendly game had slowly disappeared, and nowadays fierce competition was the order of the day.

There was no love lost between Michael and Peter, and the recent election, was hard fought, with promises from both to favour anyone that had voted for them.

Peter has captained the Hurricanes for the past 17 years with modest success, whilst Michael knew, that with his engaging personality, as well as his undoubted talent with a bat, having scored over 1,500 runs in each of the past four seasons, and was well on his way again this year to surpassing that figure. He strongly believed that with his drive, and modern thinking, he could steer the club forward. After all it was now 1976, with the mini recession a distant memory.

Michael won the captaincy by a very narrow margin, after two recounts, and then immediately installed his brother Morris, as his vice captain. The brothers were born to be cricketers, as their cricket mad parents had christened them both with the immortal initials M.C.C. after the imperious Club of the same name; Marylebone Cricket Club, the doyen of all cricket clubs. Clive was their middle name.   Their background was that the family were re- housed from a rough and dangerous estate in Harlesden, North West London, some years ago, where they attended the local comprehensive school. The brothers were bright boys, and managed to get into Birmingham University. Michael graduated with a 2.1 in economics, whilst Morris, just about scraped through with a 2.2 in History, and was now teaching it.

Michael was 26 , tall, slim, with an almost handsome face, with laughter lines around his smoky grey/green eyes. He had a natural ability to make you feel as if you were his best and only friend.   Morris, some 2 years younger, was also about 6' tall, but his torso showed signs of acquiring a beer belly, even at this early age. For some reason his attitude to life was totally the opposite of his brother. He was the one born without the happiness gene! He could often be seen brooding over trivial things. The one real passion in his life, apart from the opposite sex, was his gleaming red convertible MGB, with his personalised number plate MCC 100, that he drove as if he were Nikki Lauder, the current formula 1 champion. The car purred smoothly like a sleek metal dragon. He called it his 'Pulling machine'.

Michael, was currently dating Samantha Billings, who worked in the cricket club office, and they both were serious enough about their relationship, that she moved in with him to his cottage on the edge of the village. Morris was not at all pleased, as it was he that had first dated her, being friends from university, but she 'ditched' him in favour of his elder brother. She had hurt Morris very badly.

On the other hand, Peter, now aged 51, had served his Country with distinction in both Iraq and Afghanistan. He was in effect Lord of the Manor, and whilst he only played at it, he was a well respected pillar of the community. He was tall and willowy with an elongated thin face, deep blue piercing eyes that looked out from behind Billy Bunter style glasses, that he wore on the end of his Roman nose. Beneath which, was a most magnificent handlebar moustache. The hair on his head, once wavy , was now waving goodbye. "Grass doesn't grow on a busy street", he would say if anyone jibed him about his follicle demise.

The estate, was run by downtrodden Mellor, his fathers' manager, who quite frankly, was well past his 'sell by date', and should have retired years ago. Because of his age, he had been demoted to 'head cook and bottle washer', and was always seen wearing his long gamekeepers coat, with his hands stuffed deeply into his 'poachers' pockets, whatever the weather. He was suffering from lung cancer, and was told by his doctors that his time on earth was limited. Nonetheless, Peters' reluctance to change bore its' own fruit - a poorly run business, with money oozing out of the family coffers at an alarming rate. "Got to keep up appearances, he mentioned to Mellor. See to it that the rents are collected weekly, rather than monthly, as cash flow is a little bit tight at the moment. Only a temporary blip". "The villagers won't like change", he replied. "Just do as I say, bellowed Peter, jabbing the stem of his spittle filled pipe at him. "YES SIR, emphasized Mellor , mockingly touching two fingers to the peak of his tweed cap, I'll see to it right away."

"How many tickets have been sold for the 175th anniversary Ball?", Michael enquired of John the clubs' managing secretary. "All 500, John replied, a complete sell out, and at £25 a head we will have £12,500 from the ticket sales alone. On top of that I expect to raise another £1,500 in profit from the bar, and if we are lucky enough perhaps a further £2000 from the raffle". "That's fantastic, enthused Michael, we can do an awful lot with that."

"You haven't forgotten the extra gate revenue when we entertain Middlesex in the Gillette Cup, on the same day are you"? "No I haven't, but let's put it down as a bonus. We are insured, against the match being cancelled, I hope". "Yes, although the premium is exorbitant it will be well worth it, if it doesn't not take place.

"You know how important the match is to both myself and Morris, as I have heard a little whisper, that Middlesex County Cricket Club are going to be looking at both of us, with the possibility of gaining a playing contract with them, next season. I hope that we both play well, but unfortunately, there will only be one contract". I could certainly do with a secure income, as my current firm have announced that cut backs are in the offing, and whilst nothing certain has yet been decided, I know that I am one of the staff that they will be looking at carefully." "Surely not, how many accountants, like you are there in the firm? "12 including newly qualified staff, but I know that with the three day week only just behind us, the prospects don't look great".

"You will be bringing Sam with you, to the Ball wont you?, said John, she certainly is more than arm candy, isn't she? He chuckled. She could light up my scoreboard, anytime". "Get out of here you dirty old man", replied Michael. "It does my heart good, to just look at her. I promise not to touch". Michael playfully put his boot up Johns' arse and shoved him out of the door. "See you on Friday night. John answered back. I suppose that because of your current situation with Sam, that Morris won't be at the ball." "Correct" said Michael.

"Net practise at 5.00 tonight and again, same time, on Friday, called out Morris, we all need to be in good 'nick' for the big match on Saturday". "No problem at all", the crowd of players called back. "We'll take them on, and cause one of the biggest upsets in the history of the competition", said Michael. "Don't forget, said Morris, this will be my last match for two weeks, as I'm off on holiday on Sunday, taking my little beauty, topless, I hope, pointing at the MGB, on a tour of Wales. You know how the Welsh birds are just gagging for it"?

Very generous praise was heaped upon the committee and helpers of the Ball. "The club looks absolutely fantastic" said Michael on Friday night, after the final net session., The Grand Marquee was decked out in splendid bunting and wonderful decorations, and the club flag above the main door to the Manor House, stood out proudly in the gentle breeze that was blowing a warm summer evening to a close. Mellor, and his trusty mower, was putting the finishing touches to the wicket, that he would roll into a perfect pitch the following morning at dawn. All was set fair for the morrow, and as the club emptied, and the gates locked, a peaceful hush descended on the playing fields of battle.

Beneath a cloudless, star filled night sky, two cloaked figures emerged from the tree lined avenue, just inside the estate. "Shush", be careful where you are treading, we don't want to alert anyone in the Manor House, do we?". "No, boss, sorry, whispered the second intruder. "Look, as I've said before, this is going to be 'easy peasy', just remember your role and we can't fail". They quietly crept along the grass area of the outfield, not wanting to disturb the gravel on the drive, until they reached the side door of the wooden pavilion, that the players emerged from during a match. "I've got the spare key, said the first villain, but to make it look like a break in, you had better jemmy the lock, as quickly and quietly as you can". His mate, who was a gigantic figure of a man, stepped forward, and easily broke the hasp, holding the padlock, and softly with gloved hands, placed it carefully on the ground. Before the alarm could sound, the leader went to the control panel, punched in the four numbers, and they were in. They quickly disappeared into the pavilion . "Follow me, closely, and look at the torch light. Don't trip over anything on the floor." They made their way in single file, until they reached the main office. "Break it open, the leader ordered, and yet again mincemeat was made of the door. Pointing at the picture of the Manor

House, the leader said, "The safe is behind the painting, the combination is 1 0 8 1 -the year the Club was founded but backwards. Got it?" "Not only have I got it, but I've also got the bundle of notes". "Let's get out of here now. Meet at my place in say two weeks, Monday, let the dust settle. I'll let you know when."

Saturday morning, the birds started singing lustily and the dawn chorus was in full swing, when John arrived at the front door of the Club at 7 .00. The sun was already starting to warm up, and the ground and club, looked a picture. "All of our hard work, in staging the match and putting on the Summer Ball, was worth the effort", he thought. He strolled, happily towards his office, and was a little concerned that the alarm did not sound. "Probably, in all of the excitement, forgot to set it last night." He opened the club door, and walked with a jaunty air to his office. He stopped abruptly. "What the hell has happened here?" His first instinct was to push the damaged door open with his bare hand, but quickly thought, that he might contaminate any evidence that may be embedded in the door, so he put his shoulder to it, and shoved it open. "BOLLOCKS", he yelled, seeing the safe door hanging open, and the complete contents cleared out. "We've been robbed".

He carefully removed his handkerchief, and held it in his hand, that picked up the receiver, and dialled 9 9 9. When it was answered, he told the operator that he wanted the police, as there had been a robbery at the Hurricane Cricket Club. He was transferred to the police dispatcher. "We'll, send someone down as soon as possible, but that may not be for some hours, as there has been a serious crash on the M1 motorway, and all of our officers are at the scene helping with the other emergency services." What should I do to secure the area, said John, as we are expecting a large crowd for our Gillette Cup match against Middlesex today". "Oh, I see, said the police dispatcher, you ought to know, that the coach carrying the Middlesex team, has been involved in the crash with a sports car. It's likely that it will take several hours, maybe all day, to clear the debris from the Motorway. I doubt whether there will be any match today. The sports car has been crushed as if it were made from an egg box. There are two fatalities. Motorway madness. When will they ever learn"?

The match, of course was cancelled, out of respect for the coach driver and an unidentified person that unfortunately died. The Summer Ball went ahead as planned and was, despite the tragedy, a roaring success.

Sunday, came, and so did the police. Inspector East, and Constable Lane appeared on the scene at 8.00, as arranged and brought along the forensic team. John related his story to them, whilst they made copious notes. "Any idea how much money was in the safe?, sir", asked the inspector. "Not too sure, but there was at least £2,000 in cash, the sum that we had agreed to pay the caterers, and the band. On top of that there was probably another £3,000 in cash, that we took from late payers". "Any one that you might suspect?" "Well, said John, it looks to me like an inside job . The alarm was deactivated as well as the safe not being damaged, and therefore, someone who knew the combinations, has to be a prime suspect." Who knew the numbers, apart from you, sir?" John, rubbed his chin in thought, "there is my secretary, Sam; the Chairman, Ashley Jones, and the club captain, Michael Carson". "Is that all?". "Yes it is.   Err Sorry, no, I forgot about Peter Proctor, you know him, our former captain.   I have been very remiss, and didn't change the combinations, when he was not re-elected."

"Alright, then, lets' be having them in here for initial questioning. Lane, go and round them up, whilst I question Mr Secretary, here", Inspector East said menacingly. "Y..you don't think that I have anything to do with this do you? stammered John, I've been a loyal servant of this club for the past 22 years, and my record is exemplary". "We have to eliminate you from our enquiries, so if you have nothing to hide, then you have nothing to worry about".

Over the next 3 hours, Sam, Ashley and Michael, were quizzed, quizzed and quizzed again, until Inspector East, had no further questions for them. "You are all free to go" he told them, but you are still under suspicion until I have further evidence from forensics. Where, Lane, is Colonel Parker, may I ask?" "I'll get Mellor, in and you can ask him directly", was Lanes' reply. " The Colonel is away 'on business'. Somewhere abroad, I understand , said old Mellor, but 'e don't tell me nuffin these days. Should be back on Saturday comin".

Forensics, could not come up with anything that pointed out the perpetrator. There were no finger prints, other than those that one would normally expect to find in a busy club; no footprints as the ground was hard and firm; no items of clothing that may have snagged on something, in fact nothing at all. Unless the police could pin something on Peter, it looked like a dead end.

In the circumstances, due to several of the travelling Middlesex team being incapacitated by injury, both sides agreed not to re-arrange the match, and therefore forfeit it. Michael was not offered a playing contract at Lords', by Middlesex; the missing money was never recovered................................but the Hurricane Cricket Club did not lose financially, as the Insurance Company paid out for the cancellation of the Match.

The red MGB sports car, involved in the fatal accident was finally identified by part of the missing number plate C 1 0, together with the squashed and severely mangled chassis number. It was registered to a London based Vicar.

Ten days later, a Memorial service was held for old Mellor, who had gone to the great grounds man's home in the sky. One of his dying wishes was that he be cremated in his tatty old working clothes, cap and all, and his ashes scattered on the wicket.....................However, unknown to anyone, the proceeds of the robbery were in his poachers pocket, and he and the money literally went up in smoke.

A BUSINESS PROPOSITION

It was late one Thursday afternoon, towards the end of 1989, when the phone rang in my first floor office in St John's Wood High Street. I picked up the hand set. "Quintin Delahunte, is on the phone the receptionist announced, and he's been trying to contact you for the past few days". " Find out what it is about?, I enquired, as I am currently in a Directors meeting". The 6 Directors from the various branch offices of the successful Estate Agency business , always met towards the end of the week to discuss and report how each office was performing. These meetings had been instigated by the new owners of the business, a Nationally known Insurance Company, who had bought it, along with other multiple Estate Agencies, in order for them to be able to sell insurance to the vast mailing lists that we all possessed.

The meeting lasted about an hour, where the new game of Office Politics was now being played. The original owners of the business, having been very well rewarded financially by the takeover, were quite happy to see out their 12 month contracts, whilst the younger directors were jostling each other, trying to manoeuvre themselves into positions of power, once the regime had altered. "Anyone coming to the pub for a swift half?, it's been a hell of a week", I enquired of my colleagues. As usual, all of the Directors, made their excuses, and left me to contemplate whether they had genuine reasons for not wishing to have a sociable drink, or whether there was something more sinister, as my department had not been performing very well of late. The New Homes and Land division had been, top dog for the last three years, earning serious fees for the Company, as well as for the individual members of this specialised team, that I had carefully put together since being given the opportunity of starting it from scratch, some years earlier. The department was the envy of all of our competitors.

"I'll join you for a bevy, said Jimmy. You don't want to be drinking on your own". Jimmy was tall, dark and swarthy, with masses of jet black hair, on both his head and face with never a strand out of place. He was in his early 40s' had been a director of the Company for about a year, having joined us from his previous Company, in Scotland, which had also been the subject of a takeover.

We made our way to The Red Lion Pub, at the busy roundabout by Lords' Cricket Ground. "What'll you have Jimmy?" "Just a half of best bitter, please, you know how Sandy is about my being late for supper" he replied. "Let's sit over there" I said, pointing to the quiet table at the back of the pub. We took our drinks and put them on the small table, that had hundreds of names carved in it by people, over the years.

"You weren't your usual self this afternoon", said Jimmy, what's up? "I can't play these political games, and it has been getting to me, lately, I replied. The Insurance Company have set such strict rules, that is inhibiting my free spirit. They want to know where I am going, what I am doing, keep a log of my mileage and petrol costs, and how long each of my appointments are taking. I understand their need to keep a close eye on the regular staff, but even when I mention that my side of the business is entrepreneurial , and there are no set rules, they still are not satisfied, even when I bring in a deal that no one had believed possible. I've just about 'had it 'with them. The only perk seems to be the key to the executive toilets!". "I know exactly how you feel, said Jimmy. This takeover is following the exact pattern of my previous Company. If you ask me, the writing is on the wall. They are trying to reduce their costs, and taking out one of the highest earners is how they tend to do things, you had better watch your back" . "Thanks for the word of warning, Jimmy, please keep this conversation under your hat." Of course I will. I must be off now, thanks for the drink".

It was only 6.30, and I still had a mound of work to catch up with, and I, possibly foolishly, went back to the office. As usual, everyone had left, and the office was deserted. I was just about to lock the door behind me, when a short, balding, chubby, bespectacled well dressed fellow, pushed past me. Breathlessly, he had obviously been running, he asked, " Are you still open?" "I'm sorry, but the residential sales department closes at 6.00, and unless someone is on their way back, you've missed them today. Let me look at the appointments diary, and I'll check". "No need, it's the head of developments that I really need to see, I've been chasing him for about a week now, but the bastard is not returning my calls, but I have to see him. I have left loads of messages, but he can't be bothered to return them, I'm sure it's because he has never heard of me". Putting on my best Poker face, knowing it was me that this little chap was after, and not wishing to delay my day any longer, "I'll take a message, I said, and make sure that he calls you tomorrow. Who shall I say you are"? He handed me a beautifully embossed business card. "Quintin Delahunte, he said, my mobile number is on the card". He turned around and left me wondering what was so urgent.

In a rare moment of indecision, I called after him, "It's me, you want to talk with, so come on in, and we'll go to my office". His face went the colour of a ripe strawberry, "You sod, he said, don't wind me up, let's go".

He followed me up to the first floor, I switched on the fluorescent lights, that flickered slowly into life. I must remember to get a new tube fitted soon, before it blows, I thought.

"Sit down, I offered, you look like you could do with a drink". "Please. Have you any water?" I went to the dispenser, and filled a plastic cup with his drink. He gulped it down, "Got another one?" I poured another cupful, and handed to him. "We went to the two seat settee . "You can call me Quintin, he said, by way of introduction. "I do know that you have been driving my receptionist mad, for the last few days, what's your story? "I suppose that you ought to have all of the facts, so I shall start at the beginning. Please don't interrupt, and keep any questions until I have finished." I agreed.

"I have a business proposition for you, he started, and I think that by the time that I have finished telling my story, you and I will have reached an agreement". "My parents started me off in life, with what at the time I thought was a distinct disadvantage, by naming me Quintin. What a name to be lumbered with, especially at a Council school in the middle of Bermondsey. All the kids teased and bullied me, until one day, I learnt to fight back, and fight back I did with a vengeance. It toughened me up, no end, and now I am really grateful for that early lesson in life's jungle. It's a hard hard world out there". He made himself more comfortable, crossed his legs, and picked some imaginary fluff from his trousers. He smiled nervously, and continued.

"I left my secondary school at 16 with no qualifications, but whilst I was there, I opened my own school tuck shop, and when it started to make a good profit, sold it to one of my friends for £200. With that I used the money to become an unregistered money lender at the school, charging anyone that needed a short term loan, interest at 10%. You will be amazed just how many boys, and teachers came to me for a loan. This business was fantastic and I made several thousand pounds. I eventually sold the money lending business for a very tidy sum". He took a long swig of his drink, and handed it to me. "Another one please, I'm parched". "You know how the dispenser works, help yourself". I was 'blowed' if I was going to be his wine waiter!

Coughing, as he had taken too much drink, "Its' gone down the wrong hole", he choked. Clearing his throat with a series of heavy coughs, he eventually said, "I now had serious money, and purely by chance, a mate of mine who worked in the local Estate Agents, told me about a property that could be bought for a song, but only if I had cash, as no Building Society would touch it in it's current state. I went to see this horrible flat above the mortuary, where you could smell the vapour from the nauseous embalming fluids, through the holes in the floorboards, most of which were missing. I made, what in my opinion was a derisory offer, and to my surprise, a month later, I had acquired my first property. My dad, lent me the money to give it 'a lick and a tickle', and I put it back on the market, and trebled my money. I was on the first rung of the property ladder, that has led me here today. During the next 3 years, I established a reputation for being the best buyer of unmodernised properties in the area, as I usually exchanged contracts on the same day as I saw them, and paid the estate agents a 'personal cash and therefore tax free commission' on top of the fees, that they earned from their Company."

"I bought and sold lots of flats and houses in run down areas, and am now looking to go 'up market'.   The money is just burning a hole in my pocket.   I have made arrangements with my Bank to fund me , and have many wealthy investors willing to back me, in a new Property Company. You can check me out, by contacting these referees". He handed me a very well presented leather bound dossier about him, and his existing Company, together with copies of his complete trading figures. They looked very impressive.

He had been talking for about an hour, and when he had finished, I phoned my wife to advise that, as usual, I would not be home before 9.00, and not to bother with my supper, as I would grab a salt beef sandwich from Harry Morgan's deli, across the road, on my way home.

"It's getting quite late, I said, let me make some investigations, and I promise that I shall contact you within the next day or so. Just one question for now, why are you so keen to do business with me, when there are several other people out there, who, I am sure, could do a similar job for you?" "I'm told, he replied, that you are the best, and you get properties that they don't. It's as simple as that. We could buy them cheaply, if you under value them, and trade them for large profits, and with your expertise, and my money, we will make a 'killing'." "I'm not comfortable with putting my name on a valuation, that I don't believe is it's true value", I said. "Don't worry, he grinned , showing a good set of teeth, that resembled piano keys. Perfectly white and uniform. I have a very friendly valuation surveyor, that can get over that problem", he rubbed his nose, and winked. You won't need to put your name to anything",

I had a lot to think about on the way home, not fully concentrating on the road, and was thankful that the traffic was not heavy, although I had to swerve violently to avoid a cyclist, without lights. Here was a man, that I had never heard of, and that he had suddenly entered my life. I was always open to new clients', and I suppose that I would be foolish to ignore him. He seemed to be going places, and maybe, I thought that if we were successful, I could hang onto his coat tails in a rapid rise to the very top, away from all of the machinations of my current job.

I arrived home and relayed to my wife, the conversation that I had with Quintin Delahunte. "I DON'T BELIEVE IT, she said, mimicking Victor Meldrew, the old pessimist from the TV sitcom, 'One foot in the Grave', he can't be for real. Surely, you must have heard about him, somewhere on your travels". "You would be amazed, I said, how many new clients, with money are out there just now, taking advantage of the maniacal property market, where values are increasing at an alarming rate. I blame the Banks. They are lending money to everyone, without properly carrying out due diligence, and at the moment, they are getting away with blue murder'. It will all end in tears, mark my words."

The next day, arriving in the office at 7.00, I made a list of questions that I needed the answers to larger than life Mr Delahunte, and left instructions for my P.A., Linda, to try to find the answers, whilst I was out all day. My mobile phone rang, at about mid day, whilst I was on the M4 Motorway driving to see a site in Devizes. "Hi, Quintin here, how are you doing?" The call threw me a little, as I didn't remember giving him my number. "Who is this, I queried?" "Have you forgotten already, he answered, we met last night." "How did you get this number, I only give it to special Clients', and until I can include you on that list, I should be grateful, if you would direct all of your calls to my PA at the office". I disconnected the call.

"He's as kosher as the Chief Rabbi, said Linda, as I returned to the office. Everything that you have asked me to check, comes up positive. Quite unbelievable, but everything is whiter than white. Never had such good references from anyone like these, before. I've also found out that he is in the 'huntin, fishin and shootin sect, and as a sideline, and you'll never believe this, only plays polo with Prince Charles." "Blimey, I said, I must have really pissed him off today, when I hung up on him". "Nothing to worry about, he telephoned here and told me that he had a very bad connection with your mobile phone, and would speak with you tomorrow." Not wanting to let the grass grow under my feet, I retrieved his business card from my desk and I called him on his mobile. "Sorry that we could not speak earlier today, but I was in an area, where the signal is poor. I've done some checking on you, as suggested, and would like to take our conversation further. Are you free at say 8.00 in the morning.?" Don't be daft, man, I didn't know that time of day even existed! I'm never in my bed , until at least 4.00 in the morning, and a handsome chap like me needs his beauty sleep" he giggled. "Make it 1.00 and we can have lunch at my club. The RAC Club in Pall Mall. OK with you?" "Linda, please check my diary and see if I am free for lunch tomorrow". "You've a meeting scheduled to visit Stuart at the Highgate office, but I can always alter it". "Please do so, and put me down for lunch with Quintin Delahunte. Better allow the whole afternoon."

I looked through our latest list of residential investments and development opportunities, and earmarked the ones that I thought would be of interest to him. I highlighted them on my laptop, and took a taxi to Pall Mall, arriving in plenty of time to savour the truly magnificent building that had 'money' written all over it, from the liveried Doorman, with his top hat and long coat, to the concierge, immaculately dressed in his lounge suit, that probably cost more than I could earn in a month. "I've a lunch appointment at 1.00 with Mr Delahunte, I announced, but I'm early. Where can I wait for him?" "Why don't you wait in the upper bar, and I shall direct him to you when he arrives." Thank you, may I take a look around, whilst I wait? I asked. "Of course. Donato, will you take this gentleman around the building please, and finish in time for his 1.00 lunch appointment." "Certainly, please follow me". It was only a whistle stop tour, with well known paintings adorning the Georgian staircase. Some of the paintings were, I believe originals, and I recognised some of them, from various magazines and publications that I had read in the waiting rooms of my doctor and dentist.

Quintin Delahunte, bowled in at precisely 1.00, wearing his plus fours, check socks and a beautifully tailored tweed jacket. "I understand that Donato has been looking after you". "Yes, a great tour guide, although his English still retains a charming Italian lilt. Let's have a drink, before lunch." "Just a small one for me please, as I am sure that I shall need to keep a clear head, in order for me to present some opportunities to you, that I have brought with me on my laptop", I said, patting my case gently. "Your table is ready now, Mr Delahunte, please follow me" the Maitre D announced, and proceeded to take us into the wonderfully appointed dining room, and sat us at a table by a window overlooking St James' Park.

We both ordered Asparagus with a hollandaise sauce, followed by a Fillet of Sole Veronique. I was salivating at the thought, of the meal. "Let's get down to business, Quintin said, once the Asparagus had been devoured, the next course won't be here for about 20 minutes. I know that you are trying to keep a clear head, but won't you join me in a bottle of Chardonnay ?". "Oh alright, but just a glass".

"I don't want to talk about specific properties with you today, Quintin sprang this statement on me, but to talk about you". "P... P Pardon, I stuttered. "Yes, the real reason why I have been chasing you, is because I want you to join my organisation, and source deals for me, even before they hit the market". I was taken aback, but keeping my cool, asked "Why would I want to join you, when I already have the best job in the business right now?" "I've said it before, you're the best, and I always get the best, no matter what it costs. My private investors will only deal with credible professionals, like you, and need your expertise to vet each scheme. I can see that I have shocked you, by being so forthright, and you don't have to say anything now, just enjoy the food".

The meal was outstanding, and despite the shock of the possible offer, I thoroughly enjoyed it. "When I get into the office, tomorrow, I shall dictate an offer letter to you, which I am sure that you are going to accept. Nobody pays better than me. Incidentally, I have heard that you are not too happy with your current situation, and my offer will 'knock your socks off'. Fancy a Port or a Brandy to finish the meal off nicely?" I declined, with my head spinning with the prospects of leaving my job, after 13 years, and in effect starting all over again.

As promised, a letter was delivered by hand to my home address, and with trembling hands, using my stylish paper knife carefully slit open the envelope. Here was a genuine offer tabulated in a form that was unambiguous, together with Quintin's programme of expansion over the next 5-10 years. The salary was mind blowing, and looked too good to believe . The perks were unbelievable, incentives including, Share Options, Partnership, and bonuses on top of the usual Health Care and expenses. A side letter advised that Quintin would pay for me and my family to take a 2 week break to his Villa in Barbados to celebrate, once contracts have been signed.

"I've just taken an option on a lease on first floor offices in Highgate, which will be ready for occupation in three months time, so you can see that 'it's all systems go', and I have, in anticipation of your acceptance, provisionally placed an order to purchase a new Mercedes for you. Don't take too long making your decision", he said to me.   "Thanks for the offer, I replied, I shall show it to my solicitor and take his advice ". "Great said Quintin, . I am going away tonight to Zambia, on a three week safari, staying on the Sussi & Chuma Sanctuary which is on the Zambezi River, but I really would like to know your decision by the end of my holiday. "

I arranged to see Robert, my solicitor, who had been a friend for some 20 years or so. He had grown into a bumptious old fart, in my opinion, but I trusted his judgement. I handed him the letter which he carefully read, and then read again the terms of the offer. Removing his half glasses, he pontificated, and said "The offer of a 3 year contract and salary together with Share Options are very generous, and it looks fairly water tight, but I would caution you on a couple of minor points." "What are they"? Holding his hand out in front of him, as if to stop the traffic, he continued, "If for some reason, you fail to complete your contract, and things don't work out, there is a clause restricting you from working within a geographical radius of 1 mile from the place where the office is situated, and also you will not be allowed to take any information on projects or Clients with you." "Neither of these issues cause me any problem, I replied, let's call for a contract of employment from Quintin's solicitors".

My mind was made up, I was going to 'Cross the Rubicon', and take the offer. When I arrived home, that evening, I advised my wife of my decision. "I saw Robert, earlier today, and he agrees with me that Quintin's offer is far too good to refuse, but to be aware that if it sounds too good to be true it usually is. However, he has called for a contract. We should be in a position to sign it within the next few days, and shall exchange contracts when Quintin returns at the end of the month". She threw her arm around me, and planted a great big 'smackeroo' on my lips. "Fantastic, she yelled, you really deserve it. Let's open a bottle of bubbly to celebrate". "Not yet, I cautioned, until the deal is done and dusted." Throughout my life, I have sometimes been thrown a 'curved ball', and I was not going to 'push the boat out' until I was certain.

The following morning, in pouring rain, the paper boy, as usual, came whistling up our drive, at the crack of dawn. "I must speak to the newsagent, about him, I said to my wife, he's a noisy little bugger, and he should have a little more regard for our peace and quiet." "You're becoming a grumpy old man, before your time, she said, weren't you young once?" "OK, but I'm on edge waiting for Quintin to return, so that the deal may be signed and sealed".

I removed the newspaper, and cursed when part of it got caught in the spring loaded letter box, ripping part of the front page of The Times, which we took every day, bar Sunday, as there was just too much to read, and not enough time to do so. I tried to piece it together, but the wet paper had concertinad into such a mush that the newsprint was impossible to decipher. "That does it, I screamed, as I like my newspaper delivered to me in pristine condition, I shall go round to the shop right now, and get another copy of The Times, and cancel the delivery for good. It only takes 5 minutes to walk to the local shop, and I resent paying delivery charges, when I am quite capable of collecting it myself." "Suit yourself. Why don't you buy a dog, whilst you are in this mood, at least it will give you a good excuse, when collecting the paper, to walk it", she taunted.

I stormed out of the house, into a fierce gale that was lashing rain and tossing leaves everywhere. Marched into Maddisons , and demanded to see the manager. "I am the manager, said the male, who looked about 14 years old, who approached me, how can I help you?" I waved the torn and ripped newspaper threateningly in front of him, demanding a replacement, and told him in no uncertain terms, that I was cancelling our daily delivery. "Not a problem, but I am afraid that The Times is in short supply today, they only delivered half of their normal quota, so I am very sorry, but I have none left. Why don't you take The Telegraph?" My anger had reached boiling point "If I wanted The bloody Telegraph, I would have ordered it, I ranted, causing several customers to stare at the madman in the shop. I wouldn't buy that 'Rag', even if it's the last paper in the world." "You could always try Tesco Express, the nervous manager suggested, hoping that I wouldn't turn green and rip my shirt off, ala 'The Hulk'. I didn't take any notice, and stomped out of the shop.

By the time that I had reached my front door, I was absolutely drenched, as if I had just walked out of our power shower, and my mood was blacker than ever. I stripped off all of my wet things, had a shower, made myself a cup of coffee, and sat in my dressing gown in complete isolation in my study trying to calm down. I switched on the television, and the Sky Channel was showing a sign saying that due to bad weather the signal has been lost. I nearly blew a gasket. It was not a good start to Saturday.

The TV suddenly reconnected, and as there was nothing that I really wanted to watch, switched it off, and announced "I'm going to the Library, they will have a copy of The Times, that I can read in comfort".

I arrived at the library, sat down in the area reserved for quiet reading, and picked up a copy of The Times. The headline read, DISASTER IN ZAMBIA, BRIT SLAIN. I read on "At 4.00 yesterday afternoon, gang war broke out , and shots were fired wildly by rival drug dealers, resulting in the death of a British subject, Simon Charlton, the well known Con Man that the Australian police have been chasing for the past 2 years, for property scams, who was travelling under one of his alias'.......................... Quintin Delahunte."

DEADLY SECRET

It was a wet, windy, freezing cold winter's morning, where the temperature had fallen way off the thermometer, that was swinging haphazardly in the violent gale that had gathered in an ambush to attack the unsuspecting visitor to the Harrow Cemetery, at North Harrow. Jack Frost had been out last night painting the town in sparkling white. The worn, mottled and damaged headstones were mainly unkempt as I suspected that no living relatives had remained alive to look after them, or had long forgotten who had been buried there. The little brick built prayer hall was in such a poor state of repair. I was surprised that Harrow Council had not placed a dangerous structure notice on it. They may, of course, had done so, but with the security being almost nonexistent, the vandals could well have removed it. What sort of society are we now living in? I mused.

I walked carefully along the unmade path until I found the grave of my old boss. John Henry Smith. I touched the letters with my hand, removing the moss that had quickly grown over them, just to be sure that this was the correct headstone. The moss came away easily in my gloved hand, and sure enough I was in the right spot. I was following the instructions that John Smith had left with his solicitor, when he met his untimely end, at the age of 43, only a year ago. The icy wind had chilled me to the bone, despite several layers of warm winter clothes. I automatically pulled my coat tighter around me, and tugged my fleece lined pilots' flying hat hard down over my raw ears. My red nose was lit up like a beacon.

I had brought with me a small floral tribute, but the fierce wind had snatched it from my grasp before I could secure it firmly on the grave, and watched it cavorting crazily across the barren landscape, in a pinball fashion, crashing into the headstones, completely out of control. It vanished into the unknown, under the wicked will of the wild conditions that not even a polar bear would enjoy. I must be mad.

Six months ago, we were gathered in the cramped dingy office of Mathew Reeves, the sole principal of the hundred and five year old firm of Solicitors and Commissioners of Oaths, as it had said on the fading sign above the door. The practice had been established by his grandfather, continued by his father and now Mathew was the owner of this Dickensian law firm. He had hoped that his two sons would enter the profession, but neither were interested in the Law. Mathew was in his late 50's, short and fat with a bulbous nose and a poor excuse for a moustache that looked like a hairy caterpillar perched on his upper lip. He wore a black pinstriped three piece suit, with a spotted bow tie. He reached into the pocket of his waistcoat and produced his monocle.

Mr Reeves, coughed loudly, bringing us all to order. "We are gathered here today. I thought that he was going to recite the wedding ceremony for one moment. To read the last will and testament of the dearly departed John Henry Smith". At this stage I realised that he must be a lay preacher, as these words were from the burial service. He rambled on for about ten minutes, reading out the bequests to Mrs Smith and their daughters, and then he turned to me. He peered at me through his good eye, with what appeared to be disapproval, why I know not, as we had never met, but there was something unpleasant in the way that he addressed me.

"To Gary Jones, I leave this unopened envelope, in which he, as my most trusted, and diligent member of staff, is the only person that I have complete confidence in, will find something of interest to him. He must read the instructions contained within this envelope in complete isolation, and not mention any of its contents to anyone." 'Blimey , I thought, what could be so important, and secret'? He handed me the envelope. "Thank you ladies and gentleman, that concludes today's reading", definitely a man whose vocabulary he had learnt from the bible.

I hurried off home, and in the comfort of my flat, poured myself a stiff whisky. I sat down in my favourite chair, took the paper knife, and, slit open the envelope. In JH's own handwriting it began.

"Dear Gary, If you are reading this, then you know that I am dead, the circumstances of which I am certain were not natural. I am, open brackets, now was, close brackets, a fit and healthy 43 year old, cut down in the prime of my life. Believe it or not, over the years I have unfortunately made enemies, and between you and I, not everything was strictly above board, nothing that the Inland Revenue would be interested in, but, and this is why it must remain strictly secret, my business trips to Russia were not always for commercial reasons. As my most trusted employee and, if I may say so, my friend, I am instructing you to find my murderer." Murderer, murderer it had never crossed my mind that JH had been murdered. I was shocked, as the doctor had signed the death certificate as myocardial infarction, a heart attack, which was later confirmed by the coroner.

"I was a super grass, and my business, which allowed me unfettered access to Russia, was a very suitable cover for my nefarious activities. You are aware that since 1991 Russia transformed itself from a country where entrepreneurs were classified as outlaws, to a country where entrepreneurs had no laws. I was secretly involved with the long running Swiss investigation into money laundering and tax fraud, by a ruthless and extremely well connected Moscow based crime syndicate, that I had managed to infiltrate. The police and security officials here in Britain had shown little or no interest, but one of my Russian contacts was very keen to reclaim what he had thought was his, and that's how I became involved . I was helping a Russian lawyer to investigate a £140m tax fraud carried out in Russia in 2007. London has become the home for many seriously rich and yet corrupt survivors of the former Soviet Union, looking to improve their vast wealth through huge investments in British institutions. The size of these investments makes diplomacy very difficult between our two countries."

I stopped reading, and poured myself yet another drink, not too much as I needed a clear head to take in a most incredulous story. My blood pressure had certainly gone up. What next, I wondered. I continued reading.

"You must go to Harrow Cemetery, in North Harrow and find my grave. I reserved plot number 37B, but didn't expect to die so soon. Don't go right away, leave it for a few months. In the plot to the left of mine, signifying where Brian James is buried, you will see a small statuette of an ugly gargoyle. Twist it to the right three times, and it will reveal an opening next to it. There you will find all of the evidence that I collected, and stored it where no one else could possible know. Take the contents of the letter to my solicitor, Mathew Reeves, who has instructions to pass the information onto my Russian solicitor. On the successful conviction of the head of the crime syndicate, Alexander Stepanova, you will receive a reward of £1m. I know that with your tenacity, you will bring my murderer to justice, but be very careful, the syndicate have tentacles that stretch beyond your wildest imaginations. Good luck." It was signed JH.

I read, and re read the letter so many times, that I must have read the ink off the page. It was so outrageous, that it had to be believed. I could memorize most of the important parts, so I decided to burn all of the evidence. I took out a glass ashtray, tore the letter into hundreds of pieces, and put a match to it. The flames licked the pages, and then proceeded to burn the entire contents of the ashtray, leaving only charred remains. I had read somewhere that even charred burnt paper, could sometimes be deciphered, so I put the ashes into my waste disposal unit, and switched it on. A gurgling noise devoured it completely. I went to bed, but I hardly slept a wink all night, although I must have dropped off, because the alarm on my clock radio activated at the usual time of 06.30. The last time I had looked at the clock, the numerals had ticked over to 03.39.

Today, Monday, was the day that I had put in my diary for the visit and as instructed I had waited for some months. I drove my beaten up Honda Civic to the cemetery. There were no immediate parking spots, as I had forgotten that the U3A creative writing class meets on a Monday, in the adjacent building. However, I got lucky, as one of the Council lorries moved, and I managed to park on the grass verge, next to the fence.

I had just reached the headstone, when I heard footsteps on the semi- frozen gravel path, behind me, and saw a scruffy looking tramp, who grabbed my arm and pulled me to the ground. "Who are you", I wanted to shout, but he quickly put his dirty hand over my mouth, muffling the sound that I was trying to make. "Stay down, he whispered, flashing an identity card in front of my eyes, the mob have eyes everywhere". Scott Kerr, CIA, it read. At the next instant, an unmarked car, drove slowly towards our position. "Get under this coat, he ordered, and I shall lie next to you". Two men, dressed completely in black trench coats, skinny ties, oxford shoes and fedora hats. They also wore matching Ray –Ban Wayfarer sunglasses, to keep the low watery sun out of their eyes. They looked just like the Blues Brothers. I saw that they had guns in their hands, as they got out of the car. "Where's he gone? said the first man. He was here a moment ago". "What's that? the second man said, pointing at the crumpled heap of clothes lying on the ground. It smells awful", he said crinkling up his nose at the horrible smell coming off it. "It's only a drunken old tramp with his pile of rubbish, probably looking for somewhere to sleep. He'll probably freeze to death with the snowstorm coming. Good place to die. In a cemetery", they laughed . "It's obviously no one that we are interested in. Let's go." The two men shouldered their guns, returned to the car, and went back to the boring job of looking to see who visited the grave of JH Smith.

I pushed Scott away from me. "Who are you? and more importantly who in God's name were they?" "I'm with the CIA, and we have been called in, as you Brits don't seem to want to get involved in something that could damage International relations with Russia. Those two thugs work for Alexander Stepanov. He found out that JH was a super grass, and also knows that Mr Smith managed to obtain documents that will put the Mob inside for the rest of their natural, and have been keeping an eye on everyone and everything associated with him, including this cemetery." " Let's get out of here before I freeze my arse off." I said. "Just hold up a moment, they won't give up so easily. Here they come again". The tyres scrunched over the icy ground in a slow but calculated manoeuvre, looking left, right, and straight ahead, using the powerful headlights of the car, to see if there was anyone here. After another fifteen chilled filled minutes, the car did a U-turn, and left by the wooden gates at the entrance.

I needed to thaw out and so did Scott. "It's not safe here, and by now, they will be checking out all of the vehicle number plates in the car park. I feel sorry for those U3A guys, if those thugs use unscrupulous methods of interrogation on those old folks. Get into my car." "Where is it? I asked. "Follow me on foot to my old Ford 'banger'. It's parked in a disabled bay just behind the petrol station, he said pointing towards the Texaco sign. Let's not leave together, we just can't afford to be careless. See you in five minutes." I watched him shuffle off down the road to his car. As instructed, I caught up with him five minutes later, and tried to get into the passenger side, when I realised that it was a left hand drive car. I walked around and got into it. The car smelt like a rubbish tip, only worse, as there was no fresh air in it at all. "Do you have to travel like this?" I said, wafting the disgusting air away from my nose. "It's all part of my disguise, and I just can't afford to drop my guard for a minute", he replied.

We drove for about a mile, then turned off the main road into Parsons Grove. He pressed the remote control, and the garage doors rolled open. "Give me half an hour to clean up, and then we can talk. Make yourself at home. Drink a cup of something hot. The kitchen's through here", he said pointing at the saloon style swing doors. His house was a tip, with old newspapers scattered around the well worn furniture in the lounge, unwashed crockery littering the kitchen table, and ashtrays full of cigarette ends. Basically he lived like a slob. No doubt Uncle Sam would be picking up the tab. I wondered how the Americans would react if they knew that their hard earned taxes were paying for all of this.

Fifteen minutes later, a well dressed, groomed Scott was standing next to me. "Did you get your fairy godmother to make the transformation, I queried. Are you a master of disguise?" He just laughed and asked "are you hungry, because I certainly am. I've ordered a Pizza, it should be here soon." The doorbell rang some

20 minutes later. He looked through the spy hole, and saw a young girl in leathers and a crash helmet holding an insulated bag with DOMINO'S emblazoned on it. The bell rang again, "Pizza delivery for Mr Kerr", she said. Scott opened the door and just as he took the box from her she blasted two bullets into his chest, and sped off down the path to her waiting motor bike. I instinctively ducked down behind the sofa, she hadn't seen me. I heard the roar of the bike, and slammed the door firmly shut. I was quivering like a leaf.

My first instinct was to call the police, but I went over to his prone body just to see if I could do anything to help him. He was moaning softly, but I saw no signs of any blood. He groggily heaved himself up onto one elbow. "Lucky for me that it wasn't a head shot, or you would be listening to a ghost, but my Kevlar vest saved me. I shall be badly bruised, or may have a rib or two broken, but I am still very much alive. The mob are everywhere." "I don't think that I was seen, otherwise I would be 'brown bread', I said in a shaky voice. What shall I do now?" I asked him. "Not I but WE, he answered. We're in this together." "No we're not, I said, "but they, whoever they are, don't know about our brief connection, and quite frankly, I don't wish them to find out. I'm off."

I knew roughly where I was, and now that dark was descending, I took a chance, and jumped on the passing bus and went back to the cemetery. The snow had started to fall in blizzard like conditions, and the short journey stopped at Devonshire Road, as the bus did not have the ability to get to the terminus safely, slithering and sliding across the untreated roads. I was exasperated . Every time a drop of snow falls, Britain becomes paralysed . If I were a foreign country, I would invade with snow making machines, and could take over the entire country in a bloodless coup within a few days. A little investment in snow ploughs and tons of grit would soon solve the problem.

The gates were just shutting, but I pleaded with the officious man that my car was still in the car park, and would he be kind enough to let me collect it now. I pushed a ten pound note into his freezing hand. "Certainly, sir, he said with a smile on his cracked lips, take as long as you wish". I hurried over to the car, scraped the snow from the windscreen, and drove carefully onto the Pinner Road, sending a cheery wave in his direction. He was now my best mate.

The road conditions were not quite as bad, heading South, and with the heater working overtime, I slid home safely in four hours, a journey that would have normally taken me 25 minutes. Whilst stuck in the car, my mind began to recall everything that had happened today, not least of which was how Scott Kerr, if that was his correct name, knew me, and why should he be wearing a bullet proof vest in his own home. Also if someone was sent to assassinate him, why didn't they shoot him in the head? Questions, questions, and more questions, and as yet no answers. One thing was certain, I wasn't going to stay in my flat for a moment longer than it would take me to pack a few things into my bag, take my passport and credit cards, and disappear . In effect I was on the run.

Hiding in a big city isn't as easy as it sounds, and due to the horrendous road conditions, most of the hotels were full, with workers not wishing to chance their journey home. I thought about everyone that I knew that lived close to me. I tried to reach my cousin Harry, who lived in Northwood, but my mobile phone could not get any service, due I thought to the thousands of stranded people also trying to use the overloaded networks. Purely by chance, I was now within ten minutes walk of my office, and I saw Rosemary, one of my co-workers, treading warily through the freshly falling snow. I slithered to a stop, and wound down my window. "Can I give you a lift somewhere", I asked, my words followed by my frost laden breath in the cold night air. "I was just going home, on foot, as you know how nervous I get when I am driving on the roads in snow, she answered. No thanks, I'll walk". "I'm in a quandary, I also can't get home, I lied, any chance of staying at your place, overnight?" "Well, I suppose that I could get our two boys to share and you could have one of their beds." "I wouldn't dream of taking their bed, let me sleep on the floor". "I know, she said, the settee is long enough, you can sleep on it, if you wish". I wished, and so I spent a restless night on the settee, but not because it was uncomfortable, but because of all of the day's crazy events.

Most of the snow had miraculously disappeared by morning, and I thanked Rosemary and her family for their kind hospitality. "I won't be in today, I announced, I've still got several days holiday owed to me and I have decided to get away for a few days". "Going to the sunshine ?", said Rosemary. "Certainly, I was getting good at telling 'porky pies'. I'll send you a postcard".

My mind was racing, where could I go, without leaving any trace. I couldn't use any of my credit cars, so whatever I spent would have to be in cash. My first decision was to leave my car and mobile phone at home. I then made a visit to my own bank, and withdraw £1000, which should keep me going for a couple of weeks, provided I was careful. "Good morning, the bank teller greeted me. How nice to see you again" She was certainly in the Christmas mood. " I should like to withdraw £1000 in cash please, I said, handing over my cheque. Lots and lots of presents to buy at this time of the year", I said in as cheerful way as possible. "How would you like the notes?" "In tens and twenties please". She undid the paper bands surrounding the wads of notes and carefully peeled off 35 x £20 notes and 30 x £10 notes, and slid them across to me with a smile on her face. "Happy Christmas to you" she sang out. "And to you too". I packed the new crisp notes into my inside pocket and zipped it up. I closed my windcheater. I buttoned and zipped it up as well.

Where now? My head told me to get away as far and as fast as possible, but, why was I on the run? I had nothing to hide. ' I know, I shall go and visit my new best friend at the cemetery, I thought. There must be something so important there, that people would kill for it.' He was nowhere to be seen, but I could see a machine digging new graves in the distance, so I assumed that he was one of the grave diggers. Furtively, I glanced around to see if I could spot the two thugs from yesterday, or even Scott, who may be lurking somewhere nearby, but fortunately, the coast appeared to be clear. I walked with a determined stride to the headstone of JH. Still no one in sight save a couple of large rooks, looking at me with beady eyes, hoping that I just might be their next meal. Not if I could help it. I was going to shoo them off, but thought that their exit might cause a flurry of noisy wings, alerting any spying eyes. So I just dropped to my knees, and twisted the gargoyle on the grave of Brian James. It was left three times, wasn't it, or was it right three times? I had forgotten, but nonetheless, it wouldn't move in any direction. I twisted it first one way then the other, and despite my best strenuous efforts the only thing moving was me. Getting hotter and hotter, I removed my windcheater, but knelt on it just in case, some yobo came my way and stole it.

Bingo, it moved, just a tad, but it moved. I took a breather, and put all of my remaining strength into one final effort to move the damn thing. Oops, sorry, blaspheming in a cemetery was not a good idea. It moved again and again until the gargoyle eventually gave up its hidden secret. The hole beneath it was filled with water, but in the corner was a metal box , carefully wrapped in plastic sheeting. I tugged the box which had a pale green patina, three metal hinges on the back and a clasp in the front from its hiding place. I unwrapped the plastic from it, but the lid was frozen tight. I eventually managed to open, probably Pandora's Box. There was a bundle of papers neatly tied up in red ribbon that solicitors use, with a note on it addressed to me.

"Dear Gary, I am now literally speaking to you from the grave, not mine but the adjoining one. Well done in locating these documents. This has been the easy part. 'Easy, my God, if this has been easy, I hate to think of the hard part', I thought. Be very careful, not to contact anyone other than Mathew Reeves, my solicitor, who will know exactly what to do. Yours JH".

I collected my windcheater, and walked confidently out of the cemetery, to the main road. I remembered that there is a pub with accommodation in Hatch End. I know. It's the Moon and Sixpence. I took the H12 bus, and got off in Uxbridge Road, and went to the Pub. "I need a room for tonight", I said to the lady behind the bar. "I'll call the manager, and he will sort it out for you", she replied. A middle age man, dressed in a Father Christmas outfit, complete with white beard, came out of his office and approached me. "Hello, I said, I would like a single room for tonight. Have you anything available, especially at this time of the year"? "You don't have to worry , it's not yet Christmas, so yes, there IS room at the Inn for you, he smiled. Just fill in the registration form and I shall get someone to show you your room. How will you be paying?" "Cash, if that's alright with you". "Perfectly Mr. He looked incredulously, at the form, S M I T H. "Yes" I said, having entered in all of JH's details, just in case. "Room 22, first floor on the left". I thanked him and paid over £40 for the room, and took the key and my bag upstairs.

The room was at the rear of the pub, overlooking the yard, but away from the main road. However, the London to Birmingham train, came rattling through nearby Hatch End Station, throughout the night, and the double glazing was not of good enough quality to keep the sound out. It may have suited some young couples who wanted to do a little 'train spotting', but it certainly did not suit me, having just spent two restless nights in succession. There was a small safe, in the wardrobe cupboard. I just large enough to stuff the documents into. I was not at all interested in learning their contents.

I must have been exhausted , as I slept like a log. Refreshed, I checked with public transport to plot a route to Mathew Reeves' office in the City, having used the payphone in the lobby, to find out if he would see me today. "Mr Reeves is available at 2.15, and he can spare about 15 minutes before his next appointment", his PA told me. "Fine, I'll be there" , I replied.

I collected the documents from the safe, and once again put them into the inner pocket of my windcheater, and made my way to The City for my appointment. I arrived under dark threatening pregnant skies, that looked like they were ready to drop their load of snow at any moment. The screaming sirens of emergency services were evident along every street that I travelled. City police were, as usual patrolling the streets, moving Christmas Carol singers along to avoid any potential congestion, and keep the traffic moving. I arrived in Bishopsgate, and spotted Reeves' office, just behind St Ethelburga's Medieval Church, which had recently been rebuilt following the IRA bomb attack on it in 1993.

This part of the street, were Mathew Reeves' office was located, was now cordoned off with police tapes, saying POLICE LINE DO NOT CROSS in red and black warning letters. I approached one of the officers. "What has happened", I asked, can I gain access to number 172 please, as I have a most important meeting to attend there ?" "Sorry sir, but there has been an incident in the street, and no one is allowed to cross the line", he told me in a stern voice. Any idea when I can get to my appointment? A shake of the head in the negative, gave me my answer. I went to the nearest phone box, and called his office. "Reeves and Sons, the receptionist answered, how may I help you?" "I have an appointment with Mr Reeves at 2.15 this afternoon, but can't gain access to the street". "There has been a shooting just outside my office, and there are 2 people lying on the ground, and they look seriously injured. We are now waiting for the ambulance to arrive, she replied. All meetings this afternoon have been cancelled." " I'll try again tomorrow", I said dejectedly.

I didn't want to go back to Hatch End, and found a little B & B at 196 Bishopsgate, very convenient. The room was quiet and suited my purpose ideally. There was no safe in the room, so I planned to sleep in my windcheater, with the documents safely zipped up in the pocket. No one would get hold of these, without a struggle. I watched the News on the little television in my room, and the second item was the shoot out in the City of London. "No identification has yet been made, the news reader announced, but there are clear indications that the two dead men were likely to be from overseas, by their clothes and dental work." 'The plot thickens, I thought to myself. Could it be something to do with JH'? I may never know.

I awoke to the sound of church bells ringing, on a bright clear day, with the winter sun throwing long shadows on the street. I used the payphone in the hall, and called Reeves' office to set up an appointment for 10.00. I crossed the road, which was now clear of any signs of an incident here yesterday, and walked into

Costa Coffee. I held the door open for a tall bearded man, dressed in a short woollen coat, and flat cap on his head, who had followed me in, shuffling along with his crutch supporting him . He had a folded up newspaper tucked under his arm. I ordered a large black coffee, just to get my little grey cells working, and at that moment I felt a sharp sting in the back of my leg. "So sorry, the man said, as he stumbled, and grabbed hold of me to prevent him from falling. I slipped and my crutch knocked into you". "Not to worry, I'm OK" , I replied, straightening up my windcheater. I walked over to a table and I noticed that the man was now speaking on his mobile phone, whilst quickly hobbling out of the door. He got into a taxi that sped away.

I drank my coffee, slowly, as I still had plenty of time to kill, before meeting with Reeves. I instinctively put my hand on my inner pocket, just to confirm that the bundle was still there , and thank goodness it was still intact. I felt a little groggy, when I stood up to leave, but thought that it must be because of the extra shots in my coffee.

I re-crossed the road, and pushed the bell outside Reeves' office, and was admitted by the receptionist. " I'm Gary Jones and I've an appointment with Mathew Reeves at 10.00." "Yes he is expecting you, please take a seat. If you don't mind me saying, she said, you don't look at all well, is there anything that I can get you?" Sweating like the proverbial pig, I just couldn't stop the flow. "A glass of cold water, would be fine, please". "I'll just go and get one for you" now, she replied.

By the time she returned, I was lying on the floor, shaking from head to foot, covered with sweat. "I'm going to call for an ambulance", I just about heard her say to me, as my eyes were closing and I was losing consciousness fast. The next thing that I saw was a nurse standing over me. "Where am I"? I asked feebly. "You're in Westminster Hospital, in an isolation ward, and you've been here for the past 48 hours. You may have picked up some sort of virus, but so far we have been unable to trace its origins she replied. We have been worried about you, but now that you are awake, I'll tell the doctor".

The doctor came in and started to ask me lots of questions, and all that I could think of was that sting in the back of my leg at the coffee shop. "Let me have a look at it, please roll over", he ordered. Over I rolled, and I heard a long gasp from him. "There is some sort of pellet in your leg, and we need to remove it to see if it is something sinister. I can do it now with a local anaesthetic." "Nurse get me my tweezers, and a swab, please." The little operation was over very quickly, and the pellet dropped with a clang into the metal dish. It was sent to the lab for analysis. I was still extremely weak, but not weak enough to forget why I was in this part of town. "Can you get me my windcheater please," I asked the nurse. "You're not thinking of leaving us now, are you? " "No, I just need to find something in one of my pockets". She went to the cupboard, and brought my windcheater to me. I felt the pocket, and I let out an involuntary sigh of relief. It was still there.

Later that day, the doctor returned. "You're a very lucky man, he said, the pellet had contained ricin, but fortunately for you the dose was not quite strong enough to kill you. Just a little bit stronger and I am afraid that by now you would be dead". "What are you talking about? I replied in horror, you can't be serious. That sort of thing was prevalent back in the days of communism in the mid 1970's, and I remember a Bulgarian dissident, Georgi Markov was murdered with a jab from an umbrella, that contain ricin. Surely it can't still be in use"? "Whether it is or isn't, just relax, and hopefully we can discharge you tomorrow". What a nightmare, but at least the documents were safe.

I was given the 'all-clear' by the hospital, and before I left, I telephoned Mathew Reeves. "Sorry to hear about your short stay in hospital, he said, when can you come in to see me?" "Right now, if you are free." "Yes that suits me, see you in say 45 minutes."

I was greeted by Reeves, like a long lost relative, and his concern for my welfare was really touching. I had only met him once at the reading of the will, and whilst I didn't fully recognise him, he did seem familiar. "I trust that you have all the information for me", he said. "Certainly, I replied, patting my windcheater, It's all in here". Eagerly he stepped towards me, "can I have it now?" I reached into my pocket and produced a rather battered envelope, that must have been damaged when I fell, and handed it to him. He removed the contents and spread them out on his keyhole desk, smoothing them over with his hands. "JH was a careful man, and I can see that from the way that he has wrapped up these documents." All I could see was a folded newspaper, no documents at all. We were both dumfounded. " I had nearly been killed twice now, once in the cemetery and again this week, but for what? A tatty old newspaper?"

I slumped down into his wing back leather studded chair. "Let me look at the newspaper", I said to Reeves. He almost threw it at me in anger, seeing his fees disappearing forever. " Wait a minute, I said, look at this. Inside the newspaper was a note, and a photograph of a man of Slavic descent, dressed in a Cossack hat. "I don't know him I said, do you?" "No I don't he said angrily . What does the note say?"..Thanks for the information, my colleague Todor is an expert pickpocket and he switched the documents in the coffee house. Happy Christmas. Alexander Stepanov.

TRIGGER POINTS

"Come on, get up, shouted my mother, from the kitchen below, school holidays have been over for nearly a week. As a 'responsible' teenager, it's time you moved your butt from that cesspit that you call your bed". She had been calling me constantly since 6.30, waking me up from my deep sleep, that I had fallen into in the early hours of this morning. I had not been sleeping very well lately, could it have been the death threats that my parents had been slinging at each other in all the years of their violent marriage, playing on my mind, or my reaction from having just recovered from the virus that had kept me away from my new school, for two days now? I had gone to the Doctor last week, as I could not stop sneezing, and thought that I may have early signs of Hay fever, that had affected both of my parents. "You've got a virus, Dr. Brasher, announced, go home and straight to bed. I have written a prescription for you, the tablets must be taken three times a day".

"Virus, shmirus, that's all the Doctors ever say nowadays, when they have no real clue as to what ailment the patient may have", I said when I went to the chemist to collect my prescription. "The world is getting smaller, each day, with many new strains of viruses that attack at a moments' notice . Have you been on an aeroplane lately"? the pharmacist asked. "As a matter of fact,........ NO", I replied without humour. Her face dropped. "I was only trying to help trace a possible source, like the air conditioning on the plane." "Chance would be a fine thing I said sarcastically, we haven't been able to afford a holiday abroad since I was little. We spend our Summer holidays on a Caravan site in Skegness." I shuffled out of the shop, dragging my well worn Nike trainers on the polished wood floor. My tatty designer jeans, that I bought in a Charity shop, together with my Yankees baseball cap, worn backwards, which covered my Shirley Temple style long blonde curls, were part of my daily uniform, now that I was in the sixth form, albeit a different school, as my previous one did not have a sixth form. Other girls wore denim skirts, some of them almost too short to hide their knickers. In my view they had better cover up. Not my style at all.

I walked slowly to Henrietta Barnett School, in Hampstead Garden Suburb, from Golders Green Station, along the Finchley Road, which had a long traffic jam, with cars nose to tail as far as the eye could see. Blue flashing lights and sirens could be seen and heard indicating that some impatient driver, obviously late for an appointment may have arrived early in the next world. I later learnt that due to the torrential downpour, the rain had caused a flood in the road and that my instincts had unfortunately been correct, and a man with a van, driving without a licence had wasted his life , in a collision with a cyclist. Such a dangerous road. It was a mirror image of another car crash that I had witnessed recently.

Having reached the gates of the school, which looked like a Haunted House, I walked through the well manicured gardens. "What a beautiful display of flowers, I said to the gardener, as he unwound his elderly body carefully into an upright position, how long did it take you to plant all of these"? He looked at me through rheumy eyes, deep set in his face, above huge droopy bags that I felt I could pack my weekend clothes into! With a voice as thick and as lumpy as burnt porridge he said "It's not just me, I'm part of a 5 man team. We took about 3 days". "Great job, lovely to see mature grounds like these. I am studying geography and hope, one day, to be a landscape gardener", I told him. "If you want to see some of the superb wild flowers, he said, pointing his gnarled hand to the forested area of the grounds, when you have time, why don't you take the path through the woods"? "I will", I said earnestly.

I met the Head of Geography, in her study about 15 minutes later. She was a squat woman of indeterminate age, who wore her silver white hair in a tightly twisted bun, on the top of her head. Her gown was greyish, rather than black, due I suspect to its age. Under the gown was a knitted Fair Isle jumper, that had seen its' best days many years ago. Her tights, or maybe she still wore stockings, were black patterned and fitted neatly into her sensible flat black shoes. Her large ears, supported a pair of round framed glasses. There were signs of a little beard on her chin.

"Welcome to the school, she said, looking disapprovingly at my clothes. This is a delicate matter. I don't know who advised you on our dress code, but what you are wearing is not acceptable. You must change at once. How far do you live from here"? "The bus that I take runs twice a day, once in the morning and once in the evening, and I'm afraid that I can't get home just now". "I am sorry to do this on your first day, but you will have to stay in detention this evening after school." " I can't do that, I cried, I'll miss the last bus home". "Alright, just this once, but you will have to stay in at lunchtime, today". Not a good start to life at Henrietta Barnett's I thought. I had better dress to impress, rather than wear her idea of fancy dress, when I come in tomorrow. "Your tutor today is Mr Forman, you better explain your lateness to him, she said rather huffily. Off you go." I was half expecting her to get me to sit on the naughty step.

It took me about five minutes to walk to the classroom, that was situated in the Geography building on the edge of the grounds, angrily kicking the leaves that had fallen early this year, off the gravel drive . 'What a nutty old bat, I thought, I hope that not all of the tutors are like her. She'd do well at a Halloween Party'. The red brick building, was an obvious addition to the main school, as the gleaming brass plaque of the wall told me that it was built in 2010 and opened by former pupil, Caroline Anstey, the Managing Director of The World Bank. I found the Geography department, and shyly knocked on the door. "Come in, quickly now," a loud stern voice bellowed out. I opened the door and immediately saw a very handsome man standing at the White Board. I put him at about 30 years of age, floppy brown hair, that he kept trying to push off his face with a nonchalant toss of his head, but to no avail, as it kept falling back. I was immediately seduced by his beautiful grey eyes beckoning me towards him. "Hello, how may I help you?" I was lost by his lovely manner. My knees had turned to jelly. "I'm new, sorry that I'm late, but Miss Sparrow, kept me longer than I had anticipated", I replied. "Take a seat at the table next to the window, and I don't expect you to be starring out of it, during MY lessons, he grinned. I'll take your details at the break. We had been looking at the lesson on the screen in front of you, but there has been a computer error, and the programme is not responding, so we will have a question and answer session instead". I liked his casual approach to learning, and thought that we would get on just fine.

The term flew by, and by now, I had learnt so much, that the exams were easy. "You've all done really well, announced Tom Forman, but there has been one outstanding candidate. "Cathy, please come up and accept your prize for this term." I was naturally very pleased for Cathy, as we had become bosom buddies, but was disappointed for myself. "There were only a couple of marks between the top and bottom, so, pointing at the rest of the class, you now know how hard it will be for all of you, when the real test comes in the Summer. Good writing is all in the detail.   Have a good Christmas break, and I'll see you all at the start of next term, Monday January 14th 2013.   Put it in your calendar now." I-Pads were fished out, and the date was duly entered.

When the lesson was over, I stayed behind to see if I could find out the areas where I needed to improve. "Tom, I called out, he allowed us to use his Christian name, have you got a moment, please"? "Certainly, I've always time for my students', what can I do for you"? What a leading question, as I realised that I had a school girl crush on him, and his statement could mean anything, I thought. "Where do you think that I need to improve, I'm determined to finish top of the class, next year", I enthusiastically answered . "As it's end of term, and we all finish around lunch time, why don't I take you across to Charlie's Italian Restaurant for a bite of lunch, and we can discuss it there", he said. " Fine with me as my bus doesn't leave until 5.00, we'll have plenty of time". " See you there at 1.00", he said.

I was in a fluster, and I knew that he was taking a risk to be seen out of school with me, but even though there was a generation gap between us, I hoped that we would have plenty of things in common, apart from my geography course. This was going to be a meal to remember. We arrived simultaneously, and ordered homemade Pasta, from a trainee waiter who apologised for any delay, telling us that he had managed to get the job by going part time. "It will be about 20 minutes, as we make everything fresh here", he said. Looking around the very crowded restaurant, I said, "he's an optimist , more likely to be much longer." We nibbled on the Grissini sticks and olives, and then Tom started talking about his private life. "Can you keep a secret"? " Yes", I replied. "I don't know why, I am telling you all of this, but I suppose it's nice to have someone listen to my woes". He told me that he had had a family conflict when he met his partner, and had been living with her in Mill Hill for about 3 years. They had a small baby boy, but things had not worked out well, and his partner had kicked him out, and he was now in rental accommodation in Leighton Buzzard. "I suppose that I am my own worst enemy, when it comes to the opposite sex, this is the second time that a strong relationship has ended like this. I just can't control my emotions. I suspect that I must be living in a parallel universe." I was all ears now, sitting with this very attractive man, who by his own admission was 'a bit of a womaniser'. "Were you unfaithful? I queried. "Yes I suppose I was, that's why I moved to London from Manchester in the first place. It would seem that I am attractive to women, but don't want the commitment, it 's not domestic bliss as far as I am concerned. My first partner, was planning a fabulous wedding party, she was a serial party girl. She thought that marrying me was a dead cert, but I was frightened away. It would have been a fate worse than death. I was a worried man, and had to get away as quickly as possible. She didn't want to re-marry, and I understand that she now lives with a paid companion."

I got into my new car, late at night, that I had bought following a test drive, , and took the fastest road out of the City, past the no entry sign. However it was the wrong road, and for my troubles picked up a speeding fine. To cap it all, I hit the kerb at speed and ended up with a flat tyre. I had swerved to avoid a stray cat, at the same time just missing a girl in silver shoes, who was wobbling her way through the dimly lit road towards The Tiger Lounge, just off Princess Street. I couldn't get away fast enough. When I got to London, I opened my boot and discovered that I had taken the wrong suitcase. It was the final straw."

The waiter, carrying two steaming bowls of pasta, finally arrived at our table, after wrongly placing our order in front of another couple across the restaurant. "Pilot error, sorry," he laughed, plonking the dishes on our table. Tom continued. "My life has been one long list of errors, and now that I have established myself here, I shall tread carefully from now on. I didn't mean to hurt anyone, it was my genuine mistake. You now know my guilty secrets." I couldn't believe what he was saying, and instinctively, I put my hand on his, trying to comfort him. He didn't move it, only reacted with his eyes, which told me that there would be no turning back from this adventure. He was a bad influence, but I didn't care.

"What plans have you over Christmas, he asked in a calm voice once we had finished eating, because if you haven't, we could always stay at my mother's empty cottage in Fort Mahon Plage , in Northern France, and could get to know each other better" he smiled. I knew that it was a euphemism for sex, and to be honest, I didn't mind losing my virginity to Tom, after all I was 17, and everyone my age boasted of their sexual conquests. It was a sign of the times. This could be a leap into the unknown.

We drove to France, in Toms' car, and nearly had a fight in the car park whilst waiting for the Eurostar , as a very aggressive driver tried to take our space.   We arrived at the little house, and looking over the fence could see the 8th fairway of the Belle Dune Golf Course, only five minutes' walk from the sea. What a funny coincidence, I recalled that my parents had played golf here. The house was built within the last 10 years, and was a charming two bedroom 'love nest', but I had badly read the signs, as all that happened was that we walked around the sand dunes in an Arctic blast and I learnt some interesting facts about the flora and fauna in the area. Ideal for learning, but not for loving.   I would just have to survive Christmas without Tom.   All of my best laid plans had melted like a winter wonderland in Spring. Lasting relationships are like a big win at the Casino or on the Lottery, you just have to be lucky.

I had told my parents that I was going to France with a girl friend, but Toms' second partner had reported him to the Social Services, for not paying his maintenance for her and his child for the past six months. He, according to her, had gone on the missing list. The Police were informed, and an all points bulletin was issued. Unknown to me, when you enter or leave a foreign port, your passport is scanned, and Close Circuit Television records everyone, in order for the Police to cover all entry and exit points, looking for mainly criminals, but also runaways, escaping from home. Recent pictures of missing persons are printed in the newspapers and in urgent cases shown on television. I didn't know that the Police were looking for Tom, until I looked at the local paper and saw a photograph of him with his arm around a girl, but the girl in the photo ....was not me......................................but my best friend Cathy.

REVENGE IS SWEET

"There's a killer inside all of us, but how many of us actually have the guts to kill someone, without caring too much about the consequences that may befall us?" That was the question that I put to my lower 6th form students as a project for their end of year exams. I had been teaching this year group for about, well longer than I care to remember, and would be retiring from the College in the Summer. The years had just rolled by. I was young one day, and BANG, before I knew it, I had reached the compulsory retirement age. Life in a flash. " Is this all there really is?, or had I been too involved with my job to realise that probably I had missed the boat that had carried all of my contemporaries into water that I had not yet charted, but I had plans to change all of that."

"Please sir, Jonny Lewis's hand shot up, does it have to be something that we have actually experienced, or can it be just a figment of our imagination ?" He was always the first to respond to everything that I proposed, and despite his enthusiasm and ability, he was the class geek. He knew just about everything about everything, and it was no surprise that he always came out top at the end of the exams. "I sincerely hope that none of you have ever experienced that notion in reality, I said. It's easy to say something in the heat of the moment but never really mean it". Jonny's hand shot up again. "What is it now Lewis?", I said in exasperation. "Has it ever happened to you, sir?" he asked. I dodged the question, as I looked at the clock and saw that the lesson was just about to end, which was confirmed by the loud ringing of the bell signalling not only the end of the lesson, but the term as well. "Have a good break, and I'll see you all, next term".

I had posed the homework to the class to gauge their reaction, and also to ask myself the same question, as years ago I had been on the verge of committing murder. I was never certain that I would get my revenge, I just never knew that I had the guts to commit murder. Death was far too good for this evil, thieving, vicious , spiteful bully, but I had reached the end of my tether, and I was going to rid the world of this monster, and to hell with the consequences. Just thinking about it has brought back to the surface the anger that had been brewing, all those years ago. He, basically, had got away with murder, not literally, but by manipulating all of the people around him, to cheat, lie and steal from his so called friends. He had no scruples at all. Everyone was sucked in by his outward charm. We were just too trusting of this money grabbing sycophant. Now it was my time to turn the tables on him, as I had been diagnosed with a terminal disease, and I had nothing to lose.

I had been waiting in the consulting rooms for quite a while for the results of my tests, sensing that they would not be good. The door opened and in came the dapper Indian surgeon, Mr Dhoni, the top liver consultant in England, who had pronounced my death sentence by telling me in morbid tones that the cancer in my liver was inoperable and with any luck the chemotherapy would keep me alive for anything between 1 and 2 years. Why did I need to be kept alive, because we all know that the end result can't be altered, and will come soon enough. I decided not to go through the trauma of dying slowly. "You've probably got a maximum of about six months, he told me, but in your very advanced state it may be less than 3". "Why prolong the agony ?, I want a quick end to my life." "There is always hope, he replied, as new and improved drugs are being tested daily, and, who knows just what cure may be discovered in the next two years." "I know this, I said more forcefully than I had intended, drug testing takes at least 5 years of trials before they are allowed to be used on humans, and I am sorry to say that even if a drug was discovered today, it would be too late for me." "Just think about it, with 2 extra years you could do things that you have never got around to, previously". "I've made up my mind, and I shall let nature take its' natural course".

One of the very few things that had preyed on my mind, for the past 20 years was HIM. I often managed to go for months without giving him a second thought, and then, right out of the blue, something triggers my memory, and the pure hatred returns, even more fiercely than before. I didn't care what happened to me, but I had to resolve this, once and for all. I had very little time left on this earth, and was determined to seek my revenge on him, and if I was successful, we would be sharing the same route out of this world, although which direction, at this moment was unclear. I hoped that with my actions, it would be recognised, by himself upstairs, as an act of mercy, and I would go to heaven, whilst there was no way that he would not go to hell.

I had dreamt of devious ways to kill him, but now I had to plan with precision to put into place, something that I could be certain would end his very unworthy life. But what was it to be? I could always poison him, shoot him, or drown him, but that would need co-operation from other people, and I didn't want to have anyone else involved, so scrub that option. I could place a bomb under his car, but then other innocent people might be injured, drug him, but I would need to get close enough, which wasn't really an option. I know, I'll get some Anthrax and send it to him in a letter, but how would I obtain Anthrax? I went onto 'Google' and found out that Porton Down near Salisbury in Wiltshire has a stock of it for use in combating the spread of cattle disease, but I would never be able to bluff my way into there, so rule that out. I did, however discover, that there are lots of countries in Southern Europe, as well as The Middle East, Asia and Africa, where Anthrax is more readily obtainable, but in reality Anthrax was not an option. Good idea, but no. I would like him to die in agony, knowing that it was me that had killed him, but how? I still had no answers, and my life clock was ticking faster.

Got it, I thought, as I read an advert in the local paper. 'DEADLY SNAKES FOR SALE. There is a pet shop called Fangs, Feasts and Beasts in his village which advertised that not all snakes are deadly, and with careful handling they can become a family pet. Bizarre , I shivered, who in their right minds would welcome a snake into their house, let alone a deadly one. Nevertheless, a plan had formed in my mind. I would go to the shop and buy the most deadly one that they had, together with an antidote that would protect me, if I happened to mishandle it.

The shop was in Bishops Stortford, and was not easy to find, as it was situated in a narrow side alley, just off the main shopping area, where I had managed to park my car. The shop was dark, and extremely hot as I entered, and the little bell tinkled behind me as I shut the door. It felt spooky. "Good morning sir, a man with a gravelly voice said from somewhere in the darkness. He could see me, but I had no idea where he was. Don't worry about the dark, we have to keep it dim in here as the snakes don't like too much light. They also need the temperature up to 75-80 degrees, just like their natural habitat." He emerged from the dark and stood in front of me, and I could just about make out his features in the gloom. He was short and stubby, with a huge belly, over which hung his apron. His arms were as thick as my legs, and had a series of snake tattoos running from his hands up both of them. "How may I help you?" he said in a pleasant enough voice. "I'm looking for an unusual surprise present for someone, and when I saw your advert, I thought that you might be just the person who could be of assistance". "Well, if it's a surprise present, then Old Higgins here, he said pointing at his chest, is just the man for you, he chuckled. What did you have in mind?" "The person that I am going to surprise, loves animals. He already has two Old English Sheepdogs, and a house full of cats, and I am certain that something like a snake would suit him down to the ground. Not any run of the mill snake, mind you, but probably a dangerous one, as he lives his life in the 'fast lane' and I know that he would appreciate the danger element. And what an unusual gift it would be. I'm certain that he would just love it to death."

Old Higgins drew back the black curtain that separated the front of the shop, and beckoned me into his 'inner sanctum' where there were glass cages full of writhing ,wriggling and hissing slimy looking snakes. Some appeared to be sleeping, and others flicking their forked tongues out at both of us, almost as if they were looking at us as their next meal. I backed away from the cages. "No need to be frightened, he said, they are harmless enough in the right conditions, such as these, but you have to know how to handle them properly, or you could suffer a fatal bite if you are not careful". Those words were music to my ears. This is how you do it, he said, as he slid back the lid from one of the cages, and put on his glove and placed his hand behind the head of a vicious spitting reptile. With his other hand he put what looked like a long fork towards the head of the snake. Hold it tight, and you won't get into any trouble, but hold the head away from you as this one can spit its' venom up to six feet." He went to the next cage. "That was a Cobra, and this one is even more dangerous. My eyes lit up. This is the famous Black Mamba, known as 'The Kiss of Death' in our business, being the fastest snake in the world. Its venom is deadly and can kill a grown human in anything from 15 minutes to an hour. If bitten by both of the fangs, paralysis of the respiratory muscles happens within minutes, and causes dizziness, drowsiness, and coughing. Breathing becomes very difficult, and if no antidote is immediately administered, a horrible death follows. So be extremely careful if you decide on this snake." "What do the snakes usually eat", I asked. "They normally go for warm blooded rodents such as rats, mice, voles, and squirrels, but if they are not fed regularly, they will attack young cats and dogs, and in extreme circumstances, humans."

I had made up my mind, that the Black Mamba was the snake that I would buy. With glee in my face, I said "I'll take the Black Mamba". We agreed the price which included the cage and a sack full of dead rodents. "With such a dangerous, and unusual pet, will the recipient need a Dangerous Animals permit?" "Most certainly, we have to keep a note of all of our sales and pass them to DEFRA , Department of Environment, Food and Rural Affairs, and they will issue a permit. I shall also need your details to advise them of your purchase.." "No problem, I replied, let me fill in the necessary documents. " He handed me a sheaf of papers, and I duly entered all the information, and signed where appropriate. "As this is a surprise gift, would it be possible to delay sending the details to DEFRA until after the weekend, as I shall let him have my gift on Sunday, and wouldn't want to spoil the surprise, by him having prior knowledge of my little gift to him." "It's slightly unusual, but if I post the forms tomorrow using a second class stamp, then there is no way that they will receive the documents before Monday." "Thank you very much for your very kind help, Mr Higgins. May I have your business card, please, and I shall put it with the gift, so that if he encounters any problems, he can contact you." "Don't forget this", he said, waving the small bottle of antidote at me. "I almost forgot the most important part of this sale," I said in mock horror. He handed me a copy of the forms that I had signed, together with his business card, and helped me put the parcel into the boot of my car. I didn't want it in the car with me, as God forbid, if I had an accident and the snake escaped it could attack me as well as other possible bystanders. The boot should be safe enough.

I carefully drove home, without mishap, and even thought of giving the snake a name. The name that I conjured up from the depths of my memory as I remembered Captain Beaky and his band , not forgetting Hissing Sid. That would do very nicely I thought. The final part of my plan was coming together. I knew were my victim lived, now on his own, following yet another marriage breakdown. This was the third time to my knowledge that he had led his wife down the garden path, promising the earth, and delivering absolutely nothing. Typical.

I planned to visit his house, very early in the morning, and hide in the bushes and watch his routine carefully to see if there may be a way that I could place hissing Sid into his car. This part was easy, as he now lived in a grand house hidden behind a thick hedge, which shielded it from the road. There was no gate, so it was easy for me to conceal myself, unseen by any neighbour or delivery person. I watched and waited and at precisely 6 o'clock, he stepped jauntily out of his front door, swinging his sports bag over his shoulder, obviously on his way to his daily exercise at the gym. He got into his convertible Mini Cooper, and released the roof and sped off. He repeated this exactly the next day as well.

I hadn't fed the snake, as I wanted to make sure that it was ravenous when I put it into his car. I went to my hiding spot the next morning, and sure enough he went through the same routine, but once the roof was open, I jumped out and confronted him. "Y O U", he spat out, get off my property or I'll have you arrested for trespass". " Go right ahead, I said in a voice much calmer that I actually felt, it would be good to have the police turn up to witness your demise". He didn't understand the word demise, so he wasn't really ready for my attack on him. "You are the biggest con artist and fraudster, I spoke softly at him, you have cheated and connived to swindle lots of people out of their honestly earned money, including my father, which made him take his own life when you stole fees from him of up to half a million pounds, and you cleverly hid all of the money so carefully that no one could touch you, and now you are going to pay. "Get out of my way, you're a loser, just like your old man, and if you don't get your arse out of my way I shall have no problems in running you over, and you can join him in the cemetery." He put his foot down hard on the accelerator, and aimed the car straight at me. He had a wicked grin on his face. I jumped to the side, and at the same time lifted the cover off Hissing Sid and tipped the snake onto his lap, as he sat in the driver's seat. "Bulls eye" I screamed as I hit the floor with a bang, just out of reach of the front bumper, as the snake landed on his lap. He braked hard, sending gravel stones scattering. He tried to throw the snake off him, and in doing so exposed his bare hand, and as I scrambled to my knees, I saw the two fang marks on the back of his hand, as he managed to get the snake away from him initially. Hissing Sid was in no mood to let go of his prey, and sank his teeth into many other parts of his body, causing instant paralysis. His eyes glazed over, and formed the words 'help me' but no sound came out of his rictus lips. Sid was having a veritable feast, whilst HE was dying quickly. I managed to capture the snake with the equipment that I had bought, and put him back in his cage.

I walked back to his car, and took a look at the pitiful dying thing that I saw in the driver's seat. "Now you know what it is like to be killed by one of your own". He looked at me with mysterious eyes, not quite fathoming out what I had said. "I'll spell it out for you, I said. You have always been a snake in the grass and now you will die by being killed..................... by a snake in your arse". I laughed, as I walked sedately away from the destruction of what once was a homo sapien, but only just. Revenge tasted very sweet indeed.

THE INSPECTION

CHAPTER ONE

Sally and Bert Cross, lived in a big four bedroom house on the edge of the Town, where they had been for the past 23 years bringing up their two adopted children, who had left the nest long ago and were now living their own lives on the other side of the world in both Australia and New Zealand respectively. The only contact that they had with either of them was the cursory card at Christmas, and sometimes, if they remembered, birthdays. Bert had worked, cooped up in an office in London for one of the world's largest International accountants, whilst Sally had taught at the local nursery school. They had both retired two years ago, and whilst they believed that life begins at forty, they were just bored, bored, bored. They had agreed that upon retirement, they would spend time together, doing things that they never had time to do during working days, but having visited many exhibitions, theatres and cinemas, they felt that there must be more to retirement than this. The gardening was more of something to do, rather than enjoy. Neither of them liked sport, so bowls or golf didn't come into their thoughts, nor did ballroom dancing or driving around England to discover new places. The thought of joining a gym was horrendous, as one of their fitter friends, died on the running machine, so that had put them off those places for ever. They needed something to spark them into life.

"When will this horrid winter ever stop"? Sally, pulled up the louvred blind and looked out of the kitchen window, and saw the snow sweeping across the lawn, yet again. "It's settling", she said to no one in particular, as she was clearing up the breakfast plates from the table, where she and Bert had just finished eating. The snow and fierce rain storms had lashed England for nearly two months, causing untold misery for anyone and everyone, up and down the Country. Villages had been cut off by un-passable roads, the electricity supply had been badly disrupted, and livestock had been lost in huge numbers in the snowdrifts, some 15-20' deep. "Pretty as a picture, said Bert as he re-entered the kitchen, but I'm just about fed up with our weather, be it summer or winter. It's time we got out of here and lived in a warmer, more settled climate." "Are you being serious, or are you just in yet another of your bad moods?" "No, I'm being perfectly serious, what have we got to lose by moving away, this country is in real trouble, and I can't really see how the next 20 years are going to improve the situation. We are deep in debt, and it won't be long before we tax payers are expected to bail out some other failing Institutions. We already own the Royal Bank of Scotland as well as Lloyds Bank, and I hear rumours that Barclays Bank is also holding its hand out for Government support. We don't want to be like Cyprus,

and lose upto 40% of our savings, just because the Government says so. So yes, count me in, on a move."
"My goodness, replied Sally, you are really depressed. I only half heartedly suggested that we should find somewhere warmer, but I meant as a holiday home, not to up sticks and move out permanently." They had often sat in the garden on the rare summer days, gazing up at the planes flying overhead and leaving their vapour trails in the sky, just wondering where the passengers were travelling, and imagining exotic locations, just for fun.

Bert, picked up the morning paper and turned to the weather section. The forecast for the next seven days is, yes you've guessed it, more rain, snow and freezing conditions. Who would believe that we are already a quarter of the way through the year, with no sign of Spring. He thumped the paper down onto the table. Look here, he said, pointing at the chart in the paper showing worldwide climates, the temperature in Tenerife yesterday was 25 degrees. How about finding a place there?" "If you are really serious then before we do anything, we should consider firstly where we would like to live, the language problems, and who and what we would be leaving behind", Sally reasoned. "OK, let's sit down with a pen and pad and separately write down our own thoughts, and see how they compare when we have finished. We could do it now, as there is no way that I am going to venture outside today in those biting sub zero winds".

They compiled their separate lists, and to their surprise they seemed to agree that Southern Europe was probably the best location, with nowhere being more than 4 hours or so flight away from England. Language wasn't a real problem, as Sally had learnt Spanish at school, and she believed that with a few private lessons, it would soon come back to her. Bert, a typical Englishman, thought that all foreigners should speak English, but he would be prepared to learn, if he felt it necessary. They had no immediate family to worry about, just a few friends, but that would be no real issue. "So where do you think that we should concentrate our search?", asked Sally. "Logically, I think that Spain would be good, enthused Bert". "Are we talking about moving permanently, or a holiday home"? "I think that in the first instance we should be looking to rent somewhere, short term, to see if we could adapt to that way of life, and if we did, we could then consider buying something", said Bert. "Alright, but have you any idea what part of Spain you want to live in, and if so do you have any idea of the prices?" "I know that John and Jean have had similar ideas, and are actively looking in the Marbella area.

Over the even wetter weekend, they jointly scanned the newspapers. "There are hundreds of properties for sale, but I have heard that the time to buy in Spain is now, announced Bert, as prices are near rock bottom, and with the dreadful economic situation, we could pick up something for a song". "That as may be, Sally answered, but as Spain is a big country, we really ought to concentrate on the area first, and then make one of those 'Free' inspection trips." "You're right, of course, but where would you suggest"? "Mary, at the Nursery, always takes her holidays on the Costa del Sol, so that might be a good place to start". "We have only ever been to Spain once in our lives, said Bert, but many of the guys in the office also go to the same area. Let's see what might be available." Marbella is one of the destinations that I understand is a good area for British people to live, said Sally, and if we could get onto an estate where the residents are mainly from England, then I believe that it would help us settle in more readily."

They went to the computer and looked up the agents who were handling distressed sales and found lots of opportunities in the area, and especially one that was being marketed by The Exclusive Iberian Property Overseas Group. "Look at this one, Sally. It's got 3 bedrooms, 2 bathrooms and a private swimming pool and it's well within our budget at 250,000 Euros". "My goodness, what a lovely looking house, let's get some more details" Sally was now enjoying herself, imagining them on the sun drenched terrace with a glass or two of wine, lapping up the lazy hazy days of summer, that was according to the weather records, at least 10 months long, where the daytime temperatures never dropped below 70 degrees. "What a view, enthused Bert, you can see the sea from the upper floors". "Let's phone them, and make an appointment to view. We could easily be in Spain in a couple of days".

Bert phoned the agent. "Hello, do you speak English?", he asked. " You're speaking with Sergio Gomez, came the reply, how may we help you?" "On your web site you have a 3 bedroom villa, ref 21356H, for sale, and we would like to make an appointment to view it, later this week please". "Are you registered with us Sir?" "Not yet, but I can give you all of our details now if you wish." "Please may I have them?" Bert went through all of the registration process, and at the end of the questions he asked if they could see the villa. "I'm sorry Mr Cross, but someone else has just made an acceptable offer, and the property has been withdrawn from the market for the moment. The potential purchasers have been given an exclusive four week contract, and have paid a non refundable deposit of 10%, so I would think that the deal will be completed". Somewhat crestfallen, Bert lamely suggested that if it failed to materialise, he would like to be informed. "We do, however, have other similar properties that could be of interest to you, the agent told Bert, but Bert was not interested, as in his own mind he thought that the villa would be his. "Can you put them in an e-mail to me, and we shall look through the details, and then get back to you". "The market here in Marbella, is beginning to come back to life, and the only way to buy anything is to be on the spot right now", said the very pushy agent. "I thought that the market was very flat, and we could take our time to find something suitable", Bert said. "In the past few weeks we have sold as many properties as we did all last year, and the way things are happening right now, any purchase made now will increase in value, almost overnight." The agent was so enthusiastic that he made Bert feel that if he didn't go Spain straight away, he would end up paying over the odds for something suitable. "Let me discuss the situation with my wife, and I shall get right back to you, Snr Gomez." "Please call me Sergio".

The phones were put down simultaneously. "We've got a live one here, said Sergio to his Partner. He has no real idea what is happening in this shit market and I think that if we can get him here, we can sell him the villa that we put on the web site, and make ourselves a nice profit". "I like your style Sergio, said his Partner, Maria, with a grin spreading across her face. All we have to do is to entice him here. "Why don't you call him back and offer to pay for his air fare, and accommodation for say 3 days, during which time, you can work your charm on him and his wife?" "Great idea, he replied, we shall just add this cost to the price of the property."

Bert had no need to report the conversation to Sally as she had listened on the extension telephone in the upstairs bedroom. "What a bummer, she said, I think that both of us really fell for that villa, and from what Sergio was saying, it seems that the sale is likely to go through". "I agree, said Bert, now really upset by the fact that they couldn't buy it, there must be others in the area that we could buy, after all, it is the first one that we have even looked into in some detail, and when we get there it might be a load of rubbish, falling down the mountain, and in terrible condition inside, with a leaky roof". "I know, lamented Sally, but on the face of it, it did appear to be a bargain". "Just forget it and see if there is anything else that might be suitable", a disappointed Bert replied.

"There's a Spanish Properties exhibition at the Town Hall over this weekend Bert, why don't we go and see what's on offer?" "Good idea, Bert replied in a much more upbeat mood than he really felt, what time does it start?" "It says in the advert that it is open on both Saturday and Sunday between 10.00 and 16.00, and parking is free".

The week dragged by, and at no time did the subject of the missed opportunity come up in any of their conversations. "Mum has asked us over for lunch on Saturday, and I have accepted, said Sally, it will still give us enough time to get to the exhibition". Lunch was a real pain, as Sally's mother was almost deaf, and at the end of lunch both Sally and Bert had sore throats from shouting at her. "Turn your batteries up Mum, screamed Sally, you'll be able to hear us better." "The volume is on maximum", said her mother. "Why can't you hear us then?". "I've switched them off", she replied. "Why?" asked Bert. "The batteries are so expensive, I don't want to waste them", her mother replied. Exasperated, and exhausted, they knew when they were beaten. "Just look at the time, said Bert, we have to get going or we shall miss the exhibition." "What exhibition?" Her mother asked. "You heard that you deaf old woman, didn't you?", Bert whispered. "WHAT, she said, I can't hear you". "Turn the batteries on, he whispered again, now having fun at his mother-in- law's distress. Sally gave him a look, that made him shut up immediately, and he apologised to her mother, and then they left in a hurry to get to the Town Hall before it closed for the day. As they got there, the doors were just closing, and a member of staff told them that they were closing the doors half an hour early, as there were so many people in the exhibition, that it would be impossible to see them all within the next 30 minutes. He apologised and suggested that they come back at about 15 minutes before the opening tomorrow.

Sunday morning, just for a change the rain was pouring down, as they made their way from the car park to the Town Hall, and joined a line of about thirty people, waiting for the doors to open. They were all sheltering under a selection of large umbrellas, bearing the names of well known Companies, that were being blown inside out by the strong winds. The first in line rushed through to the main hall, quickly followed by a stream of very wet property hunters, all looking for their Shangri-La. A tall sun tanned gentleman greeted them when they approached the area where all the Spanish Property companies were located. In a strong accent, he welcomed Sally and Bert, and listened to their story. "My name is Alberto Castelino of Castelino & Co, SA, and I av just the thing for you, he said, in the heart of Marbella." He showed them the video of the lovely property, and he could see their faces light up with interest. "It certainly looks very nice said Sally, but how much is it?" "We have it on an exclusive agency from the British owners who are returning to England, as his job requires him to return to London, and he is very keen to tie something up quickly, so it's on the market for 400,000 Euros". "Wow, that's far too expensive for us, we are only looking to spend 250,000 Euros, maximum, including any taxes", said Bert. "I am sure that he would take an offer for a very quick sale", said Alberto. "We haven't seen inside yet, said Sally, how could we possibly make an offer, unseen?" "Let me speak with the owner, and see what his lowest price might be, he said, and if it is within your budget, I could arrange an inspection." Alberto went to the back of the stand and proceeded to make the call to the owner. A few minutes later, he came back to Bert and Sally, with a huge smile on his face. "I've just spoken with the owner, who tells me that his very, very last figure is 275,000 Euros, which would include all of the taxes. What do you think?" "Let us go away and think about it, said Bert, we won't be too long".

"Sally, you know that we can't afford a penny more than 250,000 Euros, without having to sell our home here, and to be honest, I don't like to be rushed over such a large decision as this. We first of all don't know where it is, secondly, we haven't seen it, and thirdly, well there is no thirdly, but my view is that we let it go." "Oh, am I glad that you said that, replied Sally. I didn't like the pushy way that he was trying to get us to buy it. I agree with you". "I think that the one thing that we have learnt from this is that in order for us to make any decision, we should go to the area, suss it out for ourselves, and then approach any agent or seller via their adverts and for sale boards, and deal with everything as if we were buying a house in England. Let's not get bamboozled, just because they think that we are idiots, which we are not". "That's the best thing that you have said, about our possible move", said Sally, and she threw a relieved hug around Bert's neck, and kissed him.

They fought their way through the ever increasing throng of people at the Town Hall, and stepped out into the still pouring rain to get into their car and drive home. "Such a relief to get out of there, Bert said, do you really think that Alberto phoned the owner, or was it just a show for us to witness?" "Don't know and don't really care, said Sally, let's forget about him, and plan our next move, if there is going to be a next move." "I don't really know, but the one thing that I am sure of is that if it is still raining next week, I shall book a last minute holiday in Marbella, and we shall carry out some further investigations".

They drove home, shook off the rain from their coats and settled down in front of the television. "What's on?", asked Sally. "You'll never guess, it's only a programme called Homes in the Sun, featuring Marbella, replied Bert. Do you want me to switch it on"? "Yes, it might be interesting, said Sally. I'll join you in a minute" The programme started with an announcement, advising prospective purchasers to be very careful when buying in some areas, especially on the Costa del Sol, or as they say Costa del crime, as several companies had recently sprung up, offering homes for sale, without ever having instructions from the owners. The rogue agents find vacant houses, change the locks, and claim to be acting on behalf of the vendor. They entice unsuspecting British people to part with the full price to be paid into their shifty solicitor's account. The keys are handed over to the buyers, who move in, only to be confronted some time later by the real owners who have never agreed to sell, nor have they ever signed an escritura with a notary, and then are forced out by law, losing every penny that they have handed over. Several companies are now being actively pursued by the police, including The Exclusive Iberian Property Group. These companies may appear to have ceased trading, but their Principals, are still being sought for questioning. A reward of 25,000 Euros will be offered to anyone with information that leads to an arrest. A telephone number was displayed across the bottom of the screen.

Bert looked aghast at Sally, who returned his look of horror. "Boy, were we lucky, they could have taken us for a fortune, stuttered Bert. I'm going to phone John and Jean and warn them." Bert picked up the phone and heard the familiar bleep advising that there was a message waiting for them. He pressed the answer message. "Hola, Mr & Mrs Cross, this is Maria, of The Exclusive Iberian Property Group in Marbella. Please call me as soon as you get this message, as I have just heard that the prospective purchasers of Villa Jasmina, that you are interested in, are not going to be able to complete the purchase, due to personal reasons, which I am not at liberty to divulge, but he is willing to let you have his contract to purchase at 250,000 Euros, with the proviso that an extra 10,000 Euros in cash, is paid over to him as part settlement of his loss of deposit".

"You'll never guess who has just left us a message", said Bert, It's only Sergio's office, offering us the villa, as the current buyers are pulling out". "You heard the warning, just now about not dealing with them, so let's heed the warning", replied Sally. B..b..but there's a huge reward, and we don't want to lose the opportunity, do we?" "I suppose not", but.... her voice tailed off, unenthusiastically. Bert was now like a dog with two tails, as he had the bit between his teeth. "I'm going to call that number on the screen right now".

"Jason Drake, Fraud Squad". "Hello, this is Bert Cross, and I think that I might be able to help you with your enquiries into the whereabouts of Sergio Gomez, of the

Exclusive Iberian Property Group, and I understand that there is a reward of 25,000 Euros, which I am hoping I will be able to claim". "Quite correct, Sir, can you please come into our office in Central London, as soon as possible, to discuss this further with us" He gave the address and they agreed to meet the following day.

Bert and Sally were so excited at the prospect of the large reward, that neither of them slept a wink all night, and with adrenaline pumping they took the tube to Charing Cross, and walked to the Serious Fraud office to meet with Jason Drake. Jason Drake was older than they had expected, and looked like he had slept in his rather faded check jacket all night. The leather arm patches had a patina and had worn very thin with little holes starting to peep through. His blue shirt had a button down collar with one button missing and the thread showing where the button used to be. The striped red and white tie had the remains of breakfast on it. He was almost bald, but tried to hide it with a few long strands in a comb over, fooling no one. He had more hair in his ears and eyebrows than was on his shiny head. His pipe lay resting in an ashtray full of smoked tobacco. His office smelled like a rubbish tip, with empty cartons of food and drink spilling out of the overflowing waste bin onto the uncarpeted wooden slatted floor.

Jason Drake listened to their story. "Here's the plan, he said, sucking on his empty pipe. Phone The Exclusive Iberian Property Company and tell them that you would like to inspect the villa, tomorrow, and if it seems as good as it says, you would like to rent it for one week, with an option to purchase it at the end of the week. I know that they may not agree initially, but if they feel that you are 'on the hook', they will let you stay". "But what if they won't go along with the suggestion?" "Believe me, they will, Drake grinned. Here, he continued, giving them an untraceable telephone, call them now and make the arrangements". What about flights?, suggested Sally . "No problems, we'll get you there ".

"Hola, Maria speaking". "Hello, this is Bert Cross, I've got your message and yes we would like to inspect Villa Jasmina tomorrow at say 17.00, if you could arrange it for us please, but if we like it, we would like to rent it from the owners for a week, just to make sure that everything is in order, before we purchase it". "I'm not sure that the people who hold the current contract would let you do that", she replied. "What have they got to lose? pleaded Bert, because if we fall in love with it they can have their money next week." "I'll see what I can do, and I shall call you back in a few minutes, after I have spoken with them". Bert handed the phone back to Drake, who had been listening in on the conversation, whist recording it.

Bert's mobile phone was ringing showing 'International Call' in the display window. "It's them, he said excitedly, pointing the phone towards Drake. Hello, is that Maria?". "Yes, I have just spoken with my people, who initially refused your request, but I have managed to persuade them to let you have occupation for 7 days from tomorrow, with the proviso that if upon your inspection you do like it, you will have to sign an option to purchase and pay over the non refundable cash sum of 10,000 Euros ". "It will take us several days to lay our hands on 10,000 Euros in cash, replied Bert, but I am sure that we shall have it within 7 days. The best that we could let you have immediately would be 1,000 Euros, which I trust will be acceptable." "Please hold the line a minute, whilst I take instructions", said Maria, who pressed the 'mute' button and turned to Sergio. "They've only 1,000 Euros immediately, but they can get the balance within a few days, I suggest that we accept and get them here". "Not ideal, but the promise of 10,000 Euros within a week is far too good an offer to turn down. We'll put pressure on them as soon as they arrive. Tell them OK", said Sergio. Maria cancelled the 'mute' on the phone. "OK, the deal is on, let's meet at our offices tomorrow afternoon at 17.00. Do you know where they are?" "No, sorry we don't, but we'll take a taxi." No need said Maria, Sergio and I will meet you at Malaga airport. Is it the Easy Jet flight from Luton that you will be taking?" Drake shook his head in affirmation. "Yes, Bert said, we shall look out for you. How shall we recognise you ?" "We'll have your names printed on a display in the arrivals hall, and if there is a problem, we also have your mobile phone. See you tomorrow".

"That's all set ,what happens now?" "Our contact, Miguel, in Malaga will follow you, on arrival, and with the help of Interpol, we shall make an arrest at the villa." "What happens to us, asked Sally, we'll be in Spain without anywhere to stay, and it would be nice if we could take a little holiday, whilst we are there." "No need to concern yourself with that, if all goes to plan, we can arrange first class accommodation for a few days at one of our 'Safe houses' on the coast. Miguel will arrange it all for you."   "And the reward" chimed in Bert, when can we expect that? " "Hopefully, upon the conviction in about three to six months".

CHAPTER TWO

Luton Airport was covered in a grey swirling fine rain mist cover, when the flight number EZY 2403 took off, and headed upwards through the clouds into the bright sunshine, and took just over two hours before it started its descent into Malaga Airport. The cabin doors swung open and it was like stepping into a furnace with the temperature somewhere in the high seventy to eighty degrees, a far cry from the six to seven degrees in England. They only had hand luggage with them, and quickly cleared customs, and went out into the semi deserted arrivals hall, as all of the other passengers had to wait for their luggage to be unloaded. Immediately they saw a young couple smartly dressed , holding up a display with their names on it. "Hello, said Bert , pointing at the board, that's us". "Bienvenido to Malaga, I'm Sergio, and this is Maria. Shall we go"?

Bert and Sally, put on their sunglasses, and followed them out to the car park, and got into the sparkling white Mercedes car. "We'll go straight to the villa, said Maria, and if everything is fine, we can ask you to sign the option, over drinks on the terrace". Bert and Sally had glanced around them, as they left the airport, looking anxiously for Miguel, but they supposed that if he was a good 'tail' they would not expect to see him.

Sergio drove quickly along the highway, and within 30 minutes they saw the entrance sign welcoming them to Marbella. "That looks a little bit Arabic", said Sally as they passed underneath the archway. "This arch was paid for by the wealthy Jet Set that started to make Marbella their home in the late 1980's, answered Maria. However, there are plans for a tunnel, and the Arch is being dismantled piece by piece, and its future is still undecided." "We shall be at the villa in about fifteen minutes, said Sergio. They drove past several golf courses, being watered by the intricate system that took the desalinated water from the sea and was now used as an irrigation system on many of the courses. The sun was shining through the water, making mini rainbows everywhere. Up the mountain side, over a tarmac road, and finally into the little road that had a sign pointing to VILLA JASMINA in bold red letters. Sergio stopped the car, jumped out and unlocked the high wrought iron gates, that also had Villa Jasmina designed within them. A pair of stone carved pineapples adorned the top of the brick piers.

"Wow, and double wow, exclaimed Sally, hardly daring to believe that this was the property that they might buy. It's even better than the photographs that we have seen". The white walled two storey villa, sat towards one side of the plot, that was at least half an acre of rolling lawn, fruit trees, shrubs and flowering borders. The villa was covered in flowering mauve and pink bougainvillea . They went up the short flight of stone steps and entered the spacious hall that had an open plan staircase winding its way up to the first floor level, with full height windows onto a balcony that overlooked the swimming pool that sparkled in the sun. Beyond, there was an uninterrupted view to the sea. The three bedrooms were fully furnished and had marble floors throughout. All had en suite bathrooms. The ground floor was set out as a huge living and dining room with a wonderful modern fully equipped kitchen and separate laundry room. They were gob smacked. This was the house of their dreams, and not a cloud in the sky. "All this for 250,000 Euros, whispered Sally, it must be some sort of mistake". "Yes, replied Bert also in a hushed whisper, but let's not forget that we aren't really going to buy it, we are just here as a bait to catch the crooks".

"Well, what do you think, asked Maria, is this a great deal or not"? They didn't want to seem too keen, so they both said that they would spend the week here and then make up their minds. "No problem at all, said Sergio, but I must ask you for the first part of the option payment of 1,000 Euros, please, and get you to sign the legal agreement that I have here". He pulled out the folded document from his shirt pocket and placed it on the table on the terrace, whilst Maria, went to the kitchen and brought out a bottle of white wine and four frosted glasses. Bert put on his reading glasses, and quickly read the option agreement. He read it again more carefully, and handed it to Sally to read. "It looks alright to me", Bert announced. "Me also" said Sally, whose heart was pumping so violently, she hoped that they wouldn't notice. She handed the Agreement back to Bert. "All I need now is the money and your signatures please, Sergio replied, and naturally, I shall give you a receipt for the money. When do you think you will be able to pay over the remaining 9,000 Euros?" "Where is the nearest Santander Bank?" It's on Avenue Guadalmina, an easy taxi ride from here. "Good, I've made arrangements via my Bank in England to have the money transferred there, and I should be able to give it to you by the end of the week". "That's fine, just let us know, and we shall arrange to meet you there, as we wouldn't want you to get robbed, carrying all of that money with you through the streets of Marbella." Bert signed the top copy of the Option Agreement and counted out 1,000 Euros from his money clip, and gave the money and signed agreement to Sergio, who in return wrote a receipt for the money and handed Bert the bottom copy of the agreement.

"Here are the keys to the property, said Sergio, giving a large bunch of labelled keys to Bert. Make sure that you activate the alarm and close all of the shutters whenever you leave the villa. You just can't be too sure these days". He winked slyly at Maria. Once they had driven away, Bert asked Sally, if she had seen any sign of Miguel. "No, that's strange, as Drake said that Miguel would follow us to the villa and make an arrest here. I wonder what has happened to him?". "I'll phone Drake and see if he can throw any light onto this?" "Jason Drake, fraud squad". " Bert Cross at the villa, your man Miguel has not shown. Where is he"? "He should be there, but let me find out, and I will call you back shortly". About fifteen minutes later the phone rang. "Jason Drake here. Sorry, but Miguel didn't turn up for work today, and we can't seem to get hold of him". "So what happens now? asked Bert, as I have already parted with 1,000 Euros of my own money, and they expect me to cough up another 9,000 Euros before we leave here, which I am not prepared to do". "Don't worry, we'll think of something, and I'll get it all sorted shortly". "Not a lot that we can do just now, so let's enjoy our stay here, until we hear from Drake, again" Bert advised Sally.

"Did you hear that Maria?". They were sitting in his parked car, just down the road, listening to Bert's conversation, via a device that they had placed in all of the rooms in the villa. "Yes, I did, she answered with a scowl on her face, they won't get away with this, trying to con a con artist. What should we do?, especially as we have already paid off Miguel to go missing for a few days". "I suggest that we go back there now, and confront them, said Sergio, what's the worst that can happen? They'll have to leave the villa." "OK, let's go back", agreed Maria.

Bert and Sally were still sitting on the terrace finishing their drinks, when the white Mercedes pulled up in the drive. Sergio and Maria made angry strides towards them. "What the hell do you two think you are playing at?", yelled Sergio, taking Bert and Sally completely by surprise. These weren't the nice people that they had been dealing with only moments ago. These were two very aggressive Spaniards gesticulating wildly, shaking their fists at them. "What's all the shouting about, asked Sally in a calm voice, using her experience with rowdy children, to try and placate them. You know that we are here for a week, and we would like to enjoy some peace and quiet". "We're on to your little scheme, screamed Maria, we just heard you on the phone". Sergio swiftly grabbed hold of Sally and held her in a tight headlock. "Let her go you, you , el bandido", shouted Bert as he tried to step forward to release her, but Maria had stuck out a leg, and he tumbled over it, down the terrace steps and into the pool, cracking his head on the tiles, and leaving a large red stain on the blue water from the wound. "What have you done to Bert, Sally tried to scream, but the grip on her throat was so tight that the words hardly left her lips.

Maria looked at the floating body of Bert, shook her head sideways and drew a finger across her throat. "He's dead" she said. Sally tried to break free by kicking out at Sergio's legs. He loosened his grip slightly, and she screamed at the top of her voice, but her vocal chords recorded no sound. She passed out and slumped to the floor. "What are we going to do about this?", Maria asked Sergio. "She has seen what happened, and although we could say that it was an accident, we can't let her go, especially as the police are looking for us for fraud. I suggest that we just lock her up in the basement, and let her rot". "I've got a slightly better idea, said Maria. We know that they have arranged for at least 9,000 Euros to be in the bank soon, so why don't we get her to tell us the security number of her bank card, and withdraw the money. They may well have deposited more than 9,000 Euros, of course, and if there is any more, we'll take it all. We'll easily have enough money to get out of Spain and take the crossing into Morocco and hide out in Tangier." "Not such a silly idea after all, but how might we get her to tell us the number"?

When Sally had regained her senses, she was gagged and trussed up with some sort of rope, and was sitting on an old chair in a windowless room. Across the room Sergio and Maria slowly came into focus, and on seeing them tried desperately to free herself from her bounds, but to no avail. All that she managed to achieve was to tear the skin off her wrists and ankles, drawing blood. "Now, look here, Maria said, we won't harm you if you just tell us the password and security number of your bank account, and once we have it, and we have collected the remainder of the money, we shall send someone here to release you". They had no intention of letting her go, but just said this to try to keep her calm. " I'm going to take the gag off your mouth, so be a good girl and don't try to shout out for help, or do anything stupid, or we will have to restrain you again, which as you already know, won't be comfortable." Sally's eyes glared at them full of hatred and venom. 'I won't let you get away with this, she thought, but I need time to think how I might be able to get away, before they take the money and escape a murder charge. The gag was removed, "Water, please" she croaked through cracked lips and a sore throat. She had water poured into her mouth by Sergio's rough hands, and most of it dribbled down the front of her dress, leaving a large wet patch on her chest. She swallowed hard. "I shall ask you once, and once only threatened Sergio, and provided that you give us the correct information about your Bank account, I promise that we won't hurt you. If, however you don't, well, I don't need to tell you what will happen to you."

Sally was terrified and was shivering uncontrollably. She had to make up her mind. She sat very quietly. "Well, what's it to be then, your money or your life"?

"How can I be certain that you will let me go, once you have my money"? " You can't" barked Sergio, but you don't really have any option do you"? he smirked. "As a sign of good faith, croaked Sally, please untie me, and I shall give you what you need". "You're in no position to negotiate with us, yelled Sergio", who was now running out of patience. "Why don't you show a little human kindness to her, she can't hurt us, whispered Maria in his ear, she'll be dead within a week." "I have been persuaded by my partner that I should show some compassion to you. It must be a female thing." He walked over to the chair and produced a large curved knife, and roughly slit the bonds that were restraining her in the chair. "I've kept my side of the deal, he said, so let's have the numbers". " I can never remember them, so I have them written down in my diary, which I keep in my handbag, which I left on the terrace". "I'll get it," said Maria, as she unlocked the door. The door flew open and knocked her backwards, as a bloodied bedraggled man charged into the room swinging a heavy branch that he had picked up in the garden, and with an accurate aim, hit Sergio on the side of his face, knocking him unconscious. Maria had also been left senseless behind the wooden door. "Tie them up, he shouted at Sally, with this rope that I found in the shed". Stunned, she obeyed, and made sure that the knots were secure.

"B....B...Bert she stuttered, I thought that you were dead, seeing your body floating in the swimming pool".

"Not quite, but thankfully they didn't check to see……………………. They of course didn't know that I was the 2012 British underwater breath holding champion", he laughed.

Printed in Great Britain
by Amazon.co.uk, Ltd.,
Marston Gate.